STRANDED

What Reviewers Say About Ronica Black's Work

A Love that Leads to Home

"If you love a slow-burn romance where the characters are carefully dancing around each other while being incredibly adorable, this story is for you. It was an emotional read for me, and if you want a good heart-wrenching story, read it."—*Hsinju's Lit Log*

Freedom to Love

"This is a great book. The police drama keeps you enthralled throughout but what I found captivating was the growing affection between the two main characters. Although they are both very different women, you find yourself holding your breath, hoping that they will find a way to be together."—*Lesbian Reading Room*

The Practitioner

"*The Practitioner* by Ronica Black is the angsty sort of romance that I can easily get lost in. I wanted to fill a tub and bathe in all the feelings. Hell, if I had one of those fancy, waterproof Kindles, I just might have."—*Lesbian Review*

"The beginning of this novel captured my attention from the rather luscious description of a pint of Guinness. I cannot tell a lie, I almost immediately wanted to be drinking it. …The first scene with the practitioner also pulled me in, making me sit up and pay attention to what was happening on the digital page. The relationship was like a low simmering fire, frequently doused by either Johnnie's personal angst, or Elaine's. This book was an overall enjoyable read and one which I would recommend to people wanting characters who practically breathe off the page."—*Library Thing*

Snow Angel

"A beautifully written, passionate and romantic novella."—*SunsetX Cocktail*

"*Snow Angel* is a novella, and it flies by. It draws characters and scenes in large strokes, and it's good fun if you'd like a quick read that's particularly escapist."—*The Lesbrary*

Under Her Wing

"From the start Ronica Black had me. I loved everything about this story, from the emotional intensity to the amazingly hot sex scenes. The emotion between them is so real and tear jerking at times. And the love scenes are phenomenal. I feel I'm raving—but I enjoyed it that much. Highly recommended."—*Kitty Kat's Book Review Blog*

"*Emily*" in Women of the Dark Streets

"A darkly disturbing brush with questionable magic that leads to an astounding one-eighty-degree turnaround after an apparent attempt at suicide. Mindboggling!"—*Rainbow Book Reviews*

The Seeker

"Stalkers, child kidnappers and murderers all collide in this fast-paced, dual-plotted novel. This is not Black's first novel, and readers can only hope it will not be her last."—*Lambda Literary Review*

"Ronica Black's books just keep getting stronger and stronger. …This is such a tightly written plot-driven novel that readers will find themselves glued to the pages and ignoring phone calls. *The Seeker* is a great read, with an exciting plot, great characters, and great sex."—*Just About Write*

Flesh and Bone—*Lambda Literary Award Finalist*

"Ronica Black handles a traditional range of lesbian fantasies with gusto and sincerity. The reader wants to know these women as well as they come to know each other. When Black's characters ignore their realistic fears to follow their passion, this reader admires their chutzpah and cheers them on. ...These stories make good bedtime reading, and could lead to sweet dreams. Read them and see."
—*Erotica Revealed*

Chasing Love

"Ronica Black's writing is fluid, and lots of dialogue makes this a fast read. If you like steamy erotica with intense sexual situations, you'll like *Chasing Love*."—*Queer Magazine Online*

Hearts Aflame

"Sleek storytelling and terrific characters are the backbone of Ronica Black's third and best novel, *Hearts Aflame*. Prepare to hop on for an emotional ride with this thrilling story of love in the outback. ...Along with the romance of Krista and Rae, the secondary storylines such as Krista's fear of horses and an uncle suffering from Alzheimer's are told with depth and warmth. Black also draws in the reader by utilizing the weather as a metaphor for the sexual and emotional tension in all the storylines. Wonderful storytelling and rich characterization make this a high recommendation."—*Lambda Literary Review*

"*Hearts Aflame* takes the reader on the rough and tumble ride of the cattle drive. Heat, flood, and a sexual pervert are all part of the adventure. Heat also appears between Krista and Rae. The twists and turns of the plot engage the reader all the way to the satisfying conclusion."—*Just About Write*

"I like the author's writing style and she tells a good story. I was drawn in quickly and didn't lose interest at all. Black paints a great picture with her words and I was able to feel like I was sitting around the camp fire with the characters."—*C-Spot Reviews*

Wild Abandon—*Lambda Literary Award Finalist*

"Black is a master at teasing the reader with her use of domination and desire. Black's first novel, *In Too Deep*, was a finalist for a 2005 Lammy. …With *Wild Abandon*, the author continues her winning ways, writing like a seasoned pro. This is one romance I will not soon forget."—*Books to Watch Out For*

"This sequel to Ronica Black's debut novel, *In Too Deep*, is an electrifying thriller. The author's development as a fine storyteller shines with this tightly written story. …[The mystery] keeps the story charged—never unraveling or leading us to a predictable conclusion. More than once I gasped in surprise at the dark and twisted paths this book took."—*Curve*

"Ronica Black, author of *In Too Deep*, has given her fans another fast paced novel of romance and danger. As previously, Black develops her characters fully, complete with their quirks and flaws. She is also skilled at allowing her characters to grow, and to find their way out of psychic holes. If you enjoy complex characters and passionate sex scenes, you'll love *Wild Abandon*."—*MegaScene*

"Black has managed to create two very sensual and compelling women. The backstory is intriguing, original, and quite well-developed. Yet, it doesn't detract from the primary premise of the novel—it is a sexually-charged romance about two very different and guarded women. Black carries the reader along at such a rapid pace that the rise and fall of each climactic moment successfully creates that suspension of disbelief which the reader seeks."
—*Midwest Book Review*

"Ronica Black has proven once again that she is an awesome storyteller with her new romance, *Wild Abandon*. With her second published novel, she has crafted an erotic, sensual and well-paced tale. ...Black is a master at teasing the reader with her use of domination and desire. Emotions pour endlessly from the pages, moving the plot forward at a pace that never slows or gets dull. But Black doesn't stop there. She is intent on giving the reader more. *Wild Abandon* hints at a plot twist early on, and while we know who it involves, we do not know what will happen, and how, until the last minute, effectively keeping us spellbound."
—*Just About Write*

In Too Deep—*Lambda Literary Award Finalist*

"Ronica Black's debut novel *In Too Deep* has everything from nonstop action and intriguing well developed characters to steamy erotic love scenes. From the opening scenes where Black plunges the reader headfirst into the story to the explosive unexpected ending, *In Too Deep* has what it takes to rise to the top. Black has a winner with *In Too Deep*, one that will keep the reader turning the pages until the very last one."—*Independent Gay Writer*

"...an exciting, page turning read, full of mystery, sex, and suspense."—*MegaScene*

"...a challenging murder mystery—sections of this mixed-genre novel are hot, hot, hot. Black juggles the assorted elements of her first book with assured pacing and estimable panache."—*Q Syndicate*

"Black's characterization is skillful, and the sexual chemistry surrounding the three major characters is palpable and definitely hot-hot-hot...if you're looking for a solid read with ample amounts of eroticism and a red herring or two you're sure to find *In Too Deep* a satisfying read."—*L Word Literature*

Visit us at www.boldstrokesbooks.com

By the Author

In Too Deep

Deeper

Wild Abandon

Hearts Aflame

Flesh and Bone

The Seeker

Chasing Love

Conquest

Wholehearted

The Midnight Room

Snow Angel

The Practitioner

Freedom to Love

Under Her Wing

Private Passion

Dark Euphoria

The Last Seduction

Olivia's Awakening

A Love That Leads to Home

Passion's Sweet Surrender

A Turn of Fate

Watching Over Her

The Business of Pleasure

Something to Talk About

Passionate Pursuance novella in Decadence

The Murders at Sugar Mill Farm

The Curse writing as Alexandra Riley

The Breakdown

Stranded

STRANDED

by

Ronica Black

2025

STRANDED

ISBN 13: 978-1-63679-761-8

This Trade Paperback Original Is Published By
Bold Strokes Books, Inc.
P.O. Box 249
Valley Falls, NY 12185

First Edition: April 2025

CREDITS
Editor: Cindy Cresap
Production Design: Susan Ramundo
Cover Design By Tammy Seidick

Acknowledgments

Thank you to BSB for your continued support throughout the writing process and for allowing me to continue to write what's in this mind of mine.

A huge thank you to my friends and family for reading my early drafts and giving me honest feedback. And for putting up with my obsessiveness and overthinking when it comes to my writing. I couldn't do this without you. Truly.

And finally, a warm thank you to the readers, for continuing to hitch a ride with me on yet another adventure. You're the reason why I write.

PROLOGUE

Tanalian Mountain Trail
Lake Clark National Park and Reserve, Alaska

There was something about the fresh, crisp Alaskan air that always both enlivened and calmed Whitley Travers. She didn't pretend to understand it or even try to figure it out. She just knew the land resonated deep within her and burrowed into her marrow, grounding her for life. And it didn't seem that anything could curdle that feeling. Not even the noisy grumbles of the hikers ahead of her as they ambled up the craggy trail with her father, Rick, in the lead. She'd heard plenty of complaining before and would no doubt hear it again with the next group. Their clients often grew weary on the longer hikes and they weren't shy about voicing it.

"Come on, gang, we got about another half hour," her father said, continuing his pace.

Maria, a stout woman with a nasally voice, spoke her concern. "That long?" Her laborious pack was weighing her down while her hands were white-knuckled around her trekking poles. "I can already see the lake."

"That doesn't mean our camp is close," another client, this one called Otter, said. He sneered back at her and adjusted the oversized pack on his wiry shoulders. Otter was a know-it-all, a smart-ass, and Whit wasn't sure how he got his nickname, but to her he did indeed look like an otter with his elongated torso and narrow front teeth. This Otter, however, was neither cute nor amusing to watch.

His attitude alone was enough to put her off, and that was difficult to do, considering her father always said she had the heart of a lion and the patience of Job.

Maria didn't respond to Otter's chastising and the group carried on, just as they'd been doing the last few hours after having ignored Otter's other numerous snide comments. Whit had heard the saying about tension being so thick one could cut it with a knife, but she'd never truly understood it until this particular outing with Otter and his uncanny ability to make people uncomfortable. She hoped her father knew how to diffuse the growing strain. She mused that he did, as he seemed to know how to do just about anything. But then again they'd never had anyone like Otter as a client before. At least she hadn't been along to witness one anyway.

The aromatic fragrance of pines mingled with the rich scent of recently rained on earth as she stared at Maria's thick legs slogging through the mud in front of her. The late afternoon was cool and heavy with moisture as low-hanging storm clouds loomed overhead. Whit hoped they made camp before another downpour, otherwise they would get soaked. That would mean more complaining, and that was something she could do without.

Thunder growled in the distance, as if agreeing with her, letting her know complaining clients were indeed a pain in the backside. She smiled at that and kept walking, stopping quickly however, as Maria tripped over a stone and stumbled ahead of her. Whit quickly cupped her elbow to steady her, and once she regained her bearings, they continued on.

Whit focused up ahead this time, tired of the relentless pounding of Maria's struggling footfalls. And what a sight to behold. The lake had come into view with its smooth, dark turquoise allure, gleaming like a magical gem beneath the gathering thunderheads. Again she thought about the incredible beauty of this land with its numerous threads of thick trees, vast serrated mountains, jewel-like waters, and ever-abundant wildlife. God, how she loved it. And she loved that her father allowed her to come along on his guided excursions to experience such beauty. She'd been doing that since she was eight. Four years now. He even paid her upon return for helping out with the clients. She incessantly tucked the cash away in an old tube sock under her bed, saving up for her very own ATV. She only had a few more guided tours to work until she had enough for a used one.

Her mother, of course, wasn't crazy about her spending her hard-earned money on an ATV. But she was wise enough to know she couldn't talk Whit out of it once her father gave his permission. Besides, Whit could ride the ATV into town and run errands. Her mother would be happy with that. She just had to wait and see.

"I need to stop," Maria let out, halting in front of her. Her back arched and she was resting all her weight on her poles for support.

"What's wrong?" Jerry, Maria's ever-faithful husband, asked as he hurried back to tend to her. "You need some water?" He slid his water bottle from his belt, but she shook her head, refusing it.

"I can't go on," she breathed. "I need a break."

Whit set down her own walking poles and placed her hand on the small of Maria's back to encourage her to straighten so she could breathe better. Maria complied, but doing so seemed to cause pain as her red face contorted and a groan escaped her dry lips. "Here, let's take off your pack," Whit said. She unbuckled the heavy pack and eased it off her shoulders.

"Everything okay?" Whit's father asked from the front of the group. Without waiting for a response, he wove between hikers until he reached Jerry and Maria, a look of serious concern on his ruddy face.

"Maria's beat," Jerry said solemnly.

Her father rested his hands on Maria's shoulders and stared into her eyes. "Take long, deep breaths," he said. "Fill up your lungs."

As she did so, Whit noticed that her legs were trembling, along with her hands.

"We need to get her to camp," Whit said, giving her father a knowing look. "I'll carry her pack."

Her father nodded, understanding her silent concern. "Can you walk a little farther to camp, Maria? Without your pack? It's just ahead."

Maria bent once again, resting her hands on her knees. "I'll try."

"Keep standing straight," her father said, angling her up. "You breathe better when you're upright, okay?"

"Okay."

"We'll take it slow," he said.

"Jesus Christ, we're already going to get rained on," Otter spat. "Now we gotta slow down because of her ass?"

Blood rushed to Whit's face, just as it seemed to have rushed to Jerry's. He looked at Otter and spat back.

"Why don't you shut the hell up, Otter?"

Her father raised his palms. "Everybody calm down. Jerry, Maria, you stay back with me. Everyone else can go on to camp with Whit." He motioned for Whit to hand over Maria's pack.

Whit gave it to him and moved to walk to the front of the group. Otter cut her off, looking disgusted.

"Great, so now you're pawning us off on your kid? I paid good money for this trip and I'll be damned if I'm going to let some weak, lazy ass woman ruin it or a little kid lead it."

Her father bored a hole into Otter but didn't speak for several seconds. Whit knew he was pissed. She could tell by the firm set of his strong jaw and the pulse of the wormy vein in his temple. Otter had better watch it. Her father, once upset, couldn't be reckoned with. Many a drunk man in a bar had found that out the hard way.

"Otter, I understand your frustrations, but you need to keep them to yourself. Everyone is doing the best they can. And remember what I said about working as a team. It's just us versus nature out here. You'd be wise to remember that should you need someone's help at some point."

"Whatever, man. I'll just go myself. I'm not waiting on some fat bitch or some kid."

Jerry spun around, hands knotted into fists. "What did you say, you son of a bitch?"

Otter sneered again. "Whoa, he comes to life again. For a while there, man, I thought you didn't have a sack. I thought your wife had it in her pack."

"You motherfucker," Jerry said as he lunged at him. But her father stepped in front of him and held him back.

"Jerry, Jerry, he's not worth it," he said. "He's not worth it."

"He's talking about my wife, Rick."

"I know. And he's doing it to get a reaction."

Maria covered her face and cried. Whit tried to comfort her, unsure what else to do as her father continued to hold Jerry away from Otter. But Otter, who was unrestrained, wasn't backing down. He was still talking, still taking jabs at Jerry.

"Come on, you piece of shit. I'm right here." He pulled out a hunting knife. One with a serrated blade.

Her father, who had his back to him, didn't even see it. And that's when Jerry lunged once again, just as Otter charged, pushing her father against Otter. Her father grunted at the contact and his eyes went wide. The three men tangled on their feet for what seemed like an eternity, Jerry still trying to get at Otter, before her father slowly reached for his side and bellowed. Otter backed away slowly then, withdrawing his knife, his thin face pale. The serrated blade was slick with dark red.

"No," Whit said, moving toward her father who promptly collapsed onto the ground.

"No!" She dropped to her knees and searched his torso frantically for the wound. He was slightly reclined, lying on his hefty pack. His hand shook as he brought it forward for inspection. They both stared at the blood.

"Dad, no!" She pulled him closer to her, trying to reach the blood-soaked patch of his shirt. She pressed her hand to it and gagged at the hot surging blood against her palm. "Dad," she breathed. His wide eyes had glossed over, focused somewhere far away. "Dad, look at me." He shifted his longing gaze to her. He attempted a smile. Covered her hand with his own trembling one.

"It's okay," he said. "It'll be fine. Just get something to put pressure on the wound."

Whit looked to Jerry, who was obviously in shock. Maria, who'd been crying, was now throwing up a few steps away. "Get me something!" Whit cried.

"What?" Jerry replied.

"A shirt, a bandana, anything. Hurry!"

Jerry first unfastened, and then slid out of his pack. He fumbled with the zipper before he got it open.

"Hurry!" Whit said. The blood was spewing out of her father, oozing through her fingers. She pressed harder, causing her father to wince. Jerry fished out a shirt. She shoved the folded fabric tightly against the wound. It was soaked through in seconds. "Dad, tell me what to do." She knew help was too far away. There was no service for the cell phones, and the only way out to Anchorage or to a hospital was by plane from Port Alsworth. It was the closest community, and it was a days' hike away. They would never make it in time.

"Send for help," her father said. "To Port Alsworth." It was a hopeful suggestion at best, but he obviously had no other recourse either. Her heart sank in hearing his only proposition.

"I'll go," one of the other hikers said. His name was Pete. Next to her, he was the youngest of the group and very fit. "I can run back."

"The terrain is too steep to run," Jerry said.

Whit wanted to hear none of that. If Pete was willing to try and run she was going to encourage him to do it.

"Go," Whit said. "And tell them to send a float plane."

Pete slung off his pack, took a great deal of his belongings out of it to lighten the load, and swung it back on. "I'll hurry," he said. He took off at a brisk walk, using his poles for support on the muddy, rocky trail, following it back toward what little civilization there was.

"It'll be okay," her father said again. But now his lips were trembling, along with the rest of him. He was going into shock. Whit looked again to Jerry. "Cover him," she said. "We need to keep him warm."

"It'll be okay," her father said. His glossy eyes had that far off look again.

"Dad." She gripped his hand. The one he'd had on his wound. It was sticky with blood. "Dad." But he wouldn't look at her.

"It'll be…okay." His trembling was worse. Spittle formed at the corners of his mouth. She was losing him.

"Jerry, blanket, now!"

Jerry found a blanket and tossed it to her. She quickly tucked it in around her father.

"Hang on, Dad. Just hang on."

Slowly, as tears formed in her eyes and her throat grew tight and raw, her father's gaze shifted back to hers.

"Whit," he said.

"I'm here, I'm right here." He was looking right at her but it seemed like he couldn't see her.

He licked his dry lips. "Whit."

"Yeah, Dad, I'm here."

"Keep them safe."

She forced a swallow and clenched her eyes. "No, Dad. You're gonna be fine. You're—"

He gripped her hand. "Lead...them out."

"No." She shook her head. "You're going to do that with me. You're going to be fine."

"Lead them," he said again. His gaze drifted beyond her once again and froze.

"Dad." She blinked at him. "Dad." He wasn't moving. Wasn't breathing.

She shoved him. "Dad!" He didn't react. "Dad!" She hit him in the chest. Again and again. Jerry pulled her away, but she fought him.

"Let me go!"

"He's gone," Jerry said. "Whit, he's gone."

She angrily yanked off her pack and collapsed onto her father. "Don't leave me, Dad. Don't—" Sobs overtook her, and this time, Jerry backed away and the rest of the group stood around her quietly and let her cry.

CHAPTER ONE

Twenty Years Later
Fairbanks, Alaska
Late September

Abigail Gardner wasn't crazy about the reflection she saw in the mirror. So she quickly brushed her thick, red mane back into a loose ponytail and touched up her face with some light blush and lip gloss. It wasn't a great job but it would have to do. She put the makeup away and heaved her backpack up over her shoulder and grabbed her rolling suitcase.

"Time to go," she said softly as she double-checked her watch and then exited the airport bathroom. After bypassing more travelers and a couple of bush pilots in a heated discussion, she made her way outside and spotted her plane immediately. It was a Piper PA-18 Super Cub. She knew because she'd studied the type thoroughly before her trip, knowing she'd have to take this particular plane to reach her last destination. The other three planes she'd flown on had been bigger. They were Cessnas. But this one was smaller, a two-seater, and it made her nervous. Especially with the billowing darkly bruised clouds.

She wheeled her luggage up to the small red-and-white plane and smiled at the older man climbing out.

"You Junior?" she asked.

He gave her a quick once-over and puffed on his pipe. She could already smell the sweet, spicy tobacco.

"Who wants to know?" he asked.

She extended her hand. "Abigail Gardner. I'm your passenger."

He plucked the pipe from his mouth. "No, you ain't."

"Sorry?"

"I ain't got no passenger." He looked up at the ominous sky. "Not today. Not in this weather."

Abby laughed nervously, not liking how this conversation was going. "Weather? It's just a few thunderheads."

"It's more than that, lady. A lot more according to the weather service. No one's taking off in this."

She stared at him in disbelief, but then recalled the heated talk the two pilots had been having inside. They'd been arguing over the weather. Shit. This wasn't good. "But I have to get to Bettles. It's the only way into Cozy. I'm due there this evening."

The man closed the door to the plane and then ambled over to tighten the binds holding the plane in place.

"You won't be getting there this evening." He straightened and looked again at the sky. "Nah. Not today."

"But I have to. I must." Cozy was the last small town on her trip. She had to get there and meet her guide so she could explore its landmarks and nooks and crannies and meet the townsfolk. Those things were a necessity so she could write her article, and she needed all the time she could get.

It seemed that this old man however, this Junior, wasn't going to budge. She sighed. "I'll find another pilot then. Surely there must be someone." She glanced around and saw other tethered planes, but no people nearby.

Junior wiped his hands on his denim coveralls as if they were dirty. "Good luck with that." He began to walk away.

"Wait. You can't just leave." She hurried toward him. "My magazine…they already paid you."

"No refunds for inclement weather."

"But—"

"Look, lady, I've got to go. I want to get ahead of this storm."

She cocked her head, confused. "I thought you said you couldn't fly."

"I can't and I won't."

"Then—"

He walked away and called back over his shoulder. "I'm driving."

"To Cozy?" Hope lifted her voice and she followed him once again.

He looked at her like she was dense. "What do you think?"

"Well, can I come with you?"

This time he looked at her like she was out of her mind.

"You? With me, in my Bronco?"

"Yes." She offered her best smile, but she could feel her nerves permeating through. She just hoped he couldn't see them.

"I already got a passenger." He pointed across the tarmac to a chain link fence, where just beyond, a woman with dark hair was loading her gear into an old Ford Bronco.

Abby thought quickly. "I can pay. Handsomely." She really couldn't afford to pay him handsomely, but her magazine could, and she knew they'd do anything for this article. It was going to be the feature and they were as excited about it as she was.

Junior stopped in his tracks. He slid the pipe from his wet, liver-colored lips and studied her with tired, watery blue eyes. "Pay, you say?"

"Yes, sir. Handsomely."

"What's handsomely?"

"How's four hundred dollars?" She slung her purse forward and dug for her wallet. She fingered out the cash. It was almost all she had. But she'd worry about that when she got to Cozy. "Cash," she said, offering it to him.

He seemed to consider it a moment. Then he took the money and counted it as if to make sure she wasn't lying. "Alright then." He shoved the money down into the pocket of his coveralls. "Put your gear in the back."

"Great, thanks." She grinned so hard her face hurt. She followed him out through the fence and rounded the old SUV. There, the woman with the dark hair did a double take at her but said nothing. Abby, after doing a double take herself at the woman's natural beauty, tried to be friendly.

"Hi," Abby said, hoisting her bags into the Bronco. "I'm Abby. I'll be riding with you." She smiled again, but it, too, was ignored. The woman simply closed the back hatch and walked to the front passenger side door where she opened it and climbed inside.

Abby stared in confusion but then joined her, sliding into the bench seat behind her. The truck was cold and smelled of tobacco. The metal buckle of the seat belt was even colder. She promptly secured herself with it and waited as Junior crawled inside behind the wheel. He didn't bother fastening his seat belt, but rather took the time to stuff his pipe with tobacco and relight it with a match. Abby watched the blue flame burn down to his thick, rough-looking fingertips where it flickered and lingered. She winced as she imagined the pain, but Junior didn't seem to be bothered, waving out the flame as if it were nothing.

After a few hearty puffs that dispersed the spicy smoke throughout the cab, he fished out his keys and started the engine.

"Thanks again, Junior," Abby said, truly grateful. "I really appreciate the ride."

"It ain't no big thing," he said, reversing and heading away from the airport.

"Oh, but it is. Without this ride, I'd be stuck. And I can't afford to be stuck. I need to get to Cozy pronto."

"What's your business in Cozy?" Junior asked.

Abby was surprised he was curious, but she answered proudly. "I'm writing an article on small, out of the way towns throughout Alaska. Cozy is my last town to visit."

"Writing an article for what?" the woman asked.

Abby perked up, wondering why she was interested. "I write for a travel magazine. *Exploring Horizons.* Maybe you've heard of it?"

No answer.

The truck grew quiet. Abby wondered if she'd said something wrong. She tried explaining. "The magazine is widely read. The article should do wonders for the featured towns. You know, bring in lots of extra tourism."

More silence.

Junior glanced over at the woman but said nothing.

Abby spoke. "I'm sorry, is something wrong?"

"Whit here doesn't like lots of tourism in Cozy," Junior said.

Abby flushed. "Oh. May I ask why?"

"Because tourists ruin everything," Whit said dryly.

Abby closed her mouth. Then she tried again. "I guess I just don't understand. Tourists bring in money. Isn't that helpful?"

"Money is fine," Whit said, turning her head to look out the window. "It's everything else they bring that's the problem."

"Like what?" Abby asked softly, truly wanting to know.

But again there was silence. Eventually, Junior spoke.

"Like yammering on for one thing."

Abby took that as her cue to stop asking questions. Instead, she pulled out her phone and updated her editor, Susan, about the travel situation. It was then that she realized she had one more question.

"Uh, excuse me, Junior? About how long is the drive to Cozy?"

"About nine hours. But I know a shortcut. So we'll be there, weather permitting, in about eight. If this guy behind me will get off my ass."

Abby texted the info to Susan and then her guide in Cozy. She informed her, too, of the situation and unfortunately had to cancel their dinner plans that evening. The woman, whose name was Clair, said it was fine and asked her to check in with her when she arrived. Abby said okay and eased back into her seat to try to rest.

She'd been flying all morning. First in a Cessna and then in a larger jet to reach Fairbanks. She couldn't wait to reach her place in Cozy where she could fully relax and hopefully get some sleep. But nine hours was a long trek in the back of an old SUV with two grumpy strangers.

She found her ear buds and tucked them into her ears and put on some soft music. Then she leaned back and closed her eyes and tried to imagine she was somewhere else with someone else. Anyone, at the moment, would do. But before she could even conjure up someone in her mind's eye, she was fast asleep.

❖

She awoke some time later to heavy jostling, and it took her a moment to remember where she was.

"What's going on?" Hard rain was pelting the windshield and Junior was crouched forward, attempting to wipe the fog off the glass so he could see.

"We're in the thick of it," he said, finally having enough with trying to wipe away the moisture. "It's coming down like the dickens."

"Why is the road so rough?" Abby asked as the Bronco shimmied left to right once again.

"It's the trail," he said, pipe gripped between his teeth. "Ain't no one on it a whole lot so it's grown over."

Abby felt her stomach flip. "We're on an overgrown trail? Not a road?"

"It's a shortcut. Been taking it for years."

Abby clenched the strap of her seat belt. "Apparently, no one else has," she said.

"Just you mind your business," Junior said, removing his pipe. "I know where I'm going and what I'm doing."

Abby let out a startled noise as the truck banked back and forth, causing her seat restraints to tighten. Her purse, which she'd kept with her, flew down onto the floor behind Junior's seat, along with her phone. Her ear buds, which had stopped playing music, dropped from her ears and she quickly grabbed them and closed them into her fist.

More jostling ensued and she eyed her purse and phone and debated unbuckling her seat belt to reach down and get them. She decided to try, realizing she might need her phone in case of an emergency. She was just about to push in on the buckle when Junior started coughing. Alarmed at the fierceness of it, she glanced up at him and saw his skinny but potbellied body rack with the exertion.

"Are you okay?" she asked.

Even Whit, who was so quiet it was like she wasn't there, placed her hand on his arm in concern. "Junior?" The truck kept swaying, Junior still pressing on the gas.

He kept coughing, eventually whipping the pipe from his mouth in order to breathe better. "I'm—fine. But this asshole is still following us, riding my ass."

Abby turned to look out the back window and saw a set of headlights in the rain. The other vehicle was newer than the Bronco and it wasn't riding Junior's bumper like he claimed, but rather was several car lengths away.

"Maybe he just knows about the shortcut too," she said, facing front again.

The coughs kept coming to Junior, so he didn't bother to respond. Abby watched him closely, growing more and more concerned.

"Are you sure you're okay?" she asked.

His hand flew up to his left arm and the tendons in his neck went taut. "I'm—" but he didn't finish his sentence. Instead his eyes went wide and he grunted and the Bronco gained speed, plowing off the rugged trail into the brush, bypassing dozens of trees. Abby screamed and Whit tried for the wheel, yanking it hard to the right.

A loud, wet sound escaped Junior as his hand moved from his arm to his chest, and the truck, banking a hard right, flipped and then slid down over a ledge, coming to a shockingly hard crash upside down, slamming Abby painfully against her seat belt and then back into her seat.

She lay limp, hanging from her belt, her head throbbing. The truck sizzled and popped and then groaned like the hull of a sinking ship. The smell of the burning engine filled her nostrils, as did the smell of spilt gasoline.

"Abby," came a voice from the front.

"Yeah, it's me." Her heart raced, her head spinning from the blood rushing to it.

"We have to get out." It was Whit and she was moving, already having undone her belt. She crawled to Junior, who, she'd suddenly noticed, stunk like shit. His body was half in half out of the windshield, his right leg twisted at an unnatural angle.

"Junior," Abby said, though she knew.

"He's dead," Whit confirmed after she checked for his pulse. She crawled back to Abby. "Brace yourself." She undid her seat belt and shoved her toward the broken window of her door once she fell. "Go. Get out, now."

Abby, dizzy with a head rush, crawled through the smashed window out into the pelting cold rain. She felt Whit follow, still pushing on her backside even when they were a few feet away from the vehicle.

"Go!" Whit said to her, pulling her up into a stand. "Run!"

Abby tripped but Whit yanked on her once again and they ran, taking six to seven good steps before a loud blast came from behind and blew them forward onto the glossy wet rocks of the ravine.

Abby remained still, her body buzzing, her back and legs warm from the ensuing heat behind her. Her ears rang. She tried to push herself up, but her arms wouldn't cooperate. She tried to call for Whit, but her voice wouldn't work. So she did the only thing she could do.

She closed her eyes and prepared to die.

CHAPTER TWO

Whit opened her eyes. Fat drops of rain smacked the rocks around her and she could smell nothing but burning oil and fuel. A wall of heat pushed into her from behind. She focused and remembered Junior. Though she was sure he was dead, it still unsettled her to think of him burning in the vehicle. But there was nothing she could do to get him out. Bile rose to her throat and she shoved herself up and half walked, half crawled toward Abby, who lay just ahead of her in a limp, uncomfortable-looking heap.

Whit knelt with a hand to her shoulder. "You okay?"

Please don't let her be dead.

"Abby?" She shook her. She didn't see any life-threatening wounds. "Abby?"

"Mm?" She turned her head and looked at her with misty green eyes, her cheek marred with dirt.

"Come on, we need to move." They didn't have time to waste. They were in a ravine. One that was quickly filling with water. Whit straightened and looked back at the burning vehicle, searching for anything she could salvage. To her amazement she saw that the back hatch was open, and a nylon bag had been thrown onto the creek bed. She hurried as best she could to gather it, careful not to get too close to the heat of the flames. Then she crossed back to Abby who was attempting to sit up.

"Junior," Abby said. Whit gripped her elbow and helped her stand.

"He's gone."

"But—"

"There's nothing we can do for him."

Abby stumbled and winced. She grabbed her knee.

"You hurt?" Whit asked.

"A little."

"Can you walk?"

"Probably not well." She palmed her head. "God, I feel dizzy. And sick." She bent and retched but nothing came up.

Whit gave her a quick once-over. Her knee was most likely strained, and she was covered in minor scrapes and bruises. They both were. But that they could handle.

"Come on." She edged her to the side of the ravine. "This creek bed is going to flood. We need to find a way out."

"Doesn't look like there is one."

A loud bang came from the burning Bronco as it blew again. They crouched in defense and saw more flames. And there, at the top of the ledge, they saw an SUV, sitting with its engine idling. Whit waved her arms and screamed, "Down here! Help!" But to her shock and amazement, the vehicle reversed and drove away.

"Why is he leaving?" Abby asked, sounding panicked.

"I don't know."

"Is he going for help?"

"Probably." But she wasn't so sure. Why hadn't the driver at least signaled that he'd seen them? Whatever the reason, she had other things to focus on at the moment, like getting her and Abby someplace where they could warm up.

She hurried them along with Abby limping. The rain was cold and a nuisance. By the time they found a way out of the ravine, they were nearly soaked through.

"Through here," Whit said, leading them up an incline.

"Shouldn't we go back to the other side? You know, back to the road? Toward that other car?"

"There's not a way out of the ravine on that side. Not anywhere close anyway." That side of the ravine was steeper and more hazardous looking. There was no way they could climb out. And right now, they needed a quick way out to avoid the imminent flood.

Whit gripped Abby's elbow again and encouraged her to walk faster.

"What's the rush? We're out of immediate danger." She was wincing with every step, and though Whit felt for her, she needed her to hurry along.

"We need shelter. And a fire."

"I can't go any faster."

"We have to get out of the rain and out of these clothes before hypothermia sets in."

"Hypothermia?" She seemed alarmed.

"The temperature will continue to drop the closer we get to sunset. It will be freezing tonight, if not colder."

Abby swallowed and then nodded as if she understood. She took bigger steps, cried out, but kept going. "How far?"

"Just up here to this tree line." They continued through the brush until they came to a large cluster of trees. They stepped into their cover and Whit could smell the strong scent of pine and wet earth. "Here is good." There were plenty of dead trees nearby and one had fallen and nestled into a forked stump, making a good base for a shelter.

Abby sighed as if relieved. She was trembling and the sight caused Whit's insides to clench in fear as memories from long ago infiltrated. She forced back her fear and eased Abby down beneath the large, forked tree. "Sit here while I work."

"I should help."

"No. Just stay there."

"But how are you going to do anything? We have nothing."

Whit knelt and lifted the bag. "We have this." She pulled her buck knife out of the sheath she wore on her ankle. "And this." She held it up for Abby to examine. "I carry it everywhere." She had. Since she was twelve and had encountered a man named Otter.

She slid the knife back into its sheath and dug through the bag, which must have belonged to Junior. She rummaged through it and found a pot with a lid, a tin cup, several cans of Spam, a box of pilot bread, a single water bottle with a filter, an all-purpose knife, a compass, a fire starting kit, and some instant coffee. It wasn't his pilot survival kit, which all pilots in Alaska were required to carry, but it would do. Knowing Junior, he probably had more survival gear in the Bronco, but it had most likely burned up in the crash and the subsequent explosion.

She showed the contents to Abby, who scowled at the Spam, and then left her to get to work. She, too, had begun to shiver, her clothes cold and sticking to her. She brought some dry branches, ones she'd found and planned to use as firewood, over to a pile she made near Abby.

Whit then got busy clearing a place for a fire. She managed to find some heavy stones and she stacked them in a half circle to make a wall for the heat to reflect off of. That would hopefully keep the heat close to them as they slept. Then she piled up some of the dead wood, pulled her own fire starting tin out of her back pocket and opened it up to retrieve her ferro rod and fire plugs.

"What's that?" Abby asked softly.

"Fire starting kit."

"You carry one around?"

"Old habit." One her father taught her. Plus, as a bush pilot, and flying into very remote areas, she felt more comfortable having it on her body, along with her buck knife.

Abby pointed. "What are those pink things?"

"Fire plugs. Kindling basically."

Whit angled her ferro rod toward the pile of dead wood and single fire plug and then scraped her knife along the shaft of the rod producing a showering of sparks. The fire plug caught almost immediately, and Whit blew on it to encourage it to grow, placing more of the dead brush and wood closer to it.

"Come on," she whispered. "Burn, you bastard." She blew some more and the fire caught, igniting the brush and then some of the smaller twigs. The fire grew and soon she was able to sit back on her haunches and hold her hands out for the heat. Smoke billowed out from the flames, lots of smoke due to the damp, but at least it was a fire. She eased all the way back and patted the ground next to her for Abby to join her.

"You sure?" Abby said, tentative.

"Yes, I'm sure."

She shrugged out of her jacket and began to untie her boots. "We need to strip down and get warm ASAP."

"You mean take off our clothes?"

"Yep."

"In front of each other?"

"You got a better idea?"

"Well, no."

"Then I suggest you get to it. Before you get into real trouble with hypothermia."

Whit took off her shoes and socks and liners, and then stood and peeled off her sweater and T-shirt. She then pushed down her pants and got up to place all of her clothes along another fallen log near the fire. She stood there looking at Abby in nothing but her bra and panties.

Abby blinked at her again and she swore she saw her blush just before she glanced away. Was she really that shy? Or was something else going on?

"Do you want me to turn away while you undress?" Whit asked.

"What? No. Don't be silly. I'm fine." She stood and began to undress. Whit made herself busy tending to the fire. She was already starting to warm up just by being out of her wet clothes. And soon Abby was nearly nude just like her, in her bra and panties, kneeling by the fire, warming her body. Whit made a point not to stare, but it was difficult. Abby was an incredibly beautiful woman, with dark red hair, creamy alabaster skin, and a cute little smattering of freckles along her shoulders and nose. She wondered if she had anyone in her life. And then decided that yes, she most definitely did. A woman like that would not be single.

Her heart sank a little at the thought, surprising her. She chuckled at herself and Abby stiffened.

"What?" she asked. "Why are you laughing?"

"No reason."

"No, really. Why are you laughing?"

She was huddled by the fire, covering herself, and Whit realized that she thought she may be laughing at her.

"It's not you, don't worry. You really think I would laugh at you?"

"I don't know."

"Wow, you must be really self-conscious."

Abby glanced away and rubbed her arms.

"Sorry," Whit said, realizing she was right.

"Don't be."

"What now?" Abby asked as she continued to hug herself. Her teeth were chattering and her once red and luscious-looking lips had turned a pale blue. "I want to help."

Whit was still cold and wet and exhausted, despite the warmth from the fire. They desperately needed shelter. "Just…" She rose, frustrated that there was still work to be done, when all she wanted to do was warm herself near the flames. "Stay there." It came out harsher than she'd intended, but it got her point across so she didn't add to it or soften the blow.

Abby in turn, blinked at her. Then she threw up her hands and sank back down to the ground. Whit ignored her. She didn't have time to worry about her feelings. She had to save their lives, and taking time to teach a tourist how to make a shelter, would waste precious minutes they didn't have.

Whit built the shelter by first placing two of the larger tree trunks she'd found down into the fork of the tree, so that the roof of their shelter had three beams. Then she filled in the gaps at the top with heavily leaved branches and brush. When she finished, she built the walls of the shelter by leaning the remaining, smaller trunks and branches perpendicular against the main beams. She shoved a bunch of pine needles into the shelter to finish the job. She encouraged Abby to crawl inside.

"It's not completely dry, but it's a start."

Abby hesitated a moment, as if Whit would bite. Then she knelt and crawled inside to check it out, before emerging again. Whit eased to the ground and sat in silence to stare into the fire. She took in a deep breath, finally able to relax. They had shelter and they were getting warm.

They were safe.

If only she could ensure that would last.

CHAPTER THREE

A bby sat by the fire with her arms wrapped around her knees. Slowly, she stopped shivering. Around her, lingering rain drops glistened on the trees, dropping unceremoniously to the ground. The sound of the water dripping was soon accompanied by birds, which had begun to sing their songs again. She closed her eyes and focused on the sounds, lulled by their sweet lullaby, the crackling and popping of the fire the icing on the cake. She was tired. So very tired. And her heart tore at the loss of Junior. She barely knew the man, but losing him was traumatic nonetheless.

"What do you think happened to Junior?" she asked. "Did he have a heart attack?"

Whit was moving around the fire, feeding it more wood and placing stones next to it. Some small, some large. One very flat. For what purpose, Abby did not know. "That would be my guess."

Abby wiped her eyes as tears sprung. "You're sure he was, you know…dead?"

"I'm sure."

Abby sniffled. "Before the fire, right?"

"He was gone," Whit said, sitting next to her and dumping the contents of the nylon bag onto the ground. "The accident nearly cut him in half."

Abby covered her mouth. "Oh, God."

Whit took a can of Spam and peeled the lid. "I checked for a pulse just to be sure. There wasn't one."

Abby lowered her hand as she watched Whit fish out the slimy hunk of meat into the pot with her knife. She didn't seem at all fazed by Junior's demise.

"Aren't you upset? I mean, wasn't Junior your friend?"

"He was a friend," she said, placing the pot on the large flat rock which was balanced over the flames on other stones. "But there isn't time to be upset. I just have to take care of the matters at hand. Like making sure we're safe and warm."

"I appreciate that," Abby said, feeling a little sheepish. Whit was taking care of them. It was courageous and honorable, as well as absolutely necessary. "I wish you'd let me help."

Whit stabbed at the now sizzling meat with her knife, slicing it up. "You really hell-bent on helping?"

"I want to do my part."

Whit held up the knife. "You can cook dinner."

Abby frowned but took the knife. It wasn't what she had in mind as far as helping, but she knelt next to the fire anyway and shuffled the glistening meat around the bottom of the pot. It was beginning to radiate a scent, and though she didn't care for the heavily processed meat, or any meat for that matter, her stomach told a different story. She was hungry and the frying pork concoction smelled appetizing.

"So, I guess I'm the little woman cooking the meals while you build the shelter and do everything else?" Abby smirked. Whit seemed to fit the strong silent type, with her sinewy athletic build, and quiet, straight to the point manner. She'd done all the important work thus far, and building the shelter had taken some muscle and skill. Abby felt almost ridiculous sitting there stirring the canned meat. "I can do other things, you know. I'm not helpless."

"You don't know survival," Whit said, carefully picking up some of the smaller hot stones and putting them in the nylon bag. "Or bushcraft."

"No, but I'm capable of learning."

"See, that's the problem." With the bag full, Whit took the stones and dumped them inside the shelter where the bed of pine needles lay. Then she returned and retrieved more stones to place back by the fire. She caught Abby watching her as she worked. "They'll help dry out the bedding," she said. "And later tonight, we'll put more under the needles and they'll help keep us warm."

"Oh." It was a neat idea. One she never would've thought of.

Whit turned their damp clothes and rehung them on the fallen log. "Clothes are drying," she said. "Hopefully they'll be dry before too long. I hope by sunset, but that's wishful thinking in this weather."

"When is sunset exactly?"

Whit glanced at her watch. "In three hours."

Abby stirred the meat, trying not to stare at Whit and her body, or think about spending the night with her alone inside that shelter. She knew nothing amorous would happen, but just the idea of being so close to her left her head spinning. "I think this is done."

"Good, I'm starved." Whit sat next to her and reached for the blue-and-white box of Sailor Boy Pilot Bread. She opened the box and took out the round, white crackers.

"What's that?" Abby asked.

"Pilot bread. An Alaskan staple."

"Is it good?"

Whit shrugged. "They're pretty plain, but they fill you up." She handed a few to her and then scooped some sizzling meat onto her own cracker and took a bite. She closed her eyes as she chewed. "It's nothing fancy, but it hits the spot." She opened her eyes and gave Abby the knife, encouraging her to do the same.

Abby maneuvered some Spam out of the pot and spread it on a cracker. She took a bite and chewed quietly. Whit was right. It wasn't great, but it wasn't awful either. And right now she was just grateful to have it.

"Yeah?" Whit asked, taking the knife from her for more meat.

Abby nodded, still chewing. "Mm-hm."

"We need to find some water. Shouldn't be hard to do. I know there's a creek not far from here."

"You know where we are?" Abby grew hopeful. Maybe their situation wasn't as dire as it seemed.

"I have some idea." She made another meat-topped cracker and ate. After she swallowed she spoke. "I know we need to head north. That's our best bet."

Abby felt her body go limp with disappointment. "Does anyone know where we are?"

Whit seemed surprised at the question. "I don't think so."

"Not at all?"

"Junior was big on his shortcuts. Even when he flew. I doubt he told anyone where we were going."

"I told my contact in Cozy I was getting a ride up from Fairbanks," Abby said. "But I didn't know how to explain the shortcut. I guess I should've asked Junior exactly what road we were taking."

"You didn't know," Whit said, once again handing over the knife. "And you couldn't have known that Junior would up and die on us. Or that the vehicle behind us wouldn't help."

Abby tried to return the knife, no longer feeling like eating. But Whit gently pushed it back to her. "You need to eat. You're going to need your strength. Especially with the cold and with your hurt knee."

"I'm upset," she said. "Junior…" She shook her head, the image of him half in and half out the windshield coming to mind, along with Whit's words about him.

Whit placed a hand on her shoulder. "Try not to think about it."

"How can you not?"

Whit dropped her hand.

"I mean, you saw him. You were there. It was traumatic. The whole thing was traumatic."

Whit took the knife, which Abby still refused, and fished out more meat for her and put it on a cracker. She handed it to her. "Eat," she said softly.

"I can't."

"Try. Just one more."

"Not until you tell me how it is you're so calm."

"I told you, there's no time to be upset."

"That can't be all," Abby said. "You're…it's like you're used to this."

Whit stood and poked at the fire with a stick. It was obvious by her behavior that she didn't want to discuss it. But Abby couldn't let it go. She was just too curious. She wanted to know this stranger she was stuck in the middle of Alaska with.

"Whit?"

"Just drop it."

"I want to know."

"I said, drop it." She tossed the stick into the fire.

Abby stood alongside her. "I'm not trying to be rude. I just want to know a little more about you. Because I can't, for the life of me, understand how it is you're so at ease with this situation."

Whit flexed her jaw as she stared off into the trees. The sun had lowered and the birds were beginning to quieten. A noticeable chill was creeping in and Abby edged closer to the fire, wondering if it was just the weather or Whit's demeanor as well.

"I've been in the wild a lot," Whit said, still staring off into the woods. "So I know a lot and I've seen a lot."

Abby studied her, waiting to see if she'd continue. She did not.

"Well, I guess we're lucky then. To have your know-how."

"Luck has nothing to do with it. Things are as they are."

Abby touched Whit's arm, feeling the urge to comfort her. She seemed so far gone, so sad. But she moved away from her touch and found another stick to play with the fire.

"I'm sorry, Whit."

"For what?"

"For whatever is making you so upset."

"I'm not upset."

"Right. Because there's no time."

Whit finally met her gaze. Her dark eyes flashed in the firelight. "Right."

Abby settled onto the ground and gave up. Whit was a gorgeous woman, one full of strength and mystery. But she was also seriously closed off. She obviously had walls that Abby knew from experience would be difficult, if not impossible, to tear down. Hell, she'd be lucky if she could even peek through at some point.

She toyed with some pine needles next to her, wondering if she'd even dare to peek through. Whit obviously didn't want her to, and who knows what she'd see. Maybe she'd better back off. At least for the time being.

She continued to pluck the pine needles, now tossing them into the flames. Whit, who was staring into those same flames, remained silent. And then, just as suddenly, she was gone, walking away into the dense woods.

CHAPTER FOUR

Whit walked into the trees with no set destination in mind. She just knew she needed space, someplace away from all of Abby's lingering questions. The ground was hard on her feet, stabbing and pricking with its rough pine needles and dead bark, but she didn't care. She'd done nothing but run barefoot as a child, so the discomfort wasn't anything new. As for being nearly nude, that *was* new and the growing chill was definitely affecting her, but she needed the peace and quiet more than she needed the comfort of warmth.

Why couldn't Abby just let it go? Why did she have to ask so many questions and demand answers? It wasn't any business of hers what all she'd been through, or why it was that she was calm in the face of chaos. She knew why she was like that, a therapist many years ago had clued her in, but Abby didn't need to know. They were virtual strangers, after all.

She examined her hands in the oncoming twilight. They were shaking. Not from the cold, but from the questioning and the reality those questions made her face. She could see her father, see his wide, glossy eyes and hear his voice telling her everything was going to be fine.

Only it wasn't.

Nothing was ever fine after that and nothing was fine now.

Junior was dead, damn near cut in two, and no doubt burned beyond recognition. She and Abby were stranded, pretty much lost in the woods with freezing temperatures on the way. Things were looking grim. Grim indeed. She needed to get control of herself and stop the damn shaking.

She clenched her fists and then leaned against a thick tree to garner breath. She could handle this. She was handling it. But Abby would have to leave her alone. Otherwise, the past would come filtering back, one small image, one small sound, one small scent at a time, and she wouldn't be able to hide what it did to her. Abby would see. And that absolutely could not happen.

She set her jaw, took one last, deep breath, and walked with a newfound determination back to the campsite. Abby was stoking the fire, the twilight now settling in around her, encasing her, causing her red hair to look like a wild flame against the orange of the fire.

God, she was beautiful.

She stopped tending to the fire and plucked her clothes off the log and began dressing. Whit approached, said nothing, but did the same. The clothes were mostly dry, but they still felt cold, so she cozied up to the fire as best she could and pulled on her liners, socks and boots. Abby, thankfully, didn't say anything. They both just sat and warmed themselves by the flames.

Whit got lost in oblivion as she stared into the fire, grateful to not be thinking about anything. Eventually, she glanced upward, trying to discern any rain clouds, but she saw only hundreds of emerging stars and the faint glowing of the northern lights.

"Look," she said.

Abby followed her line of sight. She stared in obvious awe. "They're so beautiful, aren't they?"

"They are."

"I could never get tired of seeing a sky like that."

Whit felt the same. The Alaskan sky was home to her. As was the wilderness and her tiny little town of Cozy. She wished she could make Abby understand that. She didn't want any more tourism than they already had. Especially in Cozy. It was a quiet little community full of Alaskans, not teeming with people from the Lower Forty-eight. She wanted to keep it that way.

Sure, tourists paid her bills. She flew them to whatever destination they wanted, but that was away from Cozy. Far away.

"You know," she tried to explain. "Cozy is a very special place to me."

Abby turned to look at her.

"And I hope—"

A crunching noise came from the nearby brush. They froze, eyes trained into the dim forest. Whit reached for her knife and slowly stood. The hairs on the back of her neck were raised in alarm.

"What was that?" Abby whispered. Whit could hear the fear in her strained voice.

"I don't know." She walked toward the noise, but Abby called out for her.

"Don't leave me here alone!"

Whit turned back to her. "Stay there." She held out her knife. "I'm just going to go check. It'll be fine."

The words nearly caught in her throat. Her father's last words. And here she was using them on someone, trying to comfort them when she felt anything but comfort herself. She took a few more steps and then widened her stance and spread her arms. She began to shout, thinking that if it were a bear, she needed to make as much noise as possible.

"Hey! Get out of here! Get on out of here!" She took a few more hurried steps and then froze again as she heard more noise come from the brush. She relaxed however, when she realized the noise was growing faint, moving away from her. She lowered her arms, gave one last long hard look into the darkness, and then returned to Abby, who stood ramrod still and as pale as a ghost.

"What was it?" she asked.

"I don't know. But whatever it was, it's gone."

Abby embraced herself. "What if it comes back?"

"It won't. I scared it off, so it's unlikely to return."

"I wish I was as sure as you are."

Whit thought about telling her she wasn't sure at all, but decided to continue to try to put her at ease. It would do no good to frighten her and they both needed some serious rest. Sitting up all night worried about creatures in the dark would only exhaust them, and they needed their strength for tomorrow if they were going to try to start walking out of there.

"We should turn in," Whit said, rubbing some dirt in the bottom of the pot to clean it. She then rinsed it with a little water and put it and the remaining cans of food back into the polyester bag and hung it from a tree about thirty yards away. Then she added more wood onto the fire, quickly tossed more hot rocks into the shelter, and crawled inside. She dug around in the pine needles and scooted the old, now cooled rocks out of the way, then lined up the hot rocks on the ground. Next, she covered them with the bed of pine needles and made herself comfortable, looking forward to the warmth the rocks would hopefully provide.

She tucked her hands behind her head and called out for Abby. "You coming?"

Abby knelt and looked into the structure. She seemed unsure.

Whit patted the pine needles. "Come on. It's nice and warm in here with the fire and the hot stones."

Abby crawled inside and eased down next to Whit. Her breathing was short and quick and she couldn't seem to find a comfortable spot.

"You okay?" Whit asked.

"I'm fine."

"It's not the Hilton, but it's as good as we're going to get for tonight."

"It's—good."

"I'll wake and check on the fire throughout the night so we'll keep warm."

"You've done an amazing job with building the fire wall and thinking to put those hot rocks beneath the bedding. I'm sure we'll stay warm."

Whit glanced over at her and watched as the firelight played with her profile.

"Thanks," Whit said. She rarely heard such compliments.

"Thank *you*," Abby said. "For taking such good care of us." She closed her eyes and folded her hands on her chest. "I'm still scared, mind you. But I am appreciative for all you've done."

Whit chuckled. "The wilderness takes some getting used to."

"What do you think was out there?" She opened an eye as if checking to make sure that whatever it was hadn't returned and was lurking at the entrance to the shelter.

"It was probably a curious animal. Maybe a fox or something like that." She was still trying not to scare her. But Abby didn't seem to buy it.

"It's sounded big. Much bigger than a fox."

"Sounds carry at night."

Abby grew quiet. "I'm going to trust you, Whit, and try to sleep. But if I hear so much as a peep again, I'm probably going to run like hell."

"Don't worry," Whit said softly. "I'll keep an eye on the fire and the fire will keep the animals at bay."

"Swear?" She turned to look at her.

"Swear."

"Okay then. Good night."

"Night."

Abby closed her eyes once again and Whit stared out at the fire, lost in thought. The shelter was warm and they were covered from the elements, leaving them to sleep peacefully.

She awoke three times in the night, unsure as to what woke her, but glad nevertheless, so she could add more logs to the fire, which thankfully, did keep them relatively warm.

But when she awoke the next morning, Abby was clinging to her as a hard chill had settled, dispersing into the shelter. Whit was very still, listening to Abby breathing, delighting in her tight embrace. She knew she'd only clung to her because she was cold, but it felt nice nonetheless. She lay like that for as long as she could before she eased out from beneath Abby's arms and exited the shelter. The first thing she did was restart the fire, which had apparently died sometime very early in the morning. Then she piled on more wood and stood with her hands extended, trying to warm up.

When she glanced down to kick some more pine needles into the fire, she saw what looked like footprints. Alarmed, she knelt and examined them further. They were too large to be hers or Abby's.

Am I really seeing this?

She couldn't make out the tread. Just the impression in the pine needles.

Was somebody here?

If so, who?

And why didn't they wake them and try to talk to them?

A chill crept down her back as she considered the answers. Either the person wasn't friendly, or it wasn't a person at all. Neither possibility left her feeling secure.

She swallowed hard and stared off into the woods where the footprints led. Whatever it was was long gone with the light of day. But just thinking about someone or something snooping around their campsite while they were sleeping unnerved her. Seriously unnerved her. Was that the noise they'd heard in the brush last night? Was whatever it was watching them?

She rubbed her arms and tried to think. They needed to get out of there and put some considerable distance between them and this campsite today and maybe whatever it was would remain behind. That was her only hope at the moment.

She hurried to where she'd hung the nylon bag and stared in disbelief up into the tree. The bag was gone. She quickly searched the ground and the surrounding brush and found the pot, but there was no sign of the pilot bread or the cans of Spam, coffee, or mug. Just more impressions of what looked like footprints in the pine needles.

Something was seriously wrong. She knew for sure now and it couldn't be ignored.

She walked back to camp where Abby was just emerging from the shelter. She took one look at Whit and her face clouded with worry.

"What's wrong?"

"We need to go."

"Whit, what's wrong?"

Whit thought about playing the whole thing down, but she could tell Abby wasn't going to believe her. Besides, how would she explain the missing bag?

"The bag is gone," Whit said, kneeling to toss dirt onto the flames.

"What do you mean, gone? As in, someone took it?"

"Seems so."

"There's someone else here?"

"It's the only explanation."

"Well, it could be a bear or a—"

"It wasn't a bear." She shook her head. "The prints don't match."

A look of sheer terror came over Abby's face. "Prints?"

Whit stepped away from the fire and showed Abby the tracks. Her look of terror intensified.

"Whit, those are big."

"I know."

Abby glanced around as if frightened about what would emerge from the woods.

"We should go. The sooner the better."

"I don't understand. Why wouldn't they help us? Why wouldn't they—?"

"I don't know. Which is why we need to go."

Abby nodded and Whit finished extinguishing the fire. Then she found a sturdy stick and handed it to her. "To help you walk." Abby took the stick, and after they gathered the water bottle and the utility knife, they started off, walking through the woods, headed north, with Abby turning to look behind them every few steps.

Whit didn't protest, or tell her not to worry. She couldn't do that. Because the truth was, they both needed to be worried and they both needed to keep their guard up. It was the only way they would survive.

CHAPTER FIVE

Abby walked as best she could with her sore knee. Thankfully, it wasn't as painful as it had been the day before, but she was still bruised and scraped up in other places from the accident, so moving in general was not fun. But at the moment, she'd move even if her leg was broken. Anything to get away from whoever it was that had come into their campsite and stolen their food. She kept checking behind her, convinced that whoever it was, was following them. She imagined him to be lurking like a blood-crazed killer, drooling and maniacal as he grew closer. She saw no one, but it did little to ease her qualms.

She followed Whit for what felt like hours, with Whit keeping at a pace she could handle, which was nice of her. After all, Whit could just up and leave her behind if she so chose. Abby was grateful that she was still remaining by her side, trying to help them both escape this unexpected predicament. Abby forced herself onward, determined to keep up her end of the deal by staying right behind her and not complaining about the pain or the fatigue she felt. They both had other things on their mind. Way more important things. Like how they were going to survive and get away from whatever creep might be after them.

By the time Whit eventually slowed, and Abby heard the rush of water, her lips were dry and her mouth parched. Her knee throbbed and she felt like collapsing. She nearly did onto a large rock next to the amber-colored creek. "What time is it?" she asked as she massaged her knee.

Whit didn't even have to glance at her watch. "Close to three."

"We *have* been walking for hours," Abby said, mostly to herself. She went limp on the rock, thinking how much a hard, cold surface had never felt so good on her backside. And her feet. God, her feet. She swore she had blisters on her toes and heels. Big, full blisters that were torn open and raw. She unlaced her hiking boots and gently pulled them off expecting to see bloody socks. But her socks were still white, edged with dirt around the ankles. She peeled them off. She definitely had some blisters. Big, red, full ones. And they were so sore. She winced as she touched them.

"Soak them in the water for a while," Whit said nonchalantly. "The cold will help the pain and swelling."

"Seriously?"

"Yep."

Abby walked carefully to another rock, this one close to the water. She sat and submerged her feet in the water, crying out at the shock of the cold. Whit laughed.

"It's freezing," Abby said, lifting her feet out to hover above the creek surface.

"That's why it'll help."

Abby lowered her feet back into the water and clenched her teeth. "This better work."

"Pretty soon you'll be so numb you won't feel a thing."

Whit walked upstream from Abby and filled the filtering water bottle. It took a while before the filtering was complete, but once it was, she brought the bottle to Abby and encouraged her to drink. Still parched, Abby clenched the container and began to gulp, her thirst overwhelming. The cold water flooded her mouth and throat, and a bit dribbled down her chin. Whit gently tugged on the bottle.

"Not so much," she said. "Just sip it. You don't want to get sick."

Abby wanted to groan in protest, but instead she listened and sipped the cold water slowly before setting it down next to her. "So, what now?" she asked.

Please tell me we're stopping for the day.

"We set up camp," Whit said glancing around. "We've got water to drink here and we can fish."

"We're going to fish? With what?"

Whit only smiled. "First we build a fire, then the shelter, and then we fish."

Abby removed her feet from the water, having gone pleasantly numb. She took off her jacket and used it to pat them dry and then pulled her socks on before stepping back into her boots. After lacing them up, she stood and followed Whit, who was gathering firewood. Abby helped, bringing a few armloads to the pile Whit was making not far from the water.

She didn't realize how tender her hands were until she handled the dead tree limbs and rough bark. When she had to break the wood, like Whit was doing using her foot and hands, Abby winced as the bark scraped her palms.

"You should wear gloves," Whit said, noticing. "Do you have some?"

"They were in the car."

Whit moved on and kept working, now making another stack close to a set of trees, presumably for the shelter. Abby paused and examined her hands. They were cold and red, and now sore from work. But she refused to complain and instead, held her hand out to Whit expectantly.

"You hurt?" Whit tried to look at her palm, but Abby retreated.

"I want the fire starter kit," Abby said.

"Oh?"

"Sure. Why not?"

"Okay. But don't use the fire plugs. The dry brush should be good enough to get it started."

Abby took the kit and arranged wood and brush just as she'd seen Whit do the day before. She struck the ferro rod. Sparks flew and several embedded in the ball of brush. She quickly leaned in and blew lightly, encouraging a flame. At last, one came to life and she placed it beneath the pile of wood and nestled it into another, larger collection of dried brush and weeds where it caught with a whoosh and began to grow. Proud of herself, Abby angled back on her haunches and watched the flames, loving the popping and snapping sounds. She turned to search for Whit, to show her what she'd done, and she found her standing nearby watching her intently.

"I did it," Abby said, hoping it was sufficient. She never had had much confidence in her abilities, especially when it came to doing new things. She was always worried her efforts weren't good enough.

"Yes, you did." Whit continued to kick at a fallen tree, trying to break up the trunk. Abby waited to see if she'd say more. She didn't. Abby stoked the fire, concerned that maybe Whit wasn't happy with the job she'd done. If she was she would've said so, right?

Abby stood and added more wood to the flames. Whit had crossed to the shelter pile with the dead tree trunk in tow. Abby wrang her hands, unsure what to say. Should she ask if the fire was good enough? Or just move on? But what could she do next to help? Fish? Yes, maybe she could try to fish. If so, with what? What was Whit planning on using? Her bare hands?

Whit caught her staring and stopped what she was doing. "You need something?"

Abby stammered. "Just uh—wondered if—I should keep adding wood to the fire or—"

Whit's gaze flicked to the fire. "It's going pretty good right now."

It's good? I did well, then?

"Should I try and fish? While you work on the shelter?"

Whit slid her buck knife from her ankle sleeve and began hacking at the small offshoots of branches on the log. "Can't. I haven't made the spear yet."

"Oh. Right." She remained where she was, still feeling useless.

"If you want, you can gather some pine needles for the bedding."

Abby perked up. "Okay."

"And after that, I saw some mushrooms over in that thicket. They're safe to eat if you want to collect them."

"Sure." She smiled, but Whit didn't see her. She was already focused back on the log. Abby bent to gather big bunches of pine

STRANDED

needles. She brought them to Whit, who moved some of the wood so she could put them in the right place. She once again felt good in helping, but as she smiled, she recalled sleeping in the shelter Whit had made the night before. It had been warm and cozy until early morning, and at the time she'd felt relatively safe. But now she knew differently. Now she knew they hadn't been safe at all and she felt an anxiousness rise in her gut as she thought about nightfall and how they'd be exposed once again.

"Do you think we lost whoever it was?" she asked. Whit had no way of knowing for sure, but Abby was seeking comfort in any way she could find it. She prayed Whit would play along, even if it wasn't really what she thought.

Whit paused, glanced at her, and then set the broken trunk against the tree next to Abby. "I'm sure they lost interest."

Abby could've hugged her.

"We walked for hours, so I seriously doubt they followed us."

"We would've noticed," Abby said, looking back over her shoulder just for good measure.

But Whit didn't respond. Her face merely clouded as if she didn't agree with Abby's statement. The stomach churning returned and Abby left the questions alone. She didn't want to know what Whit was thinking now. She didn't think she could handle it. She was worried enough.

Whit seemed to sense her concern. "How about those mushrooms?"

"Sure. I'm on it."

"You want to pull the whole thing from the ground, but then cut away the bottom of the stem and roots." She handed over the utility knife. "Take the pot to carry them in."

But as Abby walked away, she wondered how many potfuls she should bring back. She should've asked. Dang, why hadn't she asked? She walked into the patch of thick green and heavily shaded trees and saw the mushrooms growing in the mossy earth. They were white-bodied with tan tops. Beautiful. And there appeared to be enough for a couple of potfuls. She decided she'd take one potful and tell Whit there was more if she wanted them.

She knelt and maneuvered the mushrooms from the ground. She made a small pile and when she felt she had enough, she sat and began cutting off the stems. It was quiet, peaceful work and she hummed as she cut. Soon, she had the pot full and she returned to camp to find Whit halfway finished with the shelter.

"Would you like me to help with that?" Abby asked, setting the pot of mushrooms near the fire.

"Actually," Whit said. "It would be really great if you sliced up those mushrooms and sautéed them in a little water. I could use something to eat."

Abby thought the idea sounded good, as her stomach was growling as well. So instead of being offended at being asked to cook, she simply nodded and cleaned the mushrooms and then sliced them up for the pot.

She'd never really tasted mushrooms before because the texture had always weirded her out. She wondered if she'd like these, knowing she'd definitely try them. Her protesting stomach wouldn't allow her to turn her nose up this time.

Whit finished the shelter and sat near her on a fallen log. She had a heavy, long sapling in her hand, and she began sharpening the end.

Abby watched her when she could, quite curious. She stirred the mushrooms in the pot as she watched, and the smell was starting to add to her hunger.

"Those about done?" Whit asked.

"I think so."

"Good." She propped the stick up on the log and came over to the pot. "May I?" She took the utility knife from Abby and stabbed a hunk of mushroom. After she blew on it, she popped it in her mouth and chewed. "Oh, man, that's good."

Abby couldn't help but grin. "Really?"

"Mm. You've got to try one." She plucked another one for her and held her palm under it as she offered the bite to Abby. "Careful, it's hot."

Abby blew on the piece of mushroom and briefly, oh so briefly, got lost in Whit's dark eyes. They were so much like the color of the beautiful flowing creek, she thought she could look into them forever.

"I think it's cool now," Whit said.

Abby blinked. "Oh." She opened her mouth and took the bite. She chewed. It was pretty good. It had a nutty flavor and the texture was a little tough, but not too bad. She would definitely eat them.

"What did I tell you?" Whit said, now smiling.

"You were right."

Whit returned the utility knife to her and fished out more mushroom with her own knife. Then they sat together and ate, staring at the hypnotizing fire and the beautiful whiskey-colored creek beyond that.

The moment was so nice, Abby almost forgot about the creep who'd snuck into their camp the night before. Almost.

CHAPTER SIX

It wasn't long after they'd finished eating close to half of the mushrooms, that Whit almost had the spear finished. She'd already sharpened the edge of the sapling, now she had to split it. She did that by inserting her knife at the sharpened tip and pressing down. Then she stuck a small stick, about the width of a pencil, down into the slit, forming a gap, and then sharpened both points.

She slid her knife back into its sheath and straightened to give the spear a once-over.

"It looks good," Abby said, smiling up at her.

"Let's hope it catches us some fish."

She started to walk away and leave Abby at camp, but then she thought better of it. "You want to come with?"

Abby's eyes widened. "You sure?"

"You bet."

She stood alongside her, brushed off her pants, and walked with her upstream. "Wait, you don't want me to come with you because you're worried about the creep, do you?"

Whit kept her gaze fixed ahead. "Of course not." That was exactly the reason she wanted her to come along, but she'd looked scared enough earlier. "It's bears I'm mainly worried about."

"Bears?" She sounded mortified.

Whit grinned. "Well, yeah, we need to be alert. But no, I was just teasing you."

"What should I do if I see a bear?"

"Don't worry, I should be with you to tell you what to do. And truthfully, bears usually disperse in August when the salmon aren't as concentrated."

She didn't sound comforted. "Have you ever had trouble with a bear?"

"I've seen a few. But no, never had any trouble."

That seemed to calm her woes a little and they walked in silence up the creek until the water turned darker and grew deeper.

"Over here." Whit waved her on, and they stood near some fallen logs that were partially submerged in the water. Whit put her finger to her lips to signal for quiet. Abby nodded and watched as Whit searched the water for fish. It took a while before they saw one, a large one, about a foot long, but Whit shook her head. It was too deep. She moved upstream a little more, to where it was more shallow, and made sure her shadow wasn't casting down on the water. Abby followed but stayed a couple of feet behind, seeming to sense that Whit needed to be alone in order not to scare the fish away.

Whit balanced carefully on her feet and waited. She searched the creek up and down, spotting a few fish that were too far away. Then, after a few more long minutes, a fish similar to the first one she'd seen emerged from the dark depths. She stabbed her spear into the water and pierced the fish. It wiggled furiously and she almost lost her balance and fell in. But she felt arms grab her from behind and hold her tight as she held the spear with both hands and yanked the fish from the water. She turned and dropped the spear on the rocks as the fish continued to flail.

"What kind is it?" Abby asked, releasing her.

"Rainbow trout."

Whit pulled the fish off the spear and picked up a rock to kill it. Abby turned away as Whit gave it one good whack and then returned to the creek. "You can look now." She angled her spear and got ready to strike again.

She heard Abby come closer once again. She wondered how she was going to eat the fish if she couldn't stand to watch it be hit with a rock. It was obvious she was sensitive. Whit didn't understand it, having grown up in Alaska where she'd hunted considerably for her dinner. But city folk were different. Hell, she'd seen the way she'd looked at the Spam yesterday. Whit had thought for sure she'd refuse to eat it. But she didn't. She'd eaten it and she hadn't complained. Come to think of it, she hadn't complained all day today and Whit knew her knee had been hurting. Kudos to her. Abby was putting most of the tourists she'd come to know to shame.

Whit saw another fish come close to the surface. This one a little bigger than the other. She made her move and stabbed the water. She missed.

"Damn it." She sidestepped and waited once more. It took another fifteen minutes, but finally another fish came slowly out of the depths. She surged at it, plunging her spear into the water. She hit the fish and it flailed wildly. This time she was ready and she pulled it up out of the water and onto shore right away, not wanting to risk losing it. She dropped the spear and, to her surprise, Abby handed her a rock.

Whit took it and finished off the fish. Then she cleaned and deboned both trout on a rock at the edge of the water. When she was finished, she tossed the rock in the creek and washed her hands. Then she spiked both fish on the spear and she and Abby returned to camp.

The fire was still burning though it needed tending to. Abby took charge and handled that while Whit got busy setting a flat rock over the flames. She placed the fillets on the surface of the rock and sat down as they began to sizzle. Abby joined her after she set the pot of the remaining mushrooms near the fire once again to warm them up.

"Did we get lucky?" she asked. "Catching those fish?"

"A little." Whit poked at the lean fillets with her knife. "Sometimes it takes longer. And, of course, sometimes you catch nothing at all. But these waters…" She stared off at the rushing creek. "I'm guessing we'll continue to be lucky."

"I hope so."

"Try not to worry about it."

"Ha. Right. Easier said than done."

Whit raised an eyebrow at her and Abby explained.

"I'm a little worried about tonight and the shelter. If he wanted to, the creep could get to us."

Whit chewed her bottom lip as she considered what to say. "If you think about it, anyone could get at you, regardless of what kind of shelter you're in. Even if we were in a cabin, for instance, the man could still get in. He could kick in the door, or break a window. If there's a will there's a way."

"Great, thanks. Now I'll never feel safe again." She picked at the mushrooms, her posture slack as if she were defeated.

Whit felt responsible and tried to soothe her. "Sorry, I just thought that knowing that might make you feel better about the shelter. I mean, he can't get to us without making noise. I'll even make a makeshift door if you like. It'll block some of the heat off the fire though."

Abby continued to play with the mushrooms. "Just do whatever you think is best. I'll be fine."

"I want you to feel safe."

"Yeah, well, I don't. Not out here anyway."

"I'll be right next to you and I have my buck knife." She held it up, showing off its dangerous curve and razor-like sharpness.

Abby looked at the knife, and then offered a resolute smile. "I'm glad you're with me," she said. "I'd be completely doomed on my own."

"Most people from the Lower Forty-eight would be. So don't beat yourself up about it."

"How is it you know so much? You said you spent a lot of time out in the wilderness?"

Whit debated how much to tell her. She didn't want to mention her father's murder, or get into the whole fiasco of the immediate aftermath and the trauma it had caused. She just wanted to sit there in peace and eat her fish by the fire and enjoy the rush of the creek.

"Growing up here, you spend a lot of time outdoors. Hunting, fishing, hiking. So I know my way around the wilds of Alaska."

"Thank God," Abby said, spearing a mushroom to take a bite. "Do you enjoy it? Spending time outdoors like this?"

"Well, not totally like this. I'd like to have a few more provisions and know my way to rescue, if you know what I mean. But yes, I suppose I do feel quite comfortable in the wilderness."

"Who taught you all this?" she asked.

Whit turned the fish. "My folks."

"Really? They must know a lot."

Whit didn't respond. She couldn't. Her throat had tightened.

Abby continued, seeming not to notice. "I read a lot about the indigenous people here and how they've survived for hundreds of years off the land. It's amazing."

"They're remarkable people."

"Did you know that many of them believe in a hairy man, or bushman, or what is known as Bigfoot?"

Whit looked up and tried to hide the shock on her face. She failed.

"What?" Abby asked. "Do you?"

Whit shrugged. "I suppose I believe in something. Living here all your life, it's hard not to with all the stories and legends and everything."

"Have you ever seen one?"

Whit laughed with nerves. "You ready to eat this fish?"

Abby perked up. "You know it."

Whit motioned her over and cut a portion off for her to fork at with the utility knife. "I could make you a better fork. Just fashion one out of a stick if you like."

Abby plucked herself a bite and blew. "That would be great."

Whit took her own bite. The trout was delicious. "Mm, wow is that good."

Abby chewed. "Even better than the mushrooms."

"I'd say we've got a pretty decent dinner here. What do you think?"

"Not bad. Not bad at all." Abby scrunched her face. "It sure beats the Spam."

Whit chuckled. "Yeah, fresh trout beats that hands down."

They ate in silence for a few minutes before Abby spoke. "So you've never seen a hairy man?"

Whit swallowed. Then took a few sips of water. "I call him the bushman. And I didn't say I've never seen him."

Abby's eyebrows shot up. "So, you have seen one?"

"I've seen something."

"How many times?"

Whit focused on her fish. "A few."

"Holy shit. Are you kidding me?"

"'Fraid not."

Abby went quiet and then her face fell and her eyes went wide. "You don't think that's what's after us, do you?"

Whit blew on another bite, remaining as calm as she could. Abby obviously had a flair for the dramatic and she didn't want to feed into it. It would only frighten her more. "First of all, I don't think anyone is after us. I think whoever it was has moved on."

"Yeah but—those prints. It could've been—it was hard to tell, but they were big!"

"Abby, let's not get carried away." Though she was absolutely right. One couldn't tell from the prints they'd seen exactly who or what had made them.

"Oh, my God. Just oh, my God. I've read that they stalk people and mess with their camps sometimes. I bet it's a hairy man." She stared off into the distance and rubbed her arms.

"Like I said, let's not get carried away. We don't know anything yet."

"Yet?"

"You know what I mean. Let's just eat our supper and relax."

But Abby continued to look around as if searching deep into the wilderness for the bushman and Whit realized there was now very little she could do to comfort her. It was probably going to be a long, restless night.

CHAPTER SEVEN

The sunlight faded a couple of hours after dinner, and Abby was chilled and not just from the cold. Ever since she'd brought up the hairy man, she'd felt uncomfortable and afraid. She'd kept her gaze trained on the surrounding forest, but she'd been unable to see anything suspect. Yet every noise she heard, she turned to look, convinced the hairy man was right there, watching and waiting.

She rubbed her arms again and tossed more wood onto the fire. Whit was busy making a door for the shelter. It was a sweet gesture and Abby knew she was doing it just for her, to try to help her feel more secure. Abby knew it was a lost cause. She doubted she'd be able to sleep at all even though her eyes were growing tired and heavy and her mind was slowing down some.

Whit seemed to notice. "Why don't you turn in? I'll watch the camp for a while so you can sleep in peace."

It was a kind offer, but Abby couldn't seem to tear her eyes off her sitting across the fire, shaping wood with her knife. Her dark hair was glinting in the fire and her equally dark eyes flashing with the dance of the flames. She liked to chew her lower lip when she was pondering something or working with her hands. Abby found it somewhat sexy and she began to wonder about Whit and her sexuality. Was she a lesbian? Did she have someone? She didn't speak like she did, though she also seemed to be a rather private person.

Abby considered not asking, thinking it might be rude and put her off, but then she thought of the hairy man again and decided to ask anyway. Anything to get her mind off the mysterious creep, man or beast, that may or may not be following them

"Do you have anyone, Whit? Someone waiting for you at home?"

Whit glanced up at her, but set her knife down to fashion some branches on the skeleton of the door. "Why do you ask?"

"Just curious, I suppose."

Whit nibbled on her lip again. She didn't respond for a few long seconds. So long that Abby thought she was going to resist answering altogether.

"I do," she finally said.

Abby felt heat rise to her face and her stomach dropped as if she had just crested the high hill of a roller coaster. She did? She does? Abby forced down a swallow and then forced a smile before she poked at the fire with a nearby stick.

"Tell me about them."

"I'd rather not."

"Oh?"

Whit stood. "Door's done." She held it up. She'd fashioned it out of thick sticks, bound together in a crosshatch pattern with some sort of bendable reed she'd found near the water. Then she'd attached some heavily leaved branches to fill the gaps. "We'll crawl inside and pull this in behind us to cover the entrance. As for the back of the shelter, I already filled in with more branches, so you don't have to worry about that either."

"It's amazing," Abby whispered. "Thank you."

Whit leaned the door against the shelter and wiped her hands on her pants. "You ready to turn in? You look beat."

"I am," Abby said, suddenly feeling like she hit a wall. She massaged her face and pushed herself to a stand. She was too tired to try to pry information out of Whit. And she was too tired to think too hard about the hairy man. Right now, she just needed to sleep, and thankfully, her brain was showing her some mercy.

She gave Whit a grateful smile as she bypassed her to crawl into the shelter.

"Night," she said, as she knelt.

"Good night."

Abby eased onto the bed of pine needles and made herself comfortable. The shelter was warm and cozy and smelled of everything wilderness. The pine needles were pokey, but they also provided a nice cushion from the cold ground. She curled up on her side and closed her eyes.

"Would you like the door on?" Whit asked.

She opened her eyes and saw Whit peeking in the door. "Not if you're going to stay up for a while."

Whit walked away to sit close to the fire. Abby once again allowed her eyes to fall shut and the world to fade to black. And before she knew it, she was fast asleep.

When she woke sometime later, it was dark. So dark she once again had to think hard to remember where she was. She reached out and felt something. Someone. Her breath caught in her throat before she realized it was Whit. She exhaled and tried to slow her heart rate, but then she heard something nearby. A snap. Then another. As if someone were outside walking and stepping on twigs.

Panicked, she shook Whit and whispered. "Whit, Whit, wake up!"

"Wha?" Whit turned over and Abby squeezed her shoulder.

"I hear something. Something outside. Like walking around."

They sat up and listened. Another snap, this one farther away. "See!"

Whit scooted toward the door.

"Wait! What are you doing?" Abby clenched her forearm.

"I'm going to go see. Now let me go." She pulled her arm free, pushed the door out with her foot and allowed some of the dwindling firelight to seep inside the shelter. Abby watched as she retrieved her knife and crawled out, leaving Abby behind. Once again panicked, this time by Whit's absence, Abby hurried out after her and stood outside near the dying fire. Whit was already gone, having disappeared into the darkness. Abby was alone and terrified. Absolutely scared stiff. She couldn't move. She just stood and waited, ears piqued.

What she heard only frightened her more. Rustling and snapping and cracking. Someone or something crashing through the woods. She knew one of them had to be Whit, but the other…she tried not to think about it. The sounds grew distant, until eventually, there were none.

She grabbed a stick, the biggest one she could find, and sank down onto the nearby fallen log that Whit favored. She dropped her head into her hand and trembled, trying not to cry. What if Whit didn't come back? What if the creep, whatever it was, got her? Would he then come back for her too?

This was a nightmare. *I'm in a nightmare.*

She looked up at the star-spattered sky. *Why did I come here?* She knew the statistics about all the people that went missing in Alaska every year. It wasn't comforting and now she understood exactly how easily it could happen. She could disappear in the giant arms of the hairy man and no one would ever know what happened to her. It would be another Alaskan mystery.

Tears fell down her face. She was doomed. Running would be useless. It was dark and she didn't know which way to go. Besides, her knee was hurt and if they were really being hunted, whoever or whatever it was would eventually find her.

I'm going to die.

She didn't bother wiping her tears, but rather let them fall. She thought about adding more wood to the fire, to at least warm herself, but she was still too scared to move. A large fire would draw more attention to her, making her easily seen from within the woods.

She sniffled and tried to stifle her cries as she thought of Whit and what was happening to her. She hadn't even heard her scream. The creep probably attacked stealthfully, taking her out before she could even mutter a word.

Movement came from the blackness of the trees. Rustling. Snapping. Cracking. Her heart thudded and then rose to lodge in her throat like a heavy, cold stone. She sat erect, staring intently, waiting for the creep to emerge. The crashing grew closer. She thought she might wet herself. She clenched her eyes and prayed.

"Please, God, make my death quick."

CHAPTER EIGHT

Whit neared the edge of the tree line and stumbled over what felt like a root. She fought for balance, careful to keep her knife outstretched and away from her body. She managed to fall against the rough bark of a tree where she stilled for a moment, to regain her breath and bearings, thinking how lucky she was she didn't cut herself with her blade. Running off half-crazed into the night with a sharp knife in her hand probably hadn't been the wisest of moves, but then again she'd been frightened, and worse, Abby had been frightened. Whit realized then that she'd do anything to protect her, even chase a madman or a wild creature off in the dark, with little regard to her own safety.

She listened keenly for any more sounds of whatever had been sneaking around their camp. She heard nothing, only silence, so she knelt and sheathed the blade and then slowly crept back toward camp and the trickling of the creek. Whatever she'd been pursuing had retreated quickly, too quickly for her on her blind trek after it, so she'd given up and made her way back, following the path of crushed brush she'd crashed through. The skin on her hands stung from scratches and her palms were sore from all the woodworking she'd done with dry bark. But other than that, her belly was full and she had the fire and a shelter to keep her warm at night, so she couldn't complain. Now if only they could find their way to help.

She spotted an orange flicker ahead and emerged from the woods. It took a moment for her eyes to adjust, but when they did, she saw Abby sitting ramrod straight next to the dwindling fire, a look of complete terror and anguish on her face.

She immediately stood when she saw Whit. "Oh, thank God!" She hurried to her, limping along, and slammed into Whit with a fierce embrace. "I was so worried. So scared."

Whit froze, her arms at her side, stunned at the sudden show of affection. Abby drew away and held her face. "Are you okay? Did he hurt you?"

"Who?" Whit gently gripped Abby's hands and lowered them. The feel of her skin on her own was too much, and she had to remain in control. She couldn't allow her body to speak for her. She needed her mind leading the way right now, not her involuntary reactions to a beautiful stranger.

"The creep," Abby said. "Whoever was here."

Whit released her incredibly soft hands and sidestepped her to walk back to the fire. Abby followed.

"I'm not sure what it was," Whit said, choosing a stick to stoke the fire. "It could've been anything." She spoke with conviction, but a part of her wondered if she was right. While she hadn't seen what she'd been chasing, it did sound rather big and powerful the way it clawed through the brush.

"You mean it wasn't the creep?" Abby stood near her, face ashen, eyes wide. She was twisting her fingers like a nervous schoolgirl awaiting punishment.

"Probably not." What was the use in scaring her? She tossed more wood onto the flames and sank down onto the log.

Abby seemed to melt with relief and she sat next to her. "That's the best thing I've heard all day."

Whit savored the heat and examined her hands in the firelight. She thought about the emergency bag of Junior's and wondered why it didn't have a light source in it. Then she remembered she had her phone. She felt for it in her back pocket and slid it out. She knew she had no service, that was a given, but she'd totally forgotten about the flashlight feature. She powered it on and turned on the light. "Well, what do you know."

"I wish I had mine," Abby said. "But it fell in the car just before the crash."

"This won't last long with my low battery, but it'll be nice to have if we need it again sometime soon."

Abby rubbed her palms on her jeans as if she were anxious. "Can I maybe use it now? I need to pee."

Whit passed her the phone and waited to see if she'd ask her to go with her. She had the evening before, too afraid to go on her own. Whit had stood watch with her back to her, giving her some privacy at least.

But Abby didn't ask this time. She just walked away slowly, shining the light ahead of her into the tree line where she promptly disappeared. A few short minutes later, she reappeared, flashlight off and returned the phone to Whit.

"Thanks."

Whit tucked the phone back into her pocket.

Abby headed for the shelter. "I'm going back to bed."

"I'll stay up for a bit. See to the fire."

Abby crawled into the small lodging and settled in. Whit stared after her, lost in the pressing heat of the flames. She was still too wound up from her excursion to turn in. She had too much to consider, too many decisions to make. The first being whether or not they stayed there at the site another day. They could use the rest, and some more fish. She could build a makeshift smoker and smoke whatever extra they caught and take it with them on their continued journey. That all sounded well and good, but what about the "creep" as Abby called him? Man or beast, if that was what had been snooping around tonight, then they should definitely move on. But then again, they hadn't shaken him today, so who was to say they'd shake him if they left again?

She kicked a burning log. It broke into chunks of glowing embers and created more heat. She closed her eyes as it massaged her face. They were better off staying another day. Chances were, she couldn't get them to help any sooner if they left tomorrow and they really needed a food source for their trek out. Decision made, she opened her eyes and moved to settle down across the fire. She hugged her knees to her chest and looked up at the stars and the neon glow of the northern lights. Any other time she'd be reveling at the beautiful night, thinking how lucky she was to live in such a magical place. But tonight, it was difficult to do. She had responsibilities to think about. Namely, the woman sleeping in the shelter behind her. And also, the woman she had waiting for her at home.

❖

Whit awoke some time later and blinked against the pale light of dawn. She was curled on her side, next to the fire, which was nearly burned out. Slim tendrils of smoke snaked their way into the cold morning air as she rose and brushed herself off. The woods were quiet, save for a bird or two just beginning to make their morning calls. She glanced back at the shelter, saw Abby still fast asleep, huddled against the chill of the dawn, and plucked more wood to toss onto the fire. She poked at the remaining embers until a flame caught the new wood and began to feed. Then she settled back down onto the log and rubbed her eyes.

From the look of the camp, it didn't seem that anything was missing or out of place. The pot remained where she'd left it, and she didn't see any footprints nearby. She sighed, thankful for small favors. Maybe last night's visitor had been just a curious animal.

Movement came from the shelter and Abby crawled out, her hair a tangle of pine needles. "Morning," she croaked, palming her cheek. She stretched like an awakening feline, all yawns and nimble grace. Whit couldn't help but stare, moved by her beauty but more amused by her morning appearance and demeanor.

"Morning. How did you sleep?"

"Hard." She toyed with the pine needles in her locks and grimaced as she tried to maneuver them out. Then, suddenly, she turned and limped away, presumably to go relieve herself. Whit decided to do the same and squatted behind a bush across from the camp. When she finished, she returned to the fire and retrieved her spear. It was time to catch some breakfast if she could.

She waited a moment for Abby to return. "I'm going to fish."

"Do you want me to come?"

"It's up to you."

"I thought I'd go get some more mushrooms."

Whit nodded. "That sounds great. We can eat those if I come back empty-handed."

Abby seemed pleased as she grabbed the pot and headed off toward the mossy thatch where the mushrooms grew. Whit walked to the creek, carefully climbing amongst the river rocks to her fishing spot. The water rushed along in the early morning light, its shimmering silver covered in wisps of cottony fog, smelling like minerals and cold copper. She stood positioned to strike and waited for a fish to swim slowly into view. It didn't take long and she was able to spear one right away. The trout wasn't as large as the two she'd caught yesterday, but it would do. She quickly removed it from her stick and readied herself for another. She had another one within fifteen minutes and proudly carried her catch back to camp after she cleaned them. Abby was sitting at the fire, slicing up mushrooms.

"Fish for breakfast," Whit said with a smile.

Abby beamed.

Whit settled down across from her on the log and arranged the slab of rock over the flames. "I've been thinking," she said as she carefully placed the fillets on the flat surface.

"Yeah?" Abby looked at her quizzically.

"I think we should stay here another day."

Abby's brow knitted with obvious concern.

"Hear me out," Whit said. "If we stay, I can catch more fish. A lot more. And I can smoke them. That way we have guaranteed food for our journey."

"But what about the creep?" She was still anxious about their visitor. Whit tried to console her.

"I don't think that was him last night. Nothing was amiss at camp this morning and we weren't disturbed again."

Abby seemed to think for a moment, stirring the bits of mushrooms in the pot with her small knife.

"Besides," Whit continued. "You need to rest your knee and we'd both benefit from not having to walk for miles today."

"There's no guarantee of food if we continue today?"

"No."

"Guess we're staying then." She offered a smile, but it didn't reach her eyes. Her trepidation was still evident, but she was trying to be a good sport. Whit was appreciative.

"It'll pay off, you'll see." Whit offered her a smile of her own, hoping to ease her qualms. But Abby glanced away and studied the pot of mushrooms instead.

The fish hissed and sizzled on the rock face and Whit watched it closely, waiting patiently to flip it. Abby began cooking the mushrooms, and soon the camp was filled with the smoky scent of cooking food. Whit's stomach grumbled in anticipation and the rising sun cast a golden glow upon them. Once again, she was moved by the beauty around her.

"It's so damn beautiful here," she said as she turned to look at the crystals of sunlight dancing along the whiskey color of the creek.

"You sound like a tourist," Abby said playfully. "Completely in awe of Alaska."

"I am in awe." Whit turned back around and poked at the fish. "It's been a while since I've been out in nature like this. Guess I'd forgotten just how wonderful it is."

"Why is that?" Abby asked. "You obviously enjoy being outdoors, so why haven't you been out in a while?"

Whit felt her face crumble and she flipped the fish with her blade. She could feel Abby watching her intently and she knew she had to give an answer.

"I've been busy and I guess time just got away from me." She *had* been busy. She just didn't want to go into detail as to why.

Abby didn't seem to believe her at first, still watching her closely with an ambiguous look on her face. But eventually, she refocused on the pot and removed it from the fire. Whit tried to breathe easy, but the topic had brought up the other woman in her life once again. Worry clenched her gut, along with the guilt of being away. She wished she could at least call. To let her know she was trying her best to get back to her. But she couldn't and her heart ached, wondering what she must be thinking.

"We'll get home," Whit said softly to herself, now more determined than ever. "No matter who or what gets in our way."

CHAPTER NINE

Hours later, Whit had finished building what she called a smoker. It was an ingenious structure, framed by a tripod of timber and filled in with a vast collection of river rock and clay from the shore of the creek. The finished product looked like a tall cone and at the very top, the rock and clay were substituted with heavy branches to form the peak.

Whit straightened from adding some finishing touches. "That ought to do it," she said, wiping her hands. "Now it's time to catch some more fish."

"How long will it take to smoke them?" Abby asked, truly bewildered by all that Whit could do. She was extremely knowledgeable and Abby was once again so thankful that she was with her on this junket.

"All day and night."

"That long?"

"Smoking is a lengthy process." She stabbed the dull end of the spear into the ground as if she were a farmer proudly holding a corn rake. "Coming with?"

Abby ambled to a stand and hobbled over to her. "Wouldn't miss it."

"How are your feet?" Whit asked.

"They're still sore, but the blisters are a little better."

"Maybe you should soak them while I fish."

They walked across the river rock to the creek and Abby sat on the same stone she had before and untied her boots and carefully peeled off her socks. What she wouldn't give for a shower. She felt dirty and crusty and could only imagine how brown the water would be swirling down the shower drain.

"Guess this creek water will have to do." She bent and gathered the crisp water in her hands to splash upon her face. She gasped at the cold and scrubbed her skin as best she could, then rinsed again. Whit called to her from down the shoreline.

"Hey, don't scare the fish away."

Abby waved, feeling sheepish. "Sorry." She eased back onto the rock, gently placed her feet in the water, and dried her face with the inside collar of her sweater. She sat like that for a good while, watching as Whit pulled three fish from the creek. Whit had made a little side pool with the rocks to keep the caught fish in as she continued to try to catch more. Abby wondered how many she'd try to catch. She also wondered how many days Whit thought it would take before they reached some sort of help.

How far can I go on this knee? Abby stretched and bent her leg. It was less sore, but it stiffened up a lot when she sat. Hopefully, it wouldn't be so bad when they left again. She glanced back over at Whit and studied her as she stood braced to attack with her spear. She resembled a warrior, all astute and strong, ready for battle. Her black mane glistened in the sun and looked incredibly striking against the burnt orange of her thick, cable-knit sweater. Her snug-fitting black jeans showed off the lean muscles in her legs as she balanced, rocking a bit from her heels to the balls of her feet. She was definitely a sight to behold, and Abby wished she had her phone so she could photograph her. She wanted a picture of her just like that so she could look at it at her leisure. Never before had she been so entranced by someone. Sure, she'd seen some beautiful women before, even been with a few, but none of them compared to Whit. With her lithe, agile build, dark raven hair, and deep, amber eyes that seemed to rival the creek, she was truly someone to write home about.

Abby smiled as Whit speared the stick into the water and forked another fish. Whit laughed as she hauled it out and whooped at the size. She held it up flailing for Abby to see.

"It's huge!" Abby said. The fish was twice the size of the others.
"Whitefish!" Whit called.

Abby gave her a thumbs up. Whit grinned and removed the
fish. Abby looked back at her submerged feet, still uncomfortable
in seeing Whit finish off the fish. It was bad enough that she had
to eat them and watch her spear them, but what could she do? She
was stranded in the middle of the Alaskan wilderness and she had
to survive. So what sense did it make to complain or to refuse the
food?

I have to do, what I have to do. But eating animals did go against
her beliefs and in fact, that had been a note of contention with her
magazine when they'd first asked her to come on this trip. They'd
wanted someone to try the array of food, and when she'd told them
she was vegan, they'd originally turned their nose up at her. But she'd
explained her beliefs and the health benefits of eating plant-based
and eventually they'd conceded. She'd also, begrudgingly, agreed to
try some of the seafood. It wasn't something she'd normally do, but
she'd really wanted this opportunity and the chance to write for this
magazine full-time. Little had she known just how much fish she'd
be eating. Heck, she'd even had Spam.

Ugh, I can't believe I ate Spam. She had to admit though, it
wasn't half bad. Only if one's life was in peril that is. She was sure
it would taste different under normal circumstances.

Feet now well beyond numb, she lifted them and shifted her
legs over to the rocky shore where she patted them dry with her
jacket. Then she tucked them back into her socks and boots and
sat staring off into the wilderness. Whit was right, the beauty of
this place was awe-inspiring, and if she weren't so worried about
escaping back to civilization, she'd be more moved. But as it was,
she could only seem to enjoy her surroundings in short bursts, the
rest of the time, too concerned about danger and getting back to
safety.

She shifted her gaze from the distant area of the vast tree
line to the other, closer area. And that's when she saw something.
Movement, behind some brush. Her heart jumped to her throat, and
she was poised to move, convinced it was a bear. But upon closer

inspection, she realized it was a moose. She smiled as she watched it maneuver through the brush to feed. She turned to wave at Whit but found her already looking in the same direction. Whit smiled at her in return and raised her finger to her mouth to signal quiet.

"It's a buck," she said. "And they can be aggressive."

Abby turned back to the moose, a little nervous, and was relieved to see it walk off in the other direction. The animal was huge, much bigger than she'd ever imagined a moose to be. But it was magnificent with its wide velvety antlers shimmering in the sun, along with its beautiful hide and impossibly long legs carrying it about. She wished again for her camera.

"He's something, isn't he?" Whit said, having come to stand next to her.

"He sure is."

"Have you not seen one before?"

"Not yet I hadn't. Not in person."

Abby felt Whit's hand rest on her shoulder and her skin tingled from the touch.

"Well, now you have. You can check that off your list."

"Along with a few other choice things."

Whit chuckled. "Come on. I need to get the fire going in that smoker."

"Hey, Whit? How are we going to carry all the fish?"

She shrugged. "I'll make a basket."

"Oh. Right." She'd momentarily forgotten just how creative and deft she was with her hands. "Silly me."

They walked back to camp and Abby saw just how many fish Whit had caught already. She had six, which appeared to be trout, plus the massive whitefish. It looked as though they would be eating good for a while so far. And who knew how many more Whit would catch.

"How many are you hoping to smoke?"

"A few more."

"And we can carry that?"

"I can."

Abby settled down to watch her make the fire. "Is there anything you *can't* do?"

Whit laughed. "Take me to the Lower Forty-eight if you want to see me out of my element."

"Really? Hm. I might just have to do that." Thoughts of being with Whit back in Phoenix swirled through her mind, and she felt herself flushing at the possibilities.

"Good luck." Whit slid her fire starting kit out of her pocket and struck up a quick flame. Then she leaned in and blew on it through the small opening of the rock-and-clay structure. Abby noticed that she was only using some specific wood she'd gathered into the fire.

"Is that special wood or something?" she asked.

"Birch," Whit said. "Good smoking wood."

"Ah. I wish I could write all this down. I'm learning so much." She cocked her head. "You know, this whole adventure would make quite an article."

"You think?" She fanned the flames until a nice, thick smoke began to rise and then she backed away to collect the fish. She placed the fillets carefully inside, having to kneel on her knees and lean inside the hole to do so. Abby assumed she was setting them on the lower tier makeshift shelf she'd made with the sticks. Abby glanced away from checking out her backside, which, she had to admit, was very nice, and focused instead on stoking the other fire. She did that for a few moments until she saw Whit emerge and began building the rocks up to close off the opening.

"There," she said, standing. She'd left two smaller fillets on the log, and she quickly laid them on the flat rock to cook before she settled down on the log herself. "Don't know about you, but I'm ready for some lunch."

"Sounds good to me."

"You doing okay in eating all this fish?" Whit asked as she retrieved her knife to play with the fillets as they began to sizzle.

"What do you mean?" She hadn't complained, or told Whit she was vegan.

"I figured you weren't used to eating such cuisine seeing as how you couldn't watch me kill and clean it."

"Oh. Well, you're right. I'm not. I'm vegan. At least, I usually am."

Whit laughed. "I thought as much."

"But I'm not complaining."

"No, you're not. You've been quite the trouper. With your knee and the fish and everything."

"I can't be choosy, can I? This is about survival. And I have to eat and I have to walk. Otherwise, I'd never get out of here."

"True. But I still think you're being a real fighter. I can't tell you how many tourists I've come across who complain about everything."

"Oh?"

"They don't like the cold, they don't like the rain, they don't like all the hiking, or walking or what have you. And if they get injured? Forget it. It's over."

"Even though they came to Alaska to explore the outdoors?"

"Yep. Even so. Even when they came to go on long hiking tours, bringing all their fancy gear and everything. You'd think they came to climb Everest. But no, they'd still end up complaining."

"You took people on tours?"

Whit swallowed. "Uh, yeah. Used to."

"Well, no wonder why you're so at ease. You're pretty much used to this."

"Close."

"Why did you stop doing that? I can't imagine you got tired of the outdoors."

Whit stood suddenly and handed over her knife. "Excuse me. Call of nature." She walked off into the woods and left Abby staring after her.

Chapter Ten

Whit lingered in the brush for a while, hoping that time would change the topic of conversation once she returned to camp. She didn't want to discuss the tours she and her father used to run. She just wasn't ready. It brought up too many painful memories, ones she tried her best to bury and anytime they threatened to surface, her throat tightened and her gut churned just like they did right now.

"I'm not going to talk about it," she said softly, pacing behind the trees. She faced the campsite once again and took a deep breath. She started to walk back toward Abby, but a loud rustling caught her attention. A man slowly appeared from the woods and headed toward Abby.

Whit hurried out to head him off, heart pounding. "Help you?"

She reached instinctively for her knife, but then she remembered that Abby had it. *Shit.*

The man halted and offered a near toothless smile. "Howdy."

Whit was not amused, nor was she in the mood to be overly friendly. By the looks of him, she assumed he was a vagrant, someone living off the land. A nomad, who traveled through the wilderness during the warmer months.

Abby stood and white-knuckled the buck knife.

"I saw your smoke," the man said, shoving his filthy hands into his worn pants pockets. "Thought maybe I could rest a spell. Catch some food."

"You're welcome to fish," Whit said. "But—"

"Name's Boyd," he said, extending his hand. "Boyd Laird."

Whit reluctantly shook his rough, thick knuckled hand. "Whit."

"And she is?" Boyd said, smiling over at Abby, despite her brandishing the knife.

"A friend," Whit said.

Boyd must've picked up on her trepidation.

"I don't want no trouble," he said. Whit gauged him to be middle-aged, with slight webbing around his eyes and wild dark hair and beard threaded with white. He was on the thinner side, with baggy clothes and heavy boots. Sinewy was the word she'd used to describe him. And foul smelling. "I was just hoping for a friendly place to relax for a while." He patted his stomach. "Maybe eat something, if you could spare a fish or two. Sure smells good."

"You can have mine," Abby said.

Whit turned to look at her, shocked. But Abby had lowered the knife and she was welcoming Boyd to the fire. He happily agreed and headed toward her, slinging off his huge pack.

"Thank you, ma'am. It's been a while since I've eaten. This is much appreciated."

Boyd sat on the log where Whit usually sat and Whit grimaced but joined them, settling down near Abby, who gave her a look of "what else are we supposed to do?"

"Do you happen to have any way of contacting help?" Abby went right into asking. "We've been in an accident and we need to reach someone. Anyone."

"Nope," he said, helping himself to the cooking fish, picking it off the stone with his fingers. He chewed, groaned with pleasure, and sucked on his fingertips, making a popping sound as he slid them out of his heavily bearded mouth.

"Well, do you know how to reach help?" Abby continued.

"You head due north and you'll reach someone. That's the way I'm headed." He looked to the sky. "Gonna get our first snow soon. I can smell it. Need to get back to a village, settle in somewhere for the winter." He smiled again. "You folks don't happen to know of anywhere I can shelter, do ya?"

"No," Whit said. "We don't." She didn't like the guy and it wasn't because of his haggardly looks or his foul smell. It was something else. Maybe his ready smile, or the effortless way he was making himself right at home.

He plucked more fish and chewed loudly. "I'll find somewhere," he said. "Boyd Laird always finds his way." He chuckled and a piece of fish tumbled from his mouth to stick in his beard.

Whit glanced away, disgusted. Why wasn't Abby more concerned? This man could be their stalker for all they knew. He could've been the one who stole their food and came into their camp at night.

"How long have you been on our trail?" Whit asked, losing her patience. Who was she kidding? This *was* the man. It had to be.

Boyd blinked at her, as if truly surprised at the question. "How do you mean?"

"You know what I mean. You been in these woods long enough, you know how to pick up a trail. So how long have you been following us?"

"Ma'am, I apologize, but I don't know what you mean. I just came upon your smoke not long ago."

"We've had a fire every day, so how is it you're just now seeing our smoke?"

He blinked some more. "I don't rightly know. Maybe I wasn't close enough."

"I think you'd better be on your way."

He held up his greasy hands. "Ma'am, please. I don't mean no harm. I'm just trying to get myself a full belly and maybe some friendly company for a spell."

"There's no harm in him staying for a while, is there?" Abby said.

Whit wasn't believing a word the man said and she was more than confused with Abby's eager acceptance of him. She stood, no longer hungry, grabbed her spear, and walked off toward the creek.

She maneuvered over the rocks toward her fishing spot and heard someone following her. She whipped around, expecting it to be Boyd, perhaps on the attack, but instead she saw Abby.

"Wait up," Abby said meekly as she stumbled over to her. She caught her breath, placed her hands on her hips, and glanced back at the camp where Boyd sat, no doubt eating Abby's fillet now. "Why are you so pissed?"

"Why am I so pissed? Really, Abby?"

"Yeah, I mean—"

Whit tapped her own temple. "Don't you get it? *He's* our stalker."

"All the more reason to be friendly."

"What?"

"If we get combative with him, then he might try and hurt us. But if we humor him, he might lose interest and be on his way. I think he's just lonely."

She handed Whit her knife, but Whit tried to shake her off. "You keep it. You're the one dining with him."

"No, you need it for the fish. Besides, I really think he's harmless. And he's so skinny, I could probably bench press him."

Whit begrudgingly took the knife. "Keep your guard up. If he tries anything, scream. I'll be there in a flash."

Abby smiled. "My hero."

Whit took the knife and watched Abby walk away. She worried after her, but then resigned herself to quit. Abby felt comfortable with Boyd and she felt like she could handle herself with him physically, should it come to that. Whit had to let her be and deal with the situation on her own for now. There were fish to catch, for lunch and to smoke. Thanks to Boyd, her stomach was now protesting even though she still had no desire to eat. Her body would just have to wait. She planned to fish a while.

The next couple of hours she did just that, catching another six. Luckily, they were large enough to fill a person up. And though she'd been fortunate to catch another good batch, she'd been uncomfortable the entire time she'd tried to concentrate. Abby and Boyd had been laughing, distracting her, and making her feel sick with envy. Could the guy really be *that* funny? And could Abby really be enjoying herself *that* much? Ugh. She hated hearing them getting along so well, and hated more hearing

Boyd's raucous laugh. It ground on her nerves, like nails on a chalkboard.

She finished cleaning the fish and went back to camp. Boyd stood and offered to help her, but she kept the speared fish to herself. He held up his palms in a supposed "peaceful" gesture and returned to his seat, noble Boy Scout that he was. Whit handed her spear full of fish to Abby, ignored her confused look, and then went searching for a stump. She recalled seeing one near the mushroom growth and went to get it. After shifting it back and forth to loosen it from the underbrush, she rolled it back to camp and set it up to sit on. Then she took the fish and began carefully pulling them from the spear to set up in the smoker, leaving the biggest out for her and Abby to consume.

She felt Boyd's eyes on her as she worked to place the fillets in the smoker. Was he planning his next move? Perhaps to attack her while her back was turned? She didn't know and she wished she had some way of being warned of his advance.

She crawled out from the smoker, the bottom row now full with fish. She'd have to remove the branches from the top to fill the last two rungs. That is, if she caught enough fish to do so.

She replaced the rocks to close the opening and then settled on the stump to cook the big fish she had for her and Abby. She set it on the flat rock and gave Boyd a stern look as it began to sizzle. "That's for Abby and me. So don't get any ideas."

He leaned back as if her words had physically struck him.

"No, ma'am. I wouldn't dream of it."

Right.

She rolled her eyes and crinkled her nose. She could smell him from her position close to Abby from across the flames and she wondered how Abby could stand it. Especially since the heat from the fire only seemed to intensify the foulness. The man needed to clean up in the creek. No, wait a minute. They got their water from the creek. Filtered water bottle or not, she didn't want him bathing in their drinking water. Besides, his filth might kill the fish.

She chuckled a little at that causing both Abby and Boyd to look at her curiously.

"Nothing," she said and took the knife from Abby to turn the fillet.

Abby gave her a handful of cooked mushrooms still warm from the pot. "Thought you might like some."

"Thanks," she said. She paused as she was about to pop one in her mouth, wondering if Boyd had put his grimy hands on them. "I'm surprised there's any left."

She didn't have to look at Boyd for that one to hit home. He picked up on it at once.

"Oh, I don't like mushrooms," he said.

Whit laughed, amused. Thank God for small favors. She tossed a mushroom in her mouth and chewed. But then she wondered why a man who was claiming to be as hungry as he was would refuse food. Even Abby was eating things she normally wouldn't. It didn't make sense.

Abby was staring at her, nearly burning a hole in the side of her face.

"What?" Whit asked, but she knew. She was being a bit of an ass, but she didn't care. Boyd was a fraud. She just knew it. And Abby, even if she was only being polite to humor him, still seemed snowed over by him.

He shouldn't be sitting there with them, conversing, laughing, eating their food. Hell, he should be catching his own damn fish. Not eating what she provided. And what happened to the Spam and pilot bread he'd obviously stolen? Had that run out? Was that why he claimed to be so hungry? But wait, no, he was apparently full enough to refuse the mushrooms, so he couldn't have been that hungry. She laughed again as she tried to keep it all straight in her head. The whole thing was ridiculous. Boyd Laird and his Boy Scout routine was ridiculous.

"Are you okay?" Abby whispered.

Whit slid her eyes away from Boyd, who had glanced away from her hard stare.

"Yep, fine. How are you, Abby?" She smiled and it must've seriously weirded Abby out because her eyes widened considerably.

"I'm uh—good, thanks."

"That's wonderful." Whit edged forward to cut away a chunk of fish. Then she brought it to Abby and offered it. "Hungry? You must be after not eating earlier."

Abby took the hunk of meat and ate. "Thank you, yes, I'm hungry."

"I thought as much." Again, she shot a look to Boyd, who had the nerve to look sheepish.

He took that moment to rise. "If you'll excuse me, I need to make a trip to the little boys' room." He walked away, back behind the camp, and Abby nearly jumped on her.

"What are you doing? Are you trying to piss him off? You're being so rude."

Whit dissected a steaming piece of fish for herself. She brought the blade to her lips and dropped the food into her mouth. She chewed a good long while before she responded.

"I'm just not buying his good boy act, that's all."

"Well, I'm—I don't know. He really seems okay to me. Did you know he's ex military? A vet. And he used to be a volunteer firefighter and paramedic."

"So he says. For all we know he could be a murderer. The Alaskan wild is the perfect place to hide out for a wanted fugitive."

Abby shook her head. "Whit, come on. Really?"

"Yes, really. What kind of person lives off the land, Abby? In Alaska? Someone who doesn't want to be found, that's who."

"I think he's just a loner. A recluse."

Whit stabbed Abby another bite, but pulled it away as she reached for it. "He sure is awful outgoing and friendly to be a recluse."

Abby grabbed her wrist and brought the food to her. She plucked it off the knife and ate it, glaring at Whit.

"Funny," she said as she swallowed.

"But apparently not as funny as he is."

Abby scoffed. "Whit, come on. Just cool it, okay? Please? For me?"

Whit chewed another mushroom and watched as Boyd returned from the trees. He slowed as he neared them. "Is it okay if I rejoin you? I don't want to interrupt anything."

"Please," Whit said. "Make yourself comfortable." She popped another mushroom as she gave Abby another bite of fish. "Our casa es su casa."

He looked at Abby as if to make sure he'd heard correctly. She nodded and he sat. "Well, thank you both for the hospitality."

Abby smiled at him, but Whit could tell it was cautious. She was either not totally convinced of his nobility, or she was worried that Whit was going to piss him off and cause a fight. Whit noticed the pulse jumping in her neck. She was really worried. Whit decided to calm things down if only for Abby's sake. She finished eating, leaving the rest for Abby, and stood to grab her spear.

"I'm going to go see what more I can catch. You okay here?"

Abby nodded. "Yeah, fine."

"Okay then. Holler if you need me. I won't be too far away." She walked back to the creek, trekked across the rocky shore, and planted herself at her lucky spot. She looked back to camp and saw Abby eating and Boyd talking. She couldn't tell what he was saying, but she suspected it was more bullshit. Boyd was just rubbing Abby the right way to keep her guard down. Whatever he was up to was no good, she could feel it. But she guessed that only time would tell.

She just hoped that whatever his motive was, it wasn't something that would cost them their lives.

CHAPTER ELEVEN

Abby tried to relax again and enjoy her conversation with Boyd, but she found that her gaze kept wandering over to Whit who stood at the edge of the creek, spear poised to strike at a fish. Could she be right about Boyd? Was this overly friendly and jovial man their stalker and thief? Or worse, a killer? Gooseflesh erupted along her arms, and she rubbed them and scooted closer to the fire, hoping the heat would help. But the closer she moved, the more fierce Boyd's smell became. While she didn't want to be rude, or think ill of him because he was so dirty, she couldn't help but be disturbed by his scent. He needed to bathe in the worst way and she tried not to think about how long it had been since he'd done so. She fought plugging her nose, and smiled at him instead, as he continued to tell her yet another story about his firefighting and paramedic days. Boyd really was a hero. He'd done so much to help people, save their lives really. He couldn't be a murderer, could he? She thought again about what Whit said about his stories possibly not being true. But why make up such tales? To impress her? Why? How could that benefit him?

She poked at the fire and then finished off the last of the fish, saving the mushrooms for later, but not before first offering them to Boyd, who politely declined.

"I'm stuffed," he said. "Thanks to you two kind ladies." He smiled, showing off the prominent red and gummy gaps where teeth should be.

Abby set the pot away from the fire and brought her knees up to her chest. She was growing restless and wanted to go help Whit with the fish, even if it did slightly disturb her to watch her kill and clean them. Anything was better than sitting there, wondering if the man across from her was a killer.

But she didn't think it wise to leave him alone in the camp. She wasn't sure why, he couldn't really do anything, other than mess with the fish, but they'd see him do that if he tried. He seemed to sense her restlessness.

"You don't have to stay here with me," he said, tossing a couple of dead leaves into the fire. "I need to go see if I can hunt me down some supper anyway." He stood and wiped the seat of his pants, as if that would help his uncleanliness.

Abby joined him, wiping off her own backside. "You could always eat whatever we do," she said, feeling somewhat bad that he should have to catch his own when they obviously had plenty.

"Nah, it's best if I get my own."

He skirted the fire and scooped up his pack, giving Abby a salute. "I'll catch you later." He then disappeared back into the trees, moving as quietly as a fall breeze. Abby stared after him for a short while, making sure he didn't return, and then joined Whit at the shoreline of the creek.

"What's up?" Whit asked softly, still poised for fish with the spear.

"Boyd went off to find his own dinner."

Whit appeared amused. "Really?"

"Uh-huh."

"Well, well."

"I told you, I don't think he's so bad."

"Mm." Whit pressed her finger to her mouth as a large fish swam into view. She struck, but missed. "Damn. Thats the eighth one I've missed."

"Think they're wising up?"

"No, I think I'm just distracted."

"By?"

She looked at Abby. "What do you think? You and the Boy Scout."

"Me?"

"Yes, of course, Abby. I'm worried, okay? I don't trust him and I've been trying to keep an eye on you while I fish."

Whit cared about her. It was nice to hear, even if it didn't mean all that Abby wished it meant. Whit was just looking out for her, nothing more. Still, it made her heart race nonetheless. "I appreciate that," she said. "It means a lot."

Whit looked back to the water. "Yeah, well, I don't like the idea of you two becoming so chummy. He's bad news."

"So you say."

Whit didn't say anything more and Abby drew away to give her some space. She walked back toward the edge of the shoreline, where the water level sometimes reached land. She spotted a beautiful stone, or at least she thought it was a stone, until she picked it up and ran it over her fingertips. It was clear and prism like, with several offshoots that looked like spikes. She held it up to the sunlight and smiled. It was dazzling and she wanted to see if she could find more. She began walking along the shoreline, slowly taking in her surroundings beyond the river rocks. She headed up the creek, away from Whit, and soon was nearly out of ear shot. A glimmer of crystal caught her eye just as she turned to head back. Excited, she lifted another similar piece to the one she'd previously found and tucked it, too, in her jacket pocket. She'd have to ask Whit what they were.

She thought she saw another one, buried in the moist sand, so she knelt and dug it out. It was similar to the others, but much smaller, so she decided to leave it. She did however, find something else as she dug. It looked like…yes, it was. She pulled it from the sand and held it up for inspection. It was a clam. She quickly looked around for more, searching for air bubbles in the ground. She found more, a lot more bubbles, and after she dug another clam out to be sure that what she saw were indeed clam dens, she headed off quickly back toward Whit.

She found her cleaning another whitefish.

"Hey," Abby said.

"You sound out of breath. Everything okay?" She sliced the fish along the underbelly and Abby turned away.

"I found some clams. Lots of them."

She tossed the two she had onto the ground next to Whit. "Can we eat them?"

"Nope."

Abby turned back around. "No?"

"Could be toxic."

"Are you serious?"

"Yep."

"Damn. I thought I'd really found something that could help us out."

"It was a good idea, don't get me wrong, but yeah, we shouldn't eat them."

Abby reached in her jacket pocket. "Look what else I found." She brought out the crystal-like formations and held them out for inspection.

Whit glanced back up. "Ah, you found some quartz. Very nice."

"They're pretty, aren't they?" Abby tucked them back into her pocket.

"You gonna keep them?" She went back to deboning the fish, tossing the bony spine aside, back into the water.

"Uh-huh."

"They'll make a good souvenir."

"I thought so. If, by the end of this journey, I actually want to remember anything."

Whit chuckled. "You will."

"Swear?"

"Swear."

Whit had caught more fish while Abby was out exploring. She had three more whitefish in the tidal pool she'd built. And she was cleaning the fourth.

"Looks like your luck returned."

"Seems so."

"Well, I'll leave you to it. I'm going to go look around some more."

"Stay close. Remember this isn't a playground."

"Got it." She looked out across the creek, intent on catching the late afternoon sun's rays as it played upon the dark coppery water and spotted a bird, a very large bird, on the top branch of a tree. "Whit, look. A bald eagle. And it's so close," Abby said, amazed.

"He's watching me," Whit said, coming to a stand. "Waiting for me to leave so he can feed on the remnants."

"Really?"

"Want to see him feed?" Whit picked up a string of guts and gore. Abby had no idea what it was, or what it did for the fish, but it almost made her gag. Whit threw it down the shoreline. "Stand very still. Let's see if he goes for it."

They stood next to each other, watching. The eagle took off at once, and glided down to the ground to snatch up the pieces of food. Then he flew away, massive wings pumping.

"That was incredible," Abby said. "I've never seen a bird so big in my life. Think he'll come back?"

"Probably."

"I hope so."

Whit grabbed her spear and stabbed one of the fish in her tidal pool to bring out and clean. Abby, having seen enough guts and gore for the moment, headed off again, in search of more treasure. She walked the length of the creek, collecting more quartz bits and some pretty, colorful river rock. She wasn't sure if she was going to keep it all, but it was fun to collect. Her knee was still sore, especially when she stepped awkwardly on the rocks every once in a while, but for the most part, it wasn't too bad. How it would feel when they walked for longer periods of time, she couldn't say.

She continued her search up and down both sides of the creek for quite some time as Whit cleaned all the fish and even returned to camp to place them in the smoker. To her continued amazement, the bald eagle returned, as if it had known Whit was going away again, and took more of the fish guts. She wondered if it was perhaps feeding some little ones in a nest nearby.

As Whit went back to fishing, and the sun began its descent in the sky, Abby gave up her quest and ventured back to camp. She tended to the low burning fire and settled in to get warmed up. It wasn't long before Whit soon joined her, carrying five more fish.

"Holy shit. You caught a lot today."

"Not as much as I'd hoped."

Abby laughed. "Whit, you caught plenty. We can nibble on them a little at a time."

"I sure hope it lasts."

She slid the fish off the spear and peeled back the branches along the top of the smoker to place them inside. Once she did, she replaced the branches and then plucked away the rocks at the opening to add more wood to the fire. When she had it smoking well again, she replaced the stones and came to sit next to Abby on the stump.

"Giving up on sitting on the log?" Abby asked as she watched Whit slide the last whitefish off the spear to put on the slab over the fire.

"It's tainted."

Abby let out a hearty laugh. "You're crazy, Whit."

"At least I made you laugh."

"Why wouldn't you? You can be funny."

Whit played with the fillet with the edge of her knife. "Not as funny as *Boyd.*"

"Did I hear my name?" A booming voice came from the brush behind them and Boyd appeared, carrying something white in his arms. Abby and Whit stood, studying him closely. "I always come when called," he said as he approached.

"What's that?" Abby asked, perplexed by the white bundle. But as he grew closer, she saw that it was an animal and her heart sank. He'd found his dinner.

"Matilda," Boyd said with a smile.

"What?" Whit asked, grimacing. "Looks like a snowshoe hare to me."

It was. It was a rabbit. Abby's stomach flipped.

"She's a snowshoe alright," he walked up to Abby and bounced a little, cradling the hare. "She's already turned white for the winter."

Abby blinked. "Is she *alive?*"

"Well, sure she's alive. Here." He handed her the rabbit. It was small and obviously terrified, its ears flattened, eyes wide. She cooed at it and tried to rub its enormous feet.

"Careful," Boyd said. "She's skittish."

"Will she bite?" Abby asked.

"Hasn't yet. But even so."

Whit spoke. "Why do you have a wild hare? And furthermore, why did you bring it to camp?"

Abby's heart sank again as she considered that he might be planning on killing it to eat.

"I found her. Just like that, huddled near a tree, out in the open. She wouldn't run, so I took her. Didn't want no wild animal to get her. She's helpless."

Abby perked up and she studied the ball of fur in her arms. "She's so calm."

"My guess is, she had the tar scared out of her by something."

"Either that or she's injured," Whit said.

"Could be."

"You should have left her."

"Would you've?" he asked. "Left that poor little thing alone and helpless? At least if she could run she'd stand a chance."

"I wouldn't have brought her back here," Whit said.

Abby kissed the top of her head and rubbed her soft fur. "I'm glad you brought her," she said. "You saved her."

"Abby, you can't keep her." Whit looked pissed.

Abby didn't cave. She couldn't give up the hare. Like Boyd said, she was helpless. "I'm not letting her out of my sight."

Whit sighed and sank down on the stump. Boyd grinned. "I knew you'd like her." He eased out of his pack and sat down on the log. "Mind if I borrow your pot?"

Abby settled on the ground with the rabbit, emptied out the mushrooms, and handed the pot over. "Not at all, Boyd." She smiled at him and at the hare. She was right about Boyd. He was okay. He'd saved this little hare instead of killing it for food.

"Matilda," she said as she smiled over at Whit.

Whit shook her head at her as if warning her, but Abby ignored her.

I'm right about Boyd. I just know I am.

Chapter Twelve

Whit ate her half of the fish in silence as Boyd and Abby chatted away. Abby was keenly interested in the hare, which she, like Boyd, called Matilda. Whit didn't think it wise, seeing as how the rabbit might be injured or ill. She thought it best not to get attached. But Abby seemed to be all in. She wanted to know everything about it. Where Boyd had found it, what did it eat, etc. Whit had to hand it to him, he answered all of her questions and it was really a smart move to bring Abby the rabbit. He must've picked up on her affection for animals and her veganism.

Yep, he was slick all right, and one thing was for sure. He was all about buttering up Abby. She couldn't blame him though. Whit had been combative, even rude. So she was obviously a lost cause. But Abby? She was sweet and sensitive, and had an affinity for animals and their well-being. In short, Abby was a much easier mark.

"And they really like these," Boyd said, pulling out some birch twigs. He handed them over to Abby who set the hare down between her legs to feed. She offered the twigs to the rabbit, who didn't seem the least bit interested. "She's not eating."

"She's just scared," Boyd said. "But she'll get used to you. Give her time."

"If she doesn't starve first," Whit added, worried that Abby would have to witness the imminent death of the hare and consequently be heartbroken.

"Whit," Abby said. "Don't say that."

Whit stabbed a mushroom from the pile Abby had placed on the ground in order to give Boyd their pot. She heated it quickly in the flames and popped it in her mouth. It was hotter than expected, and she had to down some water to put out the fire in her mouth. She caught Boyd smirking, obviously amused at her pain. Her distaste for him was growing bigger by the second.

"I think that there is a leveret," he said, referring to the rabbit. "A baby. And she's probably just in shock is all."

"A leveret," Abby repeated. "And they eat twigs?"

"And bark and plants."

And sometimes even dead animals.

Whit kept that little bit to herself and she noticed that Boyd did as well. He really was playing this just right.

"It won't be hard to find her food," he said, passing Abby more twigs that he'd dug out from the bottom of his pack.

"Shouldn't she be with her mother?" Abby asked.

"Hares can do okay without their mothers at a relatively young age," Whit said, before Boyd had the chance.

"Well, that's good, I suppose," Abby said, stroking the rabbit on the head.

She was hopelessly smitten already, which was what Whit had feared would happen.

"And what are you eating?" Abby asked, pointing the question to Boyd.

He stuck his hand in one of the front pockets of his pack and brought it out full of berries. Whit rolled her eyes. She'd been planning on taking Abby berry hunting in the morning. They'd come across a few berry bushes on their hike in and Abby had thoroughly enjoyed them. Now Boyd was stealing her thunder by offering the small handful to Abby.

"Blueberries and high bush cranberries," Boyd said, grinning from ear to ear.

Abby took the berries and shot some in her mouth and groaned. "So good," she said as she chewed.

Boyd then reached back in his bag to dip out more berries. These were yellow and orange and Whit knew what they were.

"And I've got some salmon berries," Boyd said, shoving some in his mouth to gum like a cave man. He extended his hand to Abby. "Try some?"

"Thanks," she said, tossing a couple of those in her mouth to chew. "Mmm, those are nice."

"Aren't they?" Boyd said.

"Is that all you have to eat?" Abby asked as Boyd zipped up his pack to set aside.

"I had a big grouse earlier," he said.

Whit's spine straightened as a bolt of alarm surged through it. "How did you manage to get a grouse?" She hadn't seen a weapon on him, but surely he had one. A rifle at the very least, and a good hunting knife. Everyone needed those.

"I set a trap," he said.

Bullshit.

"Also caught me a squirrel."

"Aww," Abby said. "You ate a squirrel?"

He flushed, knowing he'd slipped up. "I did. Sorry, Abby."

"You sure know how to get food when you need it," Whit said, her voice full of conviction.

"I do alright."

"Makes me wonder why you claimed to be so hungry when you came walking in here earlier."

And where is your weapon, you sneaky son of a bitch?

"I suppose I do owe you an explanation," he started. "I uh—" He rubbed his hands on his britches. "You see. I've been sick."

"Sick?" Abby said.

"Yes, ma'am, I believe I had a touch of the flu or something."

Whit couldn't help but scoff. The man was laying it on thick.

"I was holed up in my makeshift shelter for three days, unable to do much of anything, including hunt."

"How do you hunt with no weapon?" Abby asked. She was obviously paying closer attention than Whit thought.

"Well, see, I lost my weapon some time back in a rapid. Tried to cross a river and lost my footing. I was lucky to survive."

"That sounds rough," Abby said.

"It was. Thankfully, I had my pack on and the supplies I lost were limited, save for my rifle. So, ever since then I've just been trapping and foraging."

Abby nodded and petted the hare. Its nose was beginning to twitch and she laughed, amused, and tried to feed it some twigs. The rabbit didn't partake, but at least it was moving a little. Whit breathed a small sigh of relief, glad it was showing signs of life. She really didn't want Abby to see it suffer and die.

"But you're feeling better now?" Abby asked.

"I tell you, that fish really helped. Gave me some strength to go off and forage and trap. So, I thank you ladies again."

"You're welcome," Abby said.

"I take it you'll be ready to leave soon, then?" Whit asked, still not buying into his bullshit.

He rubbed his forehead and pressed his dry lips together. "Well, to be honest with you, I was kinda hoping you two would let me bunk down here tonight. That way I don't have to set up a camp. See, I'm feeling a little tired from foraging all afternoon, probably because I'm still recovering a bit."

"So, you're not quite better yet," Whit said.

He shrugged. "Guess not."

"Don't you want to go build your own shelter?" Abby asked. "If you stayed here you'd have to sleep out by the fire."

"That'd be alright, Abby. I don't need much."

"But yet, you're too weak to go off and build your own fire?" Whit said.

"Whit," Abby said between clenched teeth. "You can stay here by the fire if you need to."

"Abby." Whit gave her a stern look. "We should discuss this."

"Why? He needs to stay and we can help."

Whit stared at her a moment longer, hoping to somehow inject her concerns into her mind, but then gave up. Abby was a lost cause at the moment. Hopefully, she could talk to her later when Boyd went to "use the little boys' room."

She had serious issues with him staying and she couldn't wait to share them. Would Abby listen? That remained to be seen.

The only good thing she could see when it came to Boyd was that he didn't have his rifle with him. But that didn't mean he hadn't hidden it somewhere close by. Nor did it mean he didn't have a handgun tucked away in his pack. They really just had no idea what all he had or what he was capable of. And that scared her to death, seeing as how she and Abby had nothing but a buck knife and a makeshift fishing spear.

Unfortunately for her, the sun set and Boyd remained where he was, talking their ear off, rambling on about various topics, mostly ones where he came out the hero in some way. She was so sick of hearing his goody-two-shoes tales, she actually became nauseous and had to excuse herself. She walked back into the brush, telling Abby she had to pee, and stood back away from the camp to quietly observe. She wanted to see if Boyd changed tactics, and maybe talked badly about her while she was away. But he didn't, keeping his range of focus on himself. A true narcissist to the hilt.

She returned to camp after relieving herself and tried to get comfortable on the stump, but it was hard and her backside ached. She really wanted to settle in next to Abby on the ground, but she needed to be ready to jump to her feet should Boyd choose to make his move. So the stump it was.

"Well, I'm about ready to turn in," Abby finally said, after lots more berries and stories. She gathered the rabbit into her arms and stood. "You coming, Whit?"

"Sure."

Whit joined her and headed for the shelter. She considered sleeping out next to the fire to keep an eye on Boyd, but then thought about it and realized if he were to attack while she slept so close to him, he'd have the upper hand. She was better off in the shelter where, if he came after them, he'd definitely have to make noise to get to them.

Whit crawled inside and turned and took the hare from Abby, who then scooted in next to her. Whit handed her the rabbit and then secured the door as best she could and breathed in the cool, pine scented air. "Smells so much better in here," she said, making herself comfortable on the bed of pine needles.

"Shh," Abby said, lying back next to her on her side, the hare between them. "He'll hear you."

"I don't care. He has to know he stinks, Abby."

Abby pressed her fingers to Whit's lips to shush her. "Even so, it's rude and we shouldn't say anything."

Whit swallowed the words she'd been ready to say next, so moved by the feel of her soft, warm fingertips against her mouth.

"Okay?"

Whit agreed. "Okay." At that moment, she'd say anything to appease her, her mind and body reeling with sudden desire. Abby was so tender and kind, and soft and beautiful. Truly a woman to behold. And she wondered, not for the first time, if Boyd felt the same way. If maybe he wanted her too and that's why he was laying it on so thick. That maybe in his warped mind, Abby would somehow return his affections.

Whit reached out and gripped her arm, needing to keep her close to protect her.

"What?" Abby whispered.

"I need you to sleep close to me tonight."

"Why?"

"Because I think Boyd likes you a little too much."

"Oh, no he doesn't, Whit. Come on."

"Abby, please. Just move the rabbit to your other side and curl up against me. I need to be able to feel you when you move."

"Okay, okay." She shifted the hare and then pressed her backside up against Whit so that they were spooning.

"Thanks," Whit said, liking the proximity a little more than she should. She rested her hand on Abby's shoulder and tried not to imagine them spooning after passionate lovemaking.

It's been too long since I've spooned with a woman. Way too long.

"Night, Whit."

"Night."

Whit felt Abby relax but she kept her own eyes open, too worried about their guest to close them. But the night eventually closed in on her and she was no longer able to stay awake.

When she woke it was still dark. So dark she had to sit up and kick out the door to get her bearings. Abby stirred but didn't wake, and Whit crawled from the shelter and noticed right away that Boyd was nowhere to be seen.

She pushed to a stand and looked around. Maybe he was off taking a leak. But that wasn't the case either. His pack was missing. She looked to the smoker, heart in her throat. Smoke was no longer billowing from the top, so she walked over to examine it to see if the fish were still there. She peeled off the branches and took a look inside.

The fish were gone.

CHAPTER THIRTEEN

Abby's eyes fluttered awake as she registered movement in her arms. "Hey, you," she whispered, smiling at the furry bundle trying to scurry around. She sat up and gathered Matilda close to her breast. "Good morning," she said as she kissed her. "I see you're up and at 'em." Relief washed through her at Matilda's liveliness. Maybe now she would eat. "Let's go find the others, shall we? And show them how well you're doing this morning."

Abby kicked open the makeshift door, squinted against the brightness of the day, and scooted out to find Whit by the fire, perched on the log, carving what looked to be another spear.

"Good morning," Abby said, bringing Matilda with her to the fire to sit across from Whit. "Where's Boyd?"

Whit kept scraping, face stone-like.

"Whit?"

Abby glanced around but saw no sign of Boyd. She swallowed the ball in her throat as she realized something must be wrong. "The old spear not up to par anymore?"

"Oh, it's fine," Whit said. "Or at least it was last I saw it."

"You lost it?"

Whit finally stopped working the sapling. "Of course not. That son of a bitch Boyd took it, along with all our fish."

Abby grew dizzy. She gripped Matilda tighter for some sort of grounding, but it didn't help, so she released her between her outstretched legs. "You mean, he's—gone?"

"Like the wind." Whit threw the stick down, sheathed her knife, and then collapsed her head in her hands to run her fingers through her hair.

"Whit I—I'm so sorry." She didn't know what else to say. She'd trusted Boyd for the most part. Thought he was an okay guy just down on his luck. She'd been kind to him and pretty much insisted that Whit be as well. She'd hoped he would remain kind to them in return.

"Yeah, well, sorry's not going to get us anymore smoked fish."

Abby stroked Matilda, feeling like the whole thing was her fault. Had she listened to Whit...what? Who knows what Boyd would've done had they both been hostile toward him. It could've been a lot worse. But she wasn't about to say that aloud.

"What can I do to help?"

Whit looked up, sighed, and rested her hands on her knees, causing her black hair to fall down below her shoulders and gleam in the firelight. Her dark amber eyes glinted against her olive skin and Abby found herself breathless at her raw beauty.

How can someone look so good when mad?

"You can stay here and watch the camp while I try to catch more fish today."

"We're staying then?"

"We have no choice, do we? If we leave, we risk starvation. Besides, I don't want to be close to Boyd's trail. If he's heading north, like we'll be doing, I want to remain as far behind him as possible."

Abby nodded. "Makes sense." She picked up some of the birch twigs from the night before and offered them to Matilda who began to nibble. "Look, Whit. She's eating." Abby smiled, but Whit didn't seem to be in the mood for any good news. She was still reeling from the sting of what Boyd did.

"Forgive me for not celebrating," she said as she knelt to pick up the sapling. "But I have our survival on my mind." She jerked out her knife and began working the spear again.

"I understand," Abby said softly. She glanced over to the small pile of mushrooms and berries. Boyd had left them, and the pot.

"How about I make us some breakfast?" She leaned over for the water bottle, which thankfully, had been in the shelter with them, and poured a little in the pot. Then she stirred in the berries and mushrooms and placed them on the cooking rock on the fire. "It's not IHOP or anything, but it will do, right?"

Whit grumbled.

Abby gave Matilda more twigs and a few blueberries and then retrieved the all-purpose knife from her pocket and extended the blade. She crawled to her knees, careful to go around Matilda, and stirred the food as it cooked.

"I wonder how the mushrooms will taste with the berries?" she asked, mainly to herself. But Whit surprised her by answering.

"Surprisingly, the combination's not too bad."

"No?"

"No." She chewed her lower lip as she shaped the spear.

"So, you've had it before?"

"Many a time."

"On your guided tours?"

Whit stilled, blade poised, midair. "I guess you could say that." Then she started cutting again. "But I don't want to talk about that right now."

Abby wanted to ask why, completely confused, but she refrained. "Okay." She figured the whole Boyd thing had really upset her to where she didn't want to talk much at all. It was just as well, because Abby felt guilty enough and she really didn't know what else to say to try to make the situation any better. Boyd had seriously screwed them. He'd taken nearly all their food and delayed their chance at going for help. Hopefully, they could make that up today and leave tomorrow, without any more issues.

Abby continued to stir the berries and mushrooms. "You ready for this? It's hot."

Whit shook her head. "In a minute. I want to finish this first." She planted the spear in front of her and examined the two points. Then she shoved a small piece of wood down between them as she'd done when making the previous spear and continued sharpening the ends.

Abby forked a mushroom, now coated in berry juice, and slid it off the small blade into her mouth. "Mm, you're right. This isn't bad."

"Finally realized I was right about something," she mumbled.

The comment, though said lowly, penetrated. Abby flushed, the guilt now fully surfaced. She knew she should let the dig go and not respond, but she couldn't stop herself. She had to let Whit know how badly she felt over the whole thing.

"Look, I know I was wrong about Boyd and I'm sorry. I'm really very truly sorry."

"Sorry doesn't do us any good."

"I'm aware of that. But it needed to be said nonetheless. And as for what would help…I'm at a loss. Maybe you can tell me."

Whit eyed her, though only momentarily. "You could listen to me from here on out."

Abby stifled a scoff. "You know, I'm usually a pretty good judge of character."

"Not out here you aren't."

"I was wrong about Boyd, I admitted that."

Whit finished with the spear and looked at her. Her eyes were now afire with conviction. "I'm not just referring to Boyd. I'm referring to everyone and everything that we might encounter."

"I see, so I'm to assume that I know nothing."

"Yes, when it comes to this journey and this wild country, absolutely."

"So, I'm to defer to you."

"If you want to survive."

"My God, you sound arrogant."

"I'm right. There's a difference."

Abby did scoff this time and Whit grabbed her spear and stood.

"Where are you going?"

"To catch us some food."

"Aren't you going to eat breakfast?"

But Whit had already walked away, leaving her alone with Matilda, who had happily hopped a few steps away from her as well.

"Guess you'll be off too, huh? Now that you're better."

But the hare turned and remained relatively close, eating more of the berries. Abby settled down next to her and stroked her back. "It's just me and you, kid. What shall we do?" She looked to the smoker and noticed the lack of smoke and the sloppiness of the stacked doorway. "Maybe I can work on that. Get it ready for some more fish."

It couldn't be that difficult. She stabbed more mushroom and a bit of intact berry and ate, giving some to Matilda too. Then she tried to relax and finish her breakfast before she got started. They had a lot to do today and she was intent on helping wherever she could. Now more than ever, she felt like she had to prove herself to Whit, who obviously thought she was a complete idiot when it came to…well, anything. She had to prove her wrong.

"I'll show her, huh, Matilda?" She scooped her up and nuzzled her cold little nose. Then she hugged her to her chest and got lost staring into the fire.

Sometime later, she set Matilda aside and rose to clean the pot. Just as she was about to pour water into it and go dump the remnants into the creek, she thought of Whit. "I'll be right back," she said to the hare and set off for the pebbled shoreline. She was surprised to see that Whit wasn't in her usual spot and it took her a moment to locate her. She was standing farther down shore, balanced and ready to strike. Abby froze as she did, and she brought the spear out of the water with a flailing fish on the end. Abby hurried to her, unable to suppress her grin.

"You caught one!" It appeared to be a large trout, its colorful skin sparkling in the sunlight. Abby walked up next to her as she was removing the fish from the spear.

"Caught two others as well," Whit said as she placed the trout in a new tidal pool she'd made. Abby saw the other fish in the water and surprisingly, her mouth began to water.

"Those look good," she said. "Guess I'm getting hungry."

"We'll eat soon," Whit said, grabbing her spear to stand at her perch. "I want to see if I can catch a few more first."

Abby held out the pot. "I thought you might be hungry, so I brought you what was left of the berries and mushrooms."

Whit eyed the contents and plucked a mushroom. "Thanks."

"I'll just leave it here next to you." She waited for Whit to say something more, but when she didn't, she walked away, back toward camp. Once there, she spotted Matilda exploring near the shelter, thought about wrangling her in, but decided against it. If she wanted to hop away and go live her life, she should. She shouldn't try to keep her. Feeling a little sad at the thought of losing her, she got to work on the smoker, hoping to busy her mind as well as her body. First, she rebuilt the fire, using the birch Whit had previously gathered, and leaned back on her haunches to observe the smoke the wood created. Then she rebuilt the entryway and adjusted the branches up top. When she was finished, she observed the whole structure from a distance.

"Looks pretty good to me," she said.

Whit still wasn't back, and she wasn't sure what else she could do to help. Other than gather more mushrooms, she could think of nothing. Then she spotted an errant berry on the ground. "I could pick berries. Just put them in my coat pockets. What do you think, Matilda?" But the hare was gone.

Abby sighed and willed herself to accept that it was for the best. What would she do with a wild hare? She shoved her hands in her jacket pockets, massaged the quartz she'd kept, and turned in a circle, trying to decide which direction to go. She finally headed back to the right of the shelter, feeling like she knew this area best. She wouldn't go far and she wouldn't stay long, but she had to do something to help prove herself worthy.

Now if only Whit would notice.

CHAPTER FOURTEEN

Whit caught her sixth fish, killed it and cleaned it, and then slid all the fillets on her spear to carry back to camp. She hummed as she walked but then stopped dead as she came upon the smoker. White smoke billowed out the top, seemingly ready for more fish. She glanced around for Abby, to thank her, but she was nowhere to be found.

"Must've gone to pee." She angled the heavy spear against the log and knelt to open up the smoker by un-piling the rocks. When she was finished setting the fillets, all but the largest one, on the racks, she closed the smoker back up and stood. Abby was still gone. And, come to think of it, so was the hare. Her heart raced. "I bet she went after that rabbit and got herself lost."

She circled the camp, studying the brush, looking for an entrance point. The only one she could find that looked recently trodden through was the one Abby frequented to relieve herself. She took off in that direction, found tracks well beyond the camp, and began calling for her, but there was nothing.

Whit thanked her lucky stars that her father had shown her how to track. All she had to do was keep to these markings and she should find Abby. She halted as she came upon a fork in the worn brush. One went further south, the other northwest. Confusion muddled her mind for a moment until she realized what had happened. She knelt and examined the prints. The ones she could see going northwest were smaller in both size and stride, as well as fresher. They were Abby's. The others must've been Boyd's from when he went off the day before to hunt. Whit straightened and followed the smaller tracks.

She walked for close to an hour and then the trail began to circle back and then it veered off in yet another direction.

"Abby!" she called, stopping to listen for her. A small cry came from the distance. Whit began to run, crashing through low hanging branches and thorny bushes. She called for her again, got a reply, this time closer, and picked up her speed. She plowed through more heavy brush into a small clearing and saw Abby sitting beneath a pine tree, knees pulled to her chest, crying.

"Abby!" Whit said, hurrying to her. "Are you okay? Are you hurt?"

She shook her head, wiped her face, and sniffled. "Just my knee. I think I aggravated it."

Whit knelt next to her and held her leg, trying to examine it. "Can you extend it?"

"Not all the way. Hurts too bad."

"Can you walk?"

"I think I'll need some help."

Whit helped her stand. "Go ahead and lean on me," she said. "We'll take it slow."

They headed back for the trail, pushing branches out of the way as they went.

"What were you doing way out here?" Whit asked. "You had me worried sick."

"I was looking for berries." She stuck her hand in her jacket pocket and brought out some blueberries. "See?"

"You shouldn't have wandered off."

"I thought I could find my way back. And I wasn't expecting my knee to act up."

"What would've happened if I couldn't find you? You would've frozen, or worse…"

"Boyd?"

Whit let out a breath. "Yeah." She didn't like thinking about that. Who knows what Boyd would've done had he come upon her alone.

"I'm sorry. I won't do it again."

"Please don't."

"I just wanted to help out. To show you I'm…"

"What?"

"Not useless."

Whit stopped their progress and looked at her. "I don't think you're useless, Abby." Maybe she'd been too hard on her earlier. Spoken too harshly.

"Well, I feel useless. And I feel like the whole Boyd thing was my fault."

Whit tugged her closer, trying to comfort her. She wasn't good at this kind of thing. Intimacy. Vulnerability. Empathy. Words one of her former lovers had used to describe her relationship failures. She'd been trying to prove her wrong ever since. But she still felt she wasn't very adept. "I don't think you're useless," she said again, struggling for the right words. "I just—you're a novice. You don't know all that you need to know to keep safe. So I need you to listen to me. That's all."

"I'm sorry," she said again. "I promise I'll do better."

"Don't apologize. Just don't—wander off."

"I won't. I swear."

"Okay then. We're good. Right?" She smiled at her and Abby returned it as they moved slowly along, eventually getting back to camp. Two hours had been lost for fishing, but Whit wrote them off, just glad to have Abby back safe and sound. Now she had to worry about her knee.

Whit slid out of her jacket and slipped off her heavy sweater. Then she tugged off her undershirt and walked to the creek. She stood at the water's edge and gathered a bunch of icy-cold wet rocks and secured them in the shirt, tying it off to trap them inside. Then she returned to Abby, encouraged her to roll up her pant leg, and placed the bundle on her knee. "Keep this on you for fifteen minutes at a time for the next couple of hours. When I'm done fishing, I'll get you some more cold rocks."

"Okay."

Whit settled down on the log, slipped back into her sweater and jacket, and placed the fish she'd saved for her and Abby on the hot slab. The food began to cook and Whit went to refill their water bottle. She sipped from it as the water began to filter. It was crisp and cold. A Godsend. She walked back to Abby and handed it to her. "You should hydrate."

Abby drank and Whit sank back down on the log. "Where's the hare?"

"Hm?" She seemed to be lost in thought. "Oh. Right. She wandered off. Guess she wanted to go back home."

Whit searched her face for sadness or heartache, but saw only solace.

"That's probably a good thing," Whit said.

Abby shrugged. "I suppose."

"You could always get yourself a pet rabbit. When you get home."

Abby looked at her quizzically and then laughed.

"What?" Whit said.

"Is that your idea of comforting me?"

Whit felt her skin flush. "I don't know. I just thought—"

"Oh, my, God, it is." She laughed some more. "Thank you, Whit. That was sweet."

"Well, it obviously wasn't the right thing to say. You're laughing."

"It was sweet that you tried. I get the sense you aren't good at these sorts of things."

"I can be." She thought of the woman waiting for her at home and how she cared for her and comforted her. She hadn't had any complaints, so why couldn't she do it with other women? "At least I think."

Abby laughed again. "You're too cute, Whit."

Whit continued to blush, and she stabbed at the fish. "Let's eat." She came around the fire and served Abby hers in the pot and then speared a bite for herself. "It's good, yes?"

"Mm-hm."

"You getting used to eating the fish?"

"Seems so."

"And you're liking it?"

"For now."

"But you're going to go back to veganism?"

She nodded.

"Why? I mean, why are you vegan?"

Abby took a sip of water. "Well, you know how I feel about animals. I think that's obvious."

"Yes."

"But I also do it for health reasons." She raised an eyebrow. "Want to hear more?"

"Not really."

Abby chuckled. "Didn't think so. Most people don't."

"I had a girlfriend who was vegan and I heard it all from her. So I know all about animal products being bad for you, etc."

"Ah, so you're already educated."

"And then some."

Abby looked contemplative. "What happened there? With the girl? If you don't mind my asking."

Whit was a little surprised that she didn't ask further about her sexuality, whereas a lot of people did when she told them. But Abby didn't seem struck at her confession to having a girlfriend at all. She'd just seemed to readily accept it and move on. Almost as if she'd known or even suspected. Did that mean…could that mean… Abby was gay? Butterflies took flight in her chest, fluttering her heart.

"Whit?"

"Hm?"

"Your girlfriend?"

"She moved back to the Lower Forty-eight."

Abby took a bite of fish. "Was it a mutual breakup?"

Whit poked some more at her fillet. "More or less." What should she say? That Myra told her she was cold and indifferent and in no way passionate? Or that she lacked the skills for any real intimacy? She went with the safer route, the one that didn't make her sound like a total failure as a girlfriend. "She had health issues. Which really was why she chose to become a vegan. Because of her kidney failure."

Abby straightened her spine. "Oh? And the vegan diet helped her kidneys, didn't it?"

"It took a little time, but yes. Her kidney function went up from eleven to twenty-four in less than a year."

"That's astounding! So then, why did she move away? If she was improving?"

Because she said I wasn't around enough to be a supportive partner and when I was, I was too distant.

"She wanted to be close to a certain clinic and participate in a vegan study on repairing kidney function." It was true, she wasn't lying. She was just leaving out the other stuff. That wasn't lying, was it?

She flushed again at the possibility. She didn't usually lie, and thinking that she might be doing so left her feeling awful. She needed to escape, to get away and leave this conversation altogether. Damn it, why did every conversation with Abby leave her feeling like she had to hide something because she just couldn't talk about it?

Whit shoved a last piece of fish in her mouth and grabbed her spear. "I'll fish closer to camp this time, staying on this end of the creek. So just yell if you need me."

Abby blinked up at her. "You're taking off? Already? You didn't even finish your meal."

"Gotta get back to the creek. We're losing daylight. Stay in camp, okay? No running off."

"I won't, I swear."

"And keep that bundle on that knee. Fifteen minutes at a time." She noticed that Abby didn't have a watch, so she stopped and unfastened hers. She hesitated a moment, thinking about how much the piece meant to her, but then decided that Abby wasn't likely to

lose it or damage it by just sitting there. She gave her the watch and
then realized that she probably needed to pack the fire in the smoker,
so it would keep going while she was gone. She didn't want Abby
doing it with her bad knee. She set her spear aside and tended to the
smoker, then emerged and took up her spear once again. "Smoker's
all set. You shouldn't need to mess with it. I'll be back at sunset."

"I'll be here waiting." She smiled, pressing the backs of her
hands to the bottom of her chin while batting her eyelashes. Whit
couldn't help but laugh. She waved and headed for the creek,
thinking all the while that it wouldn't be so bad to have a woman
like Abby to come home to.

CHAPTER FIFTEEN

A bby sat quietly by the fire while Whit fished into the sunset. Luckily, she could see her from where she was, so she got the chance to study her uninterrupted for hours. Whit was like a dark horse—lean, powerful, and mysterious. Abby couldn't help but be captivated, not only by her appearance, but her personality as well. She was as quiet as she was protective. Beautiful, yet guarded. And Abby couldn't shake the sense that there was a lot more to Whit than she was letting on.

"Maybe she's just a very private person." She lifted the shirt full of rocks off her leg and set it aside. It was now warm and useless, but she had to admit, it had helped with her swelling and pain. Whit definitely knew what she was doing, using the rocks as a replacement for ice. Abby flexed her leg, bending her knee again and again. It felt better already. Maybe she would be able to walk tomorrow after all.

She rolled down her pant leg and checked the time. Whit should be coming back soon and she'd have to return the watch. The black face of the stainless steel Seiko looked too large on her slim wrist, but she liked the watch regardless. It was shiny and sleek, and appeared to be older, similar to the ones she'd seen some of her friends' fathers wear when she was younger. She wondered where Whit got it. Curious, she turned it over and found an inscription.

To Rick,
The best husband
And father.

Abby ran her thumb over the engraved words. She held the watch closer, confused as to why the words were darker than the rest of the stainless steel.

"Hmm. Must be dirt."

She searched for a twig to try and dig it out. But Whit sneaked up on her.

"What are you doing?"

Abby startled and dropped the twig she'd found to palm her chest. "Oh, Jesus, you scared me." Whit must've walked up while she was inspecting the watch. She hadn't even heard her approach. "I was just going to try and clean the dirt out of the inscription on the back for you."

Whit nearly threw the fish-riddled spear against the log. "You what?" She snatched the watch away from Abby and frantically turned it over.

"I was just going to try—"

"But you didn't."

"No, not yet I—"

"Don't," she said, sitting on the log. "Don't you touch it."

Abby stared at her in confusion. "Okay, I won't."

"That's right, you won't. I'm not giving it to you again." She fastened the watch back onto her wrist and adjusted it with her fingers, as if she wanted to make sure it was resting in exactly the right spot.

"Whit, I'm sorry, I've obviously done something wrong, but I have no idea what."

Whit wouldn't look at her. "Just forget it."

"The watch…" Abby said. "It obviously means something to you. Was it your father's?"

Whit visibly swallowed as she focused on the woods behind them. "Yes."

"And you want to keep the dirt on it. I understand. It's sentimental."

Whit's gaze finally settled on hers and Abby saw a pain there so deep and so raw, it took her breath away.

"It's not dirt." She picked up a stick and stabbed at the burning logs between them, increasing the heat output significantly. Abby edged back a bit as Whit tossed the stick aside and began removing the fish fillets from the spear to place them in the smoker.

"What is it?" Abby asked softly, careful to tread lightly. "Rust?" She couldn't figure out why Whit would get so upset over rust.

Whit knelt in front of the smoker, removed the rock pile for a door, and leaned inside to set the fish on the racks. She could only place two, so she backed out and stood and peeled away the branches to place the remainder of the fillets inside. As she reapplied the branches to the top tier, she spoke.

"It's blood." She then knelt once again to rebuild the smoker door.

Abby blinked, concerned and more confused than ever. She wanted to question her further, but her mouth had gone dry. Why would there be blood on her father's watch? Had something bad happened? And why would Whit want to keep it on there?

Whit finished with the stones and rose to return to the log, where she began cooking their dinner. Abby hadn't gathered any more mushrooms, but she had collected some blueberries on her quest. She dug into her pockets and dropped handfuls into the pot. She set the pot on the slab of stone next to the cooking fish.

"Did something happen, Whit?" she asked, almost afraid of the answer. "To your father?"

"Yes." She closed her mouth and clenched her jaw. Abby could see it flexing as she maneuvered the fillet with her buck knife. Her face had lost all color and her eyes had glazed over as she stared endlessly into the fire.

"Do you want to talk about it?"

Whit was silent for a long moment.

Abby spoke. "You don't have to, of course. I just—I'm here to listen if you'd like to share. Sometimes talking about things—"

"He was murdered."

"What?" Abby choked, having swallowed wrong.

Whit came around the fire for the water bottle. She drank heartily from it and then gave it to Abby without another word.

Abby took it slowly, trying to hold her gaze, but Whit was avoidant.

"Whit," she said. "Are you okay?"

The vacant look remained in her eyes as she walked away. Abby watched as she disappeared into the woods, back where she'd disappeared once before.

"Great," Abby said. "I've run her off again." She pushed herself to a stand and hobbled as best she could over to the tree line and followed Whit into the heavily wooded forest. Nightfall was seeping in, crawling in like an approaching spider, creepy and slow, causing anticipation to build. She worried about getting lost again, but also worried about Whit. Would she be able to find her way back in the dark like she did last time? Or was she too upset?

I have to go to her. She's hurting. And if what she said is true, then she's really hurting.

Abby began to yell for her, not bothering to stop to see if she could hear a reply. She just kept on plowing through the branches and bushes scraping her skin as she walked.

"Whit! Please come back. I promise I won't ask any more questions."

She closed her eyes and turned her head as she pushed through some heavy branches, and when she came out the other side, she saw Whit bent over, picking mushrooms, and dropping them into the bottom of her sweater.

"Whit," Abby breathed, hobbling over to her. "What are you doing?"

"Getting some more mushrooms."

She sounded so nonchalant that Abby did a double take. "You're what?"

"Getting some more mushrooms."

"But you—you just left. Without a word. I thought—"

"I'm fine." She straightened and showed her the bundle of mushrooms she held in the basket she'd formed with her sweater. "I got a whole bunch."

"So you did."

Whit walked past her and headed for the trail back. Abby hurried to catch up.

"Wait for me," she said as she lingered behind her. "I can't walk that fast."

Whit didn't slow however, and Abby once again had to brave the branches and brush on her own. By the time they returned to camp, Abby's face and hands were stinging with fresh cuts. She winced, wishing for some aloe vera to spread on them.

"Can you please not do that again?" she said, eyeing her cuts.

"Do what?" Whit poured the mushrooms into the sizzling pot of blueberries.

"Just take off."

"I didn't, did I? You knew I went for mushrooms."

"No, I didn't, Whit. I didn't know what you were up to until I found you."

Whit's face dropped as if she were truly unnerved by the news.

"You didn't say anything. You just left, like you did before."

"Oh." She flipped the fish with her knife.

"Oh?" Abby said. "That's it? Just 'oh'?"

Whit dropped onto the log and ran her hands through her hair as if exasperated. "I can't promise anything," she said.

"You can't promise anything? How is that fair? You made me promise not to wander off again and I did and I intend to keep that promise. And yet, you won't do the same? What gives, Whit?"

Whit held her head in her hands. "I don't know if I can."

"Why not?"

She looked up. "Because I didn't even realize I'd done it, okay?"

Abby stared at her, dumbfounded. "I don't understand."

"Neither do I. But I don't want to talk about it, okay? Just please, leave it be for now."

Her hands shook as she clasped them together and Abby decided to honor her request. The subject of her father had obviously stressed her considerably and Abby didn't want to add to that. Whatever had happened to her father must've been absolutely awful and it still greatly affected Whit, in more ways than she realized.

Abby spoke, her voice barely a whisper. "Okay, Whit. We won't talk about it."

Whit sighed. "Thank you."

Abby could smell the cooking berries and mushrooms. "You might want to stir that pot." She'd do it herself, but her knee was aching and she didn't think it wise to move. Whit quickly stirred the pot and then gave Abby the once-over.

"You need more rocks," she said. She sheathed her knife and retrieved her phone to switch on her flashlight. Then she turned toward the creek and started to walk away but stopped. She looked back at Abby. "I'm going to the creek," she said. "I'll be right back."

Abby smiled. "Okay, thanks for letting me know."

A small grin lifted one corner of her mouth and then she was gone. Abby waited patiently for her to return and when she did, she eased the cold, wet bundle down onto her bare knee.

"Thank you."

"You're welcome."

Whit settled down once again across the fire.

"So, do you think we'll be able to leave tomorrow?" Abby asked, grimacing at the feel of the icy chill on her skin.

"I think we should. Don't you?"

"You're asking me?"

"Yes."

"I'm ready to go."

"You sure? With your knee?"

"We can't wait on my knee to feel better. As I've said before, we'd be here forever."

"Okay then, we depart at first light."

Abby smiled, though she felt anything but certain about the decision. She was worried about her ability to walk. Would she be able to keep up with Whit and if not, how much would she slow them down? Would it ruin their chances of finding help before they ran out of food?

Whit seemed to read her thoughts. "Try not to worry about it. We'll just do the best we can, alright? You keep eating that fish and build up your strength."

"Yes, ma'am."

Whit chuckled. "We'll be okay, Abby. Mark my words."

Abby hugged herself, freezing. "I hope so, Whit. But the nights are growing longer and the weather is getting colder."

"Which is why we're leaving. We would've left sooner if it hadn't been for Boyd."

"You think he'll bother us again?"

"I doubt it. Like you said, winter is fast approaching and he needs shelter."

"What if he has shelter and he just lied about it like you said?"

Whit's jaw tensed. "He's gone, Abby. Don't worry." She stood to serve Abby's half of the fillet in the pot of berries and mushrooms. "Besides, if he were still around he'd have stolen more fish when I went off to search for you today."

"That's true." Abby took the pot. "Don't you want some?"

"You go ahead. I'll just work on my fish until you're done."

She eased down on the stump and began forking herself some fillet with her knife. They ate peacefully then, both staring into the fire, watching as the logs crackled and burned and broke apart into glowing orange embers. Night fully fell, bringing with it a considerable chill and she couldn't take the feel of the rocks anymore.

"I'm freaking freezing," she said, trying to remove the bundle. But Whit stood and slid out of her jacket. "Don't," she said, resting it on Abby's shoulders. "Just wear mine for a while."

"But, Whit, it's too cold for you to go without your coat."

"I'll be fine. It's more important that we keep that knee cold."

She returned to the stump and ate more fish.

Abby watched her closely, feeling cared for and protected. Something she hadn't ever felt with a woman she was interested in.

She considered that as she watched Whit and recalled the way she'd run off without a word and didn't even realize she'd done it. There was trauma there. Serious trauma. But she wasn't the only one with deep-seated pain.

Little did Whit know, Abby had her own.

CHAPTER SIXTEEN

Whit added to the back firewall after dinner, fearing the night would be noticeably colder than it had before. Then she built up the fire and joined Abby in the shelter. They said good night and settled in, and to Whit's amazement, Abby pressed her back into her again, as she'd done the night before at Whit's request. Whit turned into her and apprehensively enveloped her in her arms, waiting to see if Abby would protest. But Abby merely snuggled into her and sighed as if content. Soon her breathing grew deep and slow, and Whit knew she was asleep. It wasn't long until Whit's eyes grew heavy as well and sleep came as easy as Abby's steady breaths.

When Whit woke, she blinked against the darkness and fought confusion. She was on her back and someone was in her arms, head resting on her chest. It took a few moments before she realized it was Abby, and that they were in their shelter, in the middle of the wilderness. She lifted her head and saw dawn's early light peeking through the door. Gently, she shifted out from beneath Abby and pushed open the door to crawl outside. The air was cold and crisp, and heavy with moisture. A frost had settled and she hurried to get the fire going. Then she managed the smoker and checked the fish. They looked good, ready to go. She removed one from the rack and set it on the stump. Then she left camp to go relieve herself but froze when she saw fresh tracks on the frosted ground. She rushed back to the smoker and removed the branches to count the fish. She counted once, came up short, and then recounted. Damn it, she was still short by four fish on the bottom rung.

She looked to the tree line. Had Boyd returned? Why? He had plenty of fish. Was it just to fuck with them?

She followed the tracks, which were once again large and nondescript, into the woods, and noted that they weren't headed north. They were headed east. If it was Boyd, he wasn't trying to escape back to civilization. He was headed somewhere else, possibly somewhere close by. She considered following the trail, but remembered her conversation with Abby. She couldn't just take off. And they had plans to leave anyway, she couldn't afford to waste time hunting down a madman. That's what Boyd was in her book. A madman. Anyone who stalked two lost souls in the woods and continuously stole from them for kicks, was seriously touched.

She quickly relieved herself and walked back to camp, her clothes slightly damp from her brief hike in the frosty fauna. Abby was standing at the fire, warming herself and picking the pine needles from her flaming red hair.

"Morning," she said, sounding like death warmed over.

"Good morning. Did you sleep well?"

"I was warm, so that's a plus."

Whit picked up the fish and settled in next to Abby on the stump. She placed the dried fillet on the hot slab to heat it up some more before lifting it to tear apart. She handed a brittle piece to Abby.

"Wanna try?"

Abby took the fish and took a small bite. She chewed a while before she spoke. "It's good." But she sounded far from convinced.

Whit chuckled. "It takes some getting used to."

Abby sipped some water and ate quietly. Whit watched her, waiting for her to complain, but she didn't.

"So, are we ready to go then?"

Whit swallowed some dried fish. "Pretty much."

"Did you ever make a basket for the fish?"

"I made a rope for the lid to the pot, so we'll just put the fish in there and I'll carry it over my shoulder."

"Will it all fit?"

"I'll break it up." And with four whole fish missing, it was going to be much easier to fit everything in the pot. But she didn't mention that to Abby. She wasn't sure exactly what to say. They should just leave and head north, and let whoever it was continue on eastward.

"Drink up and I'll fill up the water bottle before we go."

They sat for a few more minutes, eating and drinking before they rose to kick out the flames. Whit took the water bottle to the creek and filled it to filter. Then she returned to camp and got busy breaking down the smoker and removing the fish to break apart for the pot. Abby helped, packing the pot full. They nibbled on the small remainder before Whit latched on the lid and secured it with the rope she'd made out of vines. Then she put out the fire for the smoker and placed her hands on Abby's shoulders.

"You ready?"

"Yep."

Whit nodded once. "Okay then, let's do it." She took the undershirt she'd used as an ice pack for Abby and tucked the pot inside it and slung it over her shoulder like a burlap sack. She'd dried the fabric by the fire overnight and planned to use it again for Abby if they stopped near a water source.

Whit led the way, with Junior's compass in her palm and Abby close behind. They talked for the first hour, about random things, careful not to slip on the heavily frosted ground as they walked. Abby started off okay, walking at an average pace, but then began to slow about two hours in. By the fourth hour, she was in obvious distress and Whit halted near a large Sitka spruce and encouraged her to sit.

"I can keep going," Abby said, leaning on the trunk.

"Rest," Whit said, placing the water bottle and pot on the ground. "We're making good time, so there's no reason to stress your knee." She glanced around, listening keenly for the crunch of footfalls of someone following them. "I'm going to go pee." She headed off for the brush, back the way they came, to double-check for Boyd. She backtracked a short distance, and listened as she peed.

But she heard nothing. Saw nothing of suspect. She pulled up her pants, cast one last look behind her, and walked back to Abby.

"You okay?" Abby asked, settled at the base of the tree, her creamy face crimson from the cold and exertion.

"Yeah, why?"

"You were gone awhile."

"Just checking things out."

"Find anything good?"

"Nah." She roosted next to her and let out a long sigh of relief. Her legs were tingling and she couldn't imagine how Abby's knee must be feeling. "How bad are you hurting? From a scale of one to ten?"

Abby laughed. "I don't know, Whit."

"No, come on, tell me. Honestly."

"Twelve."

"Really? Shit."

"But it doesn't matter. We have to keep going."

"It does matter. I'm worried about you."

Abby shrugged. "Not much we can do."

"We can go slower."

"Yes, we'll probably have to, unfortunately. And I'm sorry about that."

"Hey, no apologies. You're injured. That's not your fault." She nudged her. "Okay?"

Abby nodded but looked solemnly down at her hands.

"And no sadness," Whit said. "You're doing great. Just look how far we've already come. We're four hours in and we've made huge progress." She handed her the water bottle and Abby took a few sips. Then Whit did the same and traded out the bottle for the pot. "You hungry?"

"We need to save it."

"We can have a bite." She gave her a small chunk and shoved one in her own mouth. "It tastes better when you're tired and hungry."

Abby jammed the piece of fish into her mouth and chewed with her eyes closed. She held her hand out for the water bottle to which Whit complied.

"That bad, eh?"

She nodded and sipped the water, swallowing loudly.

"Sorry," Whit said, taking the bottle back.

"It's okay. It's food and that's all that matters."

"Hopefully, we'll come upon some more berries or mushrooms."

"That would be nice. I really like those salmon berries Boyd—"

She grew quiet as if she'd said something wrong.

"I like those, too," Whit said. "They're good."

Abby looked at her. "Sorry, I didn't mean to bring him up."

"You can talk about him."

"I don't want to. He—stole from us and it was all my fault."

"Abby, it wasn't—"

"No. It was. I fell for his charm and he took advantage. End of story."

Whit stared into her green eyes, saw the determination and the guilt, and decided to drop it. She simply patted her hand and looked off back into the brush.

After a few minutes of sitting in silence, a bustling sound came from the direction they'd come. Whit slid out her knife and stood, telling Abby to stay behind her.

"What is it?" Abby whispered.

"Shh." Whit took a few steps toward the noise. Something or someone was definitely walking through the woods. Her heart thudded, beating in her ears, and her palms were coated in sweat, causing her to readjust her grip on the knife.

She was just about to call out, to warn whoever it was to back off, when a deer broke through and froze, black eyes focused on her. Whit relaxed and smiled.

"Oh, my, God," Abby said from behind.

"Shh, don't move."

The deer stared at her for a long moment before it bolted, running back into the woods. Whit laughed as she walked back to Abby.

"You looked really scared," Abby mused.

"I was for a second."

"Did you think it was Boyd?"

Whit tried to hide the surprise she felt at the question. "No, not especially." She flushed again at the lie.

Abby studied her closely, her gaze skimming up and down Whit's face like she was searching for any sign of deceit. Whit didn't like the scrutiny, and she broke away, needing another excuse to change the topic before she fled. "We'll see a lot more wildlife before it's over with," she said, once again picking up the pot and undershirt to sling over her shoulder.

"I'd like to see more deer," Abby said, extending her hand for Whit to help her up.

Whit did and they stood for a moment, face to face, inches apart. Whit tried to control her breathing, but her heart rate had increased tremendously.

"I'm sure we will," Whit said. "See more deer."

"Good. I look forward to it."

Whit swam in her warm gaze. "Me too."

More rustling came from behind and Whit turned to see three deer crash through the brush and dart away. She heard Abby gasp in delight.

"As I was saying," Whit said with a laugh.

Abby leaned on her, laughing as well. "That was nice, but I could do without the shit getting scared out of me beforehand. Don't they come with some sort of warning?"

"'Fraid the rustling was the warning."

"Jesus," Abby breathed, palming her heart. "I thought a giant was breaking through the woods."

Whit steadied her and brushed her hair away from her face. "Ready?" she said again.

Abby nodded and Whit led them onward, checking the compass once again to make sure they were headed north, leaving the darting deer and anything else that may or may not be lingering, behind.

Chapter Seventeen

Abby didn't know what felt worse. Her throbbing knee, or her anxiousness over telling Whit that she couldn't go on. Her body answered for her when her knee gave out and she collapsed.

"Oh, my God, Abby!" Whit knelt next to her and helped her to sit up. "Are you okay?"

Abby laughed, bemused, and a bit hysterical, she was so exhausted. "I'm just a little dizzy is all." She slurred her words and Whit held her face, making her all the more lightheaded. "You're gorgeous," Abby declared, her wits depleting quickly.

"You're delirious." Whit's grave concern for her melted Abby's heart and here she was, letting her down.

"I'm sorry," she said. "I didn't make it to the end of the day."

"Don't be silly," Whit said. "You did amazing. And obviously too much. Shit, I should've insisted we stop hours ago."

"Not your fault," Abby said. "I would've argued with you."

"Yeah, well, I need to do better. Pay closer attention. Otherwise you're not going to be able to walk at all."

"Maybe I can hop."

Whit cracked a smile. "You think? Like your hare?"

"Yes, like Matilda." She felt her face cloud. "I hope she's okay."

"I'm sure she's fine," Whit said, rising.

Abby tilted her face skyward as cold, plump drops of rain began to fall. "I think we're in trouble," she said, holding out her hands to catch the downfall.

Whit glanced up with her. "I think you're right. This is bad news." She offered Abby her hand. "Can you stand? We need to move over to that cedar for shelter until I can build us one."

Abby allowed her to lift her up and she half-hopped, half-walked over to the nearby tree. But just as she was getting ready to slouch back down onto the ground, she saw something dark through the increasing streaks of rain and heavy brush. "What is that?" she said, pointing.

Whit followed her line of sight. "I don't know. It looks like…" She began to trot toward the faded brown structure. "A cabin." She glanced back at Abby. "I'm going to go check it out."

"Be careful," Abby said. "Someone might be holed up in there."

Whit retrieved her knife and then set off for the cabin, which, from what Abby could tell, was all weather-worn dark wood, the bottom overgrown with foliage. She prayed that it was habitable though, even if only for the night. She could use the warmth and a secure place to rest without having to worry about Boyd or someone else getting to them easily.

"Please," she said. "Let it be okay."

Whit returned with her knife sheathed and her hair glossy and flattened with rain. "It's doable," she said, wiping her damp face. "Someone's been using it off and on, keeping it up to par."

"You sure that someone isn't coming back anytime soon?"

"No way to tell for sure. But there's a beam we can lock the door with from the inside and there's no one in sight." She held out her hand. "Care for a tour?"

Abby took her hand, already chilled from the raindrops seeping through the branches above her. She relished how Whit's palm felt in her own, regardless of it being cold and wet, and she shuffled with her through the trees to the rustic cabin. Whit assisted her up the two makeshift steps to the slightly warped porch and helped her in through the open door. The building was tiny and sparsely furnished, with a single window, a twin mattress on a spring frame, a two-chaired table, a splintered bookshelf full of various odds and ends, and a wood stove in the corner nestled next to a depleted pile of wood. An old, yellowed map of Alaska was pinned to the back wall next to a calendar from 1983, and the lingering scent of must and damp tickled her nostrils. But the walls were intact and the roof was seemingly good, so she was satisfied.

"Looks like a four-star joint to me," Abby said, hands on hips.

"It does, doesn't it?" Whit led her over to one of the chairs. "Check this out." She sifted through the dusty items on the bookshelf and pulled out a bottle of Jack Daniels whiskey. "We even have cups." She brought the goods to the table and poured them both a shot in the chipped, green ceramic mugs.

"This will warm us up," she said, toasting Abby. "Cheers."

Abby winced as the liquor burned its way down her throat, causing Whit to laugh. "Want another?"

"No, thanks." One was enough. God, it tasted awful and it reminded her of her college days when she used to get drunk with her friends on Jack and Cokes. Nausea slushed around in her gut. She pushed the mug away and belched softly.

"Yeah, you're right. We should probably save it," Whit said, replacing the bottle on the shelf. She picked up some books. "Hey, we've got stuff to read." She flipped through them. "Mostly old westerns, but at least it's something. And..." she said, bringing an old hurricane lantern over along with a handful of small candles. "We have light."

"Great. Looks like we've got most of what we need here." Abby blew dust off the table and settled.

"Why don't you rest while I go gather some wood?"

"You sure you don't want some help?" She knew she couldn't offer much, but she could try.

Whit gave her a look. "Don't even think about moving."

Abby consented and Whit was out the door in a flash, leaving Abby alone in the cabin. As she studied her surroundings, she saw what appeared to be two marks on the worn map, so she stood to examine it closer. Her heart lifted as she saw a spot identifying what must be their current location. But then it fell to her stomach as she saw just how far they still had to go to get to the nearest town. And Cozy may as well be a far-off dream. The other mark was farther northeast, and she wondered what it was. It wasn't close to a road or any civilization that she could see.

She resettled on the chair. "At least we're safe for now." She debated if she'd be able to make the trek out after all. Tears formed in her eyes as she thought about the little cabin being her final destination, but she quickly wiped them away when she heard Whit clamoring up the steps.

"Got some wood," she said as she breezed inside, smelling of the fresh rain and woodsy earth. "And..." she said as she straightened and dug in her pockets to pull out some dried brush. "Some kindling."

"Excellent," Abby said.

Whit frowned. "Have you been crying?"

"Of course not."

"Abby, please. I can tell." She shoved the kindling in the stove, next to the dry wood that had already been inside, and knelt before her. "What's wrong? Is it your knee? You hurting that bad?" She rubbed the moisture from her face and blinked.

Abby fought back more tears. "I'm afraid I'm not going to make it out."

"Oh, Abby. Please, don't think like that. You're going to be fine. We're going to be fine, and we're going to reach help."

Abby wanted to believe her, more than anything. But more than wanting to believe her, she wanted to reassure her that she was okay and that she was going to keep trudging along. "I'll fight," she said, willing herself to do so. "I will."

"You don't have to fight right now, okay? Right now we rest. And we rest until you feel well enough to leave again."

"But we—"

"No arguing," she said as she rose. She put a finger to her lips. "Just rest."

Abby once again acquiesced and Whit, seemingly satisfied, wriggled her fire starting kit out of her back pocket and squatted in front of the stove. She leaned in and struck the ferro rod, creating sparks that Abby could see, and then blew gently until a flame came to life. She closed the clunky-sounding door and stood. "That should get hot in no time." She slid out the accompanying chair and sat. "Ready for some fish?"

"Ugh," Abby let out before she could stop herself.

"I see you're excited."

"Totally stoked," Abby said.

"I could go look for other things to munch on. If you're okay being alone for a while?"

"I don't know, Whit." What if whoever had been here came back? What would she do?

"I need to go get more firewood anyhow, to last us through the night. I found a dry patch not far from here." But she'd obviously picked up on Abby's trepidation. "Just keep the door locked. I'll let you know it's me when I return." She dumped the dried fish on the table and readied the pot to take with her. Abby felt that nausea slosh around in her stomach again.

Whit showed her the big wooden beam that slid into place to block the door from opening. It seemed secure enough.

"Okay," Abby said, wanting to appease her.

Whit smiled. "I'll be back shortly."

Abby stood and braced herself and followed her to the door. Whit trotted down the stairs and turned to give her one last look of reassurance. "See you soon."

Abby smiled, though she knew it didn't fully reach her eyes. She was apprehensive and anxious at being left alone, but it was what had to be done. She closed the door and latched it, and then sat on the hand-crafted chair. The mattress, which rested on a metal frame, looked appealing, but she just couldn't imagine sleeping where Boyd had, regardless of how exhausted she was. So she settled in as best she could in the chair and rested her head in her arms on the table. In no time at all, as the stove began to warm, she was fast asleep.

She dreamt of the ocean, thick and heavy with white-capped waves of which she was bobbing, alone, and in a small boat. She was crying for help, searching desperately for shore, when she heard knocking. She searched desperately for the source, unable to locate it, until the boat hit something, jarring her. The knocking continued and grew louder as the waves pummeled the vessel relentlessly into the rocks, until the hull began to break apart and the water rushed in.

She cried out and sat straight up, looking around at the tight quarters of the cabin, heart in her throat. She got control of her breathing and wiped the sweat from her brow. She was still alone, save for the crackling of the fire in the stove, which was producing good heat now. Knocking came from the door, bold and forceful. She stiffened. Was that the knocking in her dream?

She stood and twisted her fingers in her hand, still feeling like she was aboard the rickety boat in her dream. Was the dizziness from sheer exhaustion? Or something else?

Someone knocked again at the door, bringing back her focus. She took a step toward the rapping but then stopped. Would Whit knock that boldly? Maybe she would if she'd been knocking awhile. She took another step. "Whit?"

Nothing.

More knocking. This time from the wall to her left. She called out again, pulse pounding. "Whit? Is that you?"

More noise, this time banging from the back wall. She froze, looking at the window, afraid to approach it. Whoever was out there would be able to see her if she did. And they'd see that she was alone. She slunk back against the wall out of sight, terrified.

Someone was out there. And by the sound of it, they were angry.

She clenched her eyes. Where was Whit? Was she okay? Had whoever it was gotten to her?

She stood very still, too frightened to move. She searched the cabin for a weapon, a stick, a stone, anything. She was alone and helpless with her bad knee and nothing to use for protection. Whit had taken the spear she'd left outside with her. Abby eyed the chair, then slid it closer to her. If worse came to worst, she could use it to strike someone.

She clung to the back of it, praying for peace. After a few long minutes with no further noise, she relaxed a little and edged toward the window. With a big breath of courage, she turned and snuck a look outside, panning hurriedly from left to right. She saw nothing but the darkening woods.

Then another knock came from the door, startling her. She turned with her hand on her heart and nearly collapsed with relief when she heard Whit call her name.

"Oh, thank God." She wobbled over and lifted the beam to open the door. Whit bounded in with an armload of firewood and the pot dangling from the rope over her shoulder. "Have you been knocking?" Abby asked, with the hope that maybe it had been Whit trying to wake her after all.

"You mean other than just now?" She deposited the load next to the stove and rested her hands on her hips, breathless. Then she walked back to the porch and brought in her spear to lean against the wall.

Abby nodded.

"No, why?" She grabbed Abby's hands. "You're trembling."

"There was knocking," Abby said, trying to calm herself. She didn't like the fact that she was shaking, nor did she like the panicked concern in Whit's gaze. "Before you came. All over the walls."

Whit's brow furrowed. "Knocking?"

"And banging."

Whit stole a glance outside. "Did you see anyone?"

"No."

Whit drew out her knife. "Lock the door. I'm going to go look around."

Abby seized her by the arm. "No! Don't go out. Please." She was still trembling, terrified Whit would walk out and disappear, never to be seen again. Besides, it was pouring rain. She could hear it slamming onto the roof, see the silver sheets of it falling through the open door.

Whit fell silent, taking her in. Finally, she nodded. "Okay." She released her to gather the remaining wood and bring it back inside. Abby quickly bolted the door as Whit dumped the pile on the floor.

"Thank you," Abby breathed.

Whit sank down into a chair and wrung out her rain-soaked hair. She was trembling slightly as well, but Abby knew it was from the cold and not fear.

"Someone really banged on the walls?"

Abby dragged her chair over to the table and joined her. "The door, the walls, everywhere. Scared me to death."

Whit seemed to think. "Had to be Boyd. He's messing with us."

But Abby wasn't so sure. The knocking, the banging, was so loud and forceful, it sounded like someone bigger than Boyd. Someone angry. Really angry.

"I don't know, Whit. I'm not so sure."

"What do you mean?"

"Well, I was asleep and having this dream—"

"Whoa." Whit leaned forward. "You were dreaming?"

"Yes, but—"

"Could you've dreamt the noise?"

"No, I—"

Whit slid some fish over and toyed with the pieces. "Let's not worry about it," she said. "Let's just focus on dinner." She passed some chunks to Abby. Then she retrieved some for herself and popped a sliver in her mouth. "Okay?"

Abby flushed, feeling brushed off. "I didn't dream it, Whit."

"Okay." She chewed. "But let's try not to think about it. For now anyway. Sorry, I couldn't find anything else to eat."

Abby stared at her dismayed. Whit had an uncanny ability to shut off when things bothered her. Abby wished, at the moment, that she could do the same.

Unfortunately, she couldn't, and she wondered just what had happened to Whit to make her be able to do so so easily.

CHAPTER EIGHTEEN

Whit wasn't sure what exactly had happened while she was out collecting wood, but whatever had happened had definitely traumatized Abby. She'd come back to find her as pale as a ghost and trembling like a leaf. And the look on her face... it was as if she'd encountered the devil himself. What seemed to upset her even more was when she'd suggested that maybe Abby had dreamt the whole thing. She'd argued with Whit, refusing to even consider that it was possible, and then she'd grown unusually quiet and all but abandoned her fish, choosing instead to just lay her head on the table and stare into oblivion. Whit feared that she might slowly be losing her.

"Want me to heat up your fish? It's better that way." She could put some in the stove on a piece of wood, no problem. In fact, she placed a few pieces on a long stick and gently set it inside the stove, nestled in the glowing ashes.

"That'll take just a few minutes," she said, resettling in her chair.

But Abby said nothing. Nor did she even blink.

"I believe you about the knocking," Whit said, wanting her to know that she was still on her side and that she could trust her. "I only suggested that you might've dreamt it because it sounded more plausible than someone harassing us. But obviously I was wrong and I apologize." Again, she didn't mention the tracks she'd seen that morning. Now it seemed that someone, namely Boyd, was indeed still stalking them, trying to make their life hell. She wondered what else he would do.

Abby remained still.

"Abby?"

Slowly her gaze shifted to Whit.

"Will you talk to me, please?" Whit said.

She sat up. "What would you like for me to say?"

"I don't know. Anything. But preferably that you heard me at least."

"I heard you."

"Great. So, what do you think? You forgive me?"

She shrugged.

"Come on, Abby. Give me a break here."

"Why should I?" Anger knitted her brow. "I had the absolute shit scared out of me, I tried to tell you about it, and you wrote it off as a dream and then refused to talk about it. How do you think that made me feel?"

Whit felt her throat tighten. "I said I'm sorry. I didn't mean to upset you."

"Well, you did, Whit. You did." She stood. "Damn it, I can't even freaking walk!" She toppled her chair and groaned.

Whit went to her. "Hey, it's okay," she said softly.

"Don't tell me everything's okay, Whit. Everything is far from okay."

"Things aren't so bad." She rested her hands on her shoulders and felt the hard tension in her muscles. "We've got a roof, and food, and a fire."

"We've got a crazy person harassing us, shitty fish to eat, a smelly cabin with a bed that stinky Boyd had lain in, and a downpour of rain outside, keeping us in. How is that okay?"

"And let's not forget my decrepit knee, or the fact that we're nearly starving, and that I'm having trouble keeping my jeans pulled up, or the fact that we have next to no water left, and no creek that we've been able to find."

Whit waited until she paused to breathe before she spoke. "Things are less than ideal, yes. But we have to find the positives in those things in order to make it through. That's what I'm doing."

"I know," she said after a brief pause, obviously exasperated. "And you do a good job of it, too. I'm just tired, Whit. And scared. And Boyd, or whoever, just sent me over the edge."

Whit led her toward the bed. "You want to lie down? Prop your knee up and rest?" Perhaps all she needed was some good sleep.

Abby stiffened. "Not on that mattress."

It was an older mattress and not very thick, but other than that, it appeared fine.

"Boyd slept on it," she said. "So it probably stinks and God knows what's living in it."

Whit laughed, unable to help herself. This was the first time Abby was voicing any complaints, and she might be right about Boyd and the mattress. She wanted to reassure her nonetheless, and Abby did desperately need to prop her leg up and rest.

Whit hoisted up the mattress. "Open the door, will you?"

Abby looked mortified. "But what about Boyd?"

"Boyd Schmoyd. If he wants to do something, let him. My guess is he's too chicken shit, so he'll stay hidden."

Abby reluctantly unlocked the door, allowing Whit to carry the bundled bed outside. Once there, she dropped it on the porch, then grabbed the end and shook it out as best she could, turning it over to do the same. Then she stood it up and smelled it. "It's musty, but it doesn't stink like Boyd." She smelled the other side. "Same."

"Are there any…bugs?"

Whit studied the mattress closely. "Nope. None that I can see." She lifted the mattress and began to carry it back inside. "I'm going to put it back unless you want to let it air out awhile."

Abby shook her head.

"Okay, then." Whit returned the bed to the frame and Abby closed and latched the door. Then she limped over to the mattress and sat, a look of sorrowful compliance on her face.

Whit couldn't hide her grin. "You look as excited about lying on that as you do about eating the smoked fish."

"They're about the same in my book. But I need to stop whining and suck it up."

"You've only whined once."

"Once is too many." She groaned and relaxed onto the bed, wincing as she positioned her hurt leg. Whit came to her side with the undershirt she'd been using to provide cold therapy for Abby's knee. She wadded it up and carefully tucked it beneath her knee.

"There. That'll elevate it a little."

"Thanks." She scooted. "You want to join me?"

"Maybe later. I want to eat some more and tend to the stove." While she did indeed need to do those things, she was really avoiding lying next to her because she could only think of spooning with her as she'd done the night before. And she didn't think she had the courage to try again at the moment.

"What's that smell?" Abby asked, her brow crinkled.

Whit turned, searching for the source. "Oh, shit, the fish!" She rushed to the stove and removed the stick with the fish on it. The dried pieces were toasted beyond what she'd intended.

"Ugh, I don't think I can eat those," Abby said.

Whit deposited them onto the table and tossed the stick back inside the stove and closed the door.

With quick fingers, she popped a piece into her mouth and chewed. It was hot, overdone, and crunchy, but she ate it anyway. They couldn't afford to waste food.

"Well?" Abby asked.

"It's awful."

Abby laughed. "Thanks for the honesty." She held out her hand. "Bring me some."

"You sure?"

"I need to suck it up, like I said. Especially if I want to keep my pants on."

Whit stilled, thinking of Abby out of her pants, but then recovered. She brought Abby some of the toasted fish.

"Don't say I didn't warn you."

Abby was watching her curiously and Whit had to remind herself that there was no way she was aware that she'd been imagining her out of her pants.

"What was that look for?" Abby asked.

Whit sat. She focused on the fish, stirring it around with her fingers, afraid to make eye contact with Abby.

"You looked weird there for a second."

"Hm? Nah, I'm fine. Just grossed out by the overcooked fish."

"If you say so."

Whit saw Abby eat the fish. She grimaced like she had with the pain in her knee, but she kept chewing, and eventually swallowed with great effort. "Ugh, my God, that's horrible." But she slid another piece in and ate it as well.

Whit smiled, amused. Abby was trying again. Being a real trouper. In the morning, if the rain stopped, she'd go out and try to find them other food sources. For now, they'd have to settle for the fish.

She took their water bottle and crossed to open the door. This time Abby didn't protest, and Whit stood at the edge of the porch and held the open filter beneath a stream of rain running off the roof. When it was full, she brought it back inside and re-bolted the door.

"We have more water," she said, hoping it would help to cheer Abby up, but as she looked over at her, she discovered her fast asleep. "Sleep well, Abby," she whispered, going back to the table. She set the water bottle down, held the filter up so it could do its job, and studied the map on the wall. She saw the X marking where they were and searched with her index finger nearby. They were still south of any noticeable help, but she did spot a water source not too far away. Tomorrow, she'd search for it. There was also another X, about a days' hike away. She wondered if it was another cabin or at least someplace to get help.

"Things aren't so bad," she said softly to herself. She sat and lowered the filter as it finished with the rainwater. They now had a full bottle of water once again. Abby would be pleased. She watched as she slept, wishing she had a blanket to cover her with. Instead, she slinked out of her own coat, feeling plenty warm with the fire from the stove, and spread it over her. Abby stirred slightly and snuggled beneath the jacket, releasing a puff of air as she did so. Whit smiled wistfully at her, tucked an errant lock of hair behind her ear, and returned to her seat.

As she watched Abby dream, she thought about what it was that was causing her to be so concerned with her well-being, when she obviously hadn't been that way with her ex, Myra, the one who'd complained.

No answer was forthcoming.

CHAPTER NINETEEN

Abby awoke to mostly darkness and a soft, rhythmical sound coming from her right. She blinked to get her bearings, then turned to find Whit snoring at the small table near the stove. Abby shifted and groaned at her sore knee as she sat up and draped her legs over the squeaky bed. Whit's coat fell onto the floor, and she knelt to pick it up, touched that Whit had shrouded her as she'd slept. Now she hobbled over to the table and eased it beneath Whit's head to serve as a pillow. But the gentle movement disturbed her and she woke.

"Mm, is it morning?" she asked as she sat up and rubbed her eyes.

The candle in the hurricane lamp had a tiny flickering flame burrowed inside it, trying desperately to hang on to life. Abby blew it out and sank into a chair.

"By the looks of it," Abby said. "I can't believe I slept that long without waking. I must've slept like a rock."

"You did," Whit said.

"Why didn't you come to bed? You could've moved me over. I wouldn't have minded."

"I wanted to let you sleep. You needed the rest."

"So did you." She lightly grazed her arm, disliking the exhausted look on her face. Whit didn't pull away; she merely eyed her hand and then met her gaze.

"Not as much as you did."

"Well, I'm rested now," Abby said, patting her arm. "So, tell me what I can do to help our situation?"

"Whoa there, cowgirl." Whit stood and stretched. "How's your knee?"

"It's not bad." It still hurt, but she was trying to downplay it. She knew that as soon as Whit saw her try to walk the gig would be up. So she confessed. "It's still sore."

"How bad?"

"Pretty bad."

Whit nodded as if she'd expected as much. "Then you should stay here. I'm going to go find that creek I saw on the map and look for berries."

Abby didn't like the idea of staying behind, but she knew it was the wise thing to do. She would only slow Whit down, and going out in search of a creek and food would most definitely irritate her knee. The disappointment she felt must've been showing on her face, because Whit rested a hand on her shoulder.

"I won't be long."

Other concerns came to mind as she looked into her maple syrup-colored irises. "You sure you'll be okay out there alone?"

Whit squeezed her shoulder. "I'll be okay. Will you?" She focused on the window, as if searching for the culprit of the knocking.

"I'm not going to lie, I'm a little anxious he'll come back while you're gone."

"I'll leave you the knife. If it'll make you feel safer."

"You need that. You're the one going out alone."

Whit chewed her lower lip. "Alright. But you keep that door locked. No matter what."

Abby didn't agree but she didn't argue either.

Whit snatched up her coat and slipped into it. Then she grabbed the empty pot and the undershirt Abby had used as a cushion for her knee, along with the spear. "Do you need to relieve yourself? Now's the time to do it, before I take off."

Abby slowly followed Whit out the door. She ambled down the steps into the frigid, frosted morning, and went to pee as Whit stood guard on the porch. When Abby returned, she found Whit studying her closely.

"You're walking a little better," she said. "But still not good enough for our journey just yet."

"I wish it would hurry and heal."

"It will. You just need more rest." She helped Abby back up the stairs. "I shouldn't be gone long. An hour or so."

"Please, be careful."

"You do the same."

Abby watched her disappear into the woods and then closed and locked the door. She added more firewood to the embers in the stove, hoping a flame would catch. But after monitoring it for a few minutes, she knew she had to do something to help it burn. She scavenged through the wood pile until she found some dry bark and brush. She chucked that in the pile of ash and stirred the contents with a stick. Soon a flame caught and the stove came to life with heat once again. She closed the door and sat at the table, enjoying the growing warmth.

With the icy temperatures of the mornings, she worried the first snow would come and then soon after that, even more. Then what would they do? Could she walk through inches of snow to get out? It didn't seem likely, considering she could hardly walk as it was. And even if they were able to leave in the snow to try to make it out, there was no telling what Boyd would do to them while they were on their way. Would he become violent and try to hurt them physically? Or would he continue to fuck with them in other ways? The dooming thoughts plagued her, and her throat grew raw with emotion. Tears threatened but she shoved them down and wiped angrily at her eyes.

A loud bang startled her. A chill ran up her spine and the hair stood up on the back of her neck. She brushed away more tears and steeled herself as more banging ensued. Whoever it was had bypassed the knocking this time and gone straight for the loud, forceful banging.

"Who's there?" she called, gripping the table so hard it hurt. More thumping, this time on the back of the cabin. The wall shook and the calendar fell to the floor. The window rattled and she feared it would crack or break altogether. Though it was small, she still had the fear that the perpetrator would be able to come through to get her. She couldn't let that happen.

She stood, gritted her teeth, and marched to the door. Before she could think long enough to change her mind, she unlatched the door and flung it open. "I'm not afraid of you, you son of a bitch!"

The banging stopped.

She stood frozen, shaking as she'd done before. Swallowing, she spoke again, more terrified than ever as she imagined the villain making his way around the cabin to get her. "Why don't you show yourself, huh? Or are you too chicken shit to face me like a man?"

She held fast to the door, gripping it so tightly she could feel the splinters digging into her fingertips. She waited in silence. An eternity seemed to pass and she felt like she might faint from fear at the slightest of movements. She stared straight ahead, too afraid to turn to scan the surrounding area. But there was only quiet. Slowly, she reversed back into the cabin and closed the door. She locked it and slid down the rear wall and fought sobbing. Eventually, she fell asleep.

Another loud series of noises jolted her awake and she rubbed her face, confused. She pushed herself up as the clamoring continued from the front of the cabin.

A knock sounded at the door and Whit called out. "Abby, it's me."

Feeling stiff, she limped over to the door and let her in. Whit took one look at her and her face clouded. "What happened?"

Abby started to shake her head, to deny that anything had occurred, but Whit grasped her shoulders and stared into her with a deadly seriousness. "Abby, what happened?"

"He came again."

"When?"

"Soon after you left."

"He's watching us. Motherfucker."

Abby didn't tell her about confronting him. She was realizing now just how stupid it was to do. He could've easily attacked her and taken the cabin back for himself. Then where would they be? Up shit's creek, that's where.

"You're safe now. He seems to be gone," Whit said after taking a look around. She picked up the pot and the wet shirt bundle. "I brought back some cold rocks for your knee, and I managed to find some salmon berries. There aren't many, but I thought it would be a nice treat for you."

"They will be, thanks." She took the pot and Whit carried the shirt full of rocks inside and locked the door. Abby scooted her back to the wall on the bed as Whit placed the cold bundle on her leg.

"Good?"

"Mm-hm." Abby opened the pot and munched on some berries. "Want some?"

"No, those are for you." She smiled and sat at the table.

"You're too good to me, Whit," Abby said. She did so much for her, going out of her way to help her, and make sure she was okay. It was very kind.

"I'm just doing what's right." She started picking at the pile of smelly fish to nibble. Then she got a thick stick to line some pieces of fish on and stuck that carefully in the stove.

"You do more than that and you know it," Abby said. She shrugged, but Abby prevailed. "I appreciate it, Whit. Truly. You're a really nice person."

"Nice," she said with a chuckle.

"Something wrong with nice?"

"No, just…" She grew quiet.

"What?"

"Nothing."

Abby could tell there was definitely something and she couldn't let it go. "No, tell me."

"It's nothing. Forget it." She opened the stove door and started fiddling with the fish-lined stick.

"No way. You don't let me get away with not telling you things. So fess up, woman."

Whit remained silent.

"Something bothered you about the word nice and I want to know what it was." Abby changed her position on the bed, and slung her legs over the side. "Otherwise, I'm going to come over there and make you tell me."

Whit chortled.

"Don't laugh."

"I'm sorry." She kept messing with the stove's contents. "It's just, that's a ridiculous statement."

"Ridiculous?" The bundle of cold rocks clamored to the floor as she stood. Whit hurried to her.

"Abby, don't." She appeared serious now in not wanting her to move. But Abby was resolute. She took a step toward her, putting a little more pressure on her knee than she'd intended, and she fell, landing in Whit's arms.

"So—rry," Abby said, bracing herself against Whit's chest. "Guess that was dumb."

Whit held her tight, staring into her eyes. "Yeah."

She didn't let go and Abby didn't try to pull away. Instead, she relaxed against her and released a breath.

"Guess I should lie back down."

"Uh-huh."

But neither moved. Abby held her breath again, heart thudding madly behind her breast. She shut her eyes as Whit inched closer. Then, at the last second, Abby widened her eyes.

"You have someone," she blurted.

Whit blinked. "What?"

"Back in Cozy. You said so yourself."

"Abby—"

"No," Abby pushed away. "I can't, Whit. Not if you're just going to go home to her."

Whit held fast but didn't try and pull her back. "I'm not. I mean, I am, but I'm not."

"What the hell does that mean?"

"It means—she's—it's not like that."

"Not like what? Serious? Is now when you tell me you have an open relationship?"

"What?" She had the nerve to look appalled. "No, of course not."

"Then what, Whit?"

Whit's eyes drifted closed. "It's not what you think."

"But you do have someone waiting for you back in Cozy?"

Whit seemed to struggle to answer. "Yes, but—"

"Forget it. I don't want to hear it." Abby pushed away fully this time and fell onto the bed. She cried out as a sharp pain shot up from her knee. Whit tried to come to her side, but she refused her.

"I'm fine," she said, more hurt than she'd care to admit, and not just from her knee. Whit tried to return the cold bundle to her leg, but Abby turned on her side to face away from her.

"Abby, come on. You need to keep your knee cold."

"Later."

"It won't be cold then."

Abby didn't want to admit it, but Whit was right. And she didn't want her to have to go back out to the creek. She flipped onto her back and raised her pant leg. "Fine."

Whit situated the shirt onto her leg and remained at her side. She seemed to be searching for something to say. "Whatever you're thinking about me, it's not true. If you'll just listen, I—"

"No, Whit. I don't want to listen. So, just leave me alone. Please."

She closed her eyes to shut her out. It apparently worked because she heard her messing with the stove again.

Abby kept her eyes closed, wanting nothing more than for sleep to come once again. Anything to stop feeling the hurt she now couldn't deny.

CHAPTER TWENTY

Whit sighed and rubbed her eyes as she set down a copy of Cormac McCarthy's *Suttree*. She'd been reading for over an hour, trying to concentrate on something other than the friction she'd had with Abby. But even McCarthy's words couldn't distract her. She knelt before the bookcase and leafed through the remainder of the books, hoping that perhaps another selection would do the trick. But nothing seemed appealing. She snacked on more fish and swallowed some water.

Abby was right, the food wasn't very tasty, but beggars couldn't be choosers. She eyed the mug sitting in front of her and decided that she'd had enough water. What she needed was a drink. She pulled the whiskey from the shelf and poured herself a generous helping. She didn't consider herself an alcoholic, but she did partake in the occasional shot or two when she was alone late at night, just as her father used to do when they'd return home from an expedition.

The thought only made her want to swallow more, so she sat and sipped and watched Abby sleep. She hoped the rest would bolster her, in more ways than one. She'd been so close to kissing her and then it had all gone to hell. But how could she explain her situation if she refused to listen? Abby had been so upset, she hadn't even given her a chance to try to tell her about her life back home in Cozy. So, how could she remedy this?

"I can't. Not if she won't listen." She took another slow sip and enjoyed the warming ache of the alcohol in her chest. She was already beginning to feel the effects as relaxation soothed her troubled mind. Maybe she should try again. Maybe Abby would wake in a better, more generous mood and she'd let her explain. Then they could rekindle that would-be kiss and who knows what that might lead to.

Another sip went down as thoughts turned over and over of her and Abby making love. She imagined them far from the cabin, in a warm, soft bed, with a roaring fire, its dancing light kissing their naked skin, while a silent snow fell outside through a large, picturesque window. Then she saw Boyd slide into view just beyond that pane of glass, lifting a gun to shoot at them. She shivered and downed the rest of the whiskey before pushing up from the table. She couldn't sit there any longer and allow this asshole to scare Abby every time she left.

She quietly opened the door to snoop for any telltale signs of their visitor and then gently closed it. The snapping of a twig came from her left and she saw movement in the brush just beyond the cabin in the tree line. She jumped off the porch and sprinted into the woods, determined to tackle the son of a bitch in a fit of rage. But the longer she ran, the farther she got from the cabin where Abby was sleeping without a locked door to keep her safe. And she wasn't gaining on whoever she was chasing, the sound of his crashing footfalls now impossibly far away. She stopped her chase and rested her hands on her knees to regain her breath.

"Fuck." She headed back to the cabin, crestfallen. How was she going to stop this guy? And why them? Didn't this asshole have anything better to do? "If it's Boyd, then I doubt it." But why would he do this? Had he been that offended over her attitude toward him? Talk about holding a grudge. But why frighten Abby? He'd liked Abby. Was it just to get to her? He had known how protective she was of Abby, so maybe it was plausible. Still, something didn't sit right with her. Boyd…he was a liar and a manipulator, yes. But someone who would do all this? For fun? She shook her head, unable to think it through.

She pushed through the brush as the cabin came into view. She cursed as she saw that, in her haste, she'd somehow left the door ajar. Abby appeared at the opening, saw her, and came trudging out. "Where were you?" She didn't look rested, and she didn't sound as though she were in a more generous mood as Whit had hoped.

"I thought I heard someone in the woods." She was almost positive it had been a *someone* and not an animal, but she couldn't be sure.

"So you took off?"

"They sounded close. I thought I could catch them."

"So, you left me? Alone and asleep with the door open?"

Whit climbed the steps, her skin burning from both the alcohol and Abby's accusations. "I thought I could catch him."

Abby turned to walk back inside, obviously pissed, but halted in front of the door. "Whit," she said, brow crinkled.

Whit came to her side. There, hastily carved in the old wood of the door, was a word that made her chest constrict so hard she found it hard to breathe. She traced the word with her finger and followed Abby's line of sight as they glanced around the front of the property.

"When did he do this?" Abby asked, her mood now considerably more solemn and quiet.

"I don't know," Whit said.

"While we were both inside? It's impossible."

"I don't know," Whit said again. Had she drifted off while drinking? Maybe she'd had more than she thought. "Maybe he did it when I ran off." She didn't like to admit that, but it made sense. Maybe she hadn't been chasing their stalker at all. Unless there were two of them. She swallowed the ball in her throat and checked the property again but saw nothing suspect.

"You mean he did this while I was in here asleep? With the door open?"

"I don't know, Abby."

"Wonderful."

"Maybe not. Maybe I drifted off while reading. I'm just not sure."

Abby staggered back inside and Whit followed, closing the door behind them. She carefully engaged the lock and stood there very still, unsure what to do. She felt responsible, and the feeling was terrible.

"I'm sorry I left you alone," she said.

"With the door wide open."

"I could've sworn I closed it, Abby."

"It still wasn't locked."

"No, no it wasn't. And it was irresponsible for me to just take off. I won't do it again."

"Just wake me first, okay? So I can bolt the door."

Whit agreed. Abby perched on the bed. "Are you going to come in?"

Whit walked slowly to the table, but she couldn't sit. She ran her hand through her hair, frustrated. She'd screwed up for the second time, left Abby alone with a certifiable mad man. What was wrong with her? First, they'd had discourse over the other woman in her life, and now this. The fantasy of making love to Abby now seemed like a far-off pipe dream rather than something that could truly happen.

"Whit, it's okay," Abby said.

"It's not. I put you in danger."

"Yes, but it's over. We have to move on."

"I can't," Whit whispered. Memories of her father clouded her mind. Otter's knife sliding from his side, all slick with dark blood. The way her father had then collapsed and stared off into oblivion with glossy, wide eyes. He'd been in danger too and she'd failed to see it, failed to stop it, and she'd lost him. She couldn't lose Abby too.

"Whit," Abby said, touching her shoulder. Whit flinched, alarmed at her sudden proximity. When had she moved?

"Sorry," Abby said gently, removing her hand. "I just…I don't want you to beat yourself up. It won't do either of us any good."

Whit couldn't look at her, she was too emotional and not used to showing her vulnerability. "You could've been killed, Abby. And if he would've hurt you…"

"Hey." Her hand was back on her shoulder. She rotated Whit to face her and lifted her chin so she'd meet her gaze. "It's over. He's not here and he didn't hurt me. Coward only had the balls to leave us a message. Took a shitty knife and made chicken scratches in the door."

"But you're upset, and rightfully so."

"I *was* upset, yes. But I'm over it now and you should be too. For both our sakes. Okay?"

Her fingers felt warm on her face and Whit wanted so desperately to taste her full lips. Abby was looking at her wistfully, wantonly, but she drew away. "How about you heat us up some fish, huh? I'm starved."

Whit smiled. "You hate the fish."

"Hate is such a strong word."

"But sometimes it's fitting."

Abby sat. "True. But it's not in this case. Especially since it's keeping me alive."

Whit gave her a look of disbelief as she lined some fish up on a stick to place in the stove. "Got anymore berries?"

"I do." She started to stand to go for the pot on the bed, but Whit went instead.

"I got it." She brought it to the table and took out a handful of the colorful berries.

"What are you doing?"

Whit dropped them in one of the ceramic mugs and set it, too, in the stove.

"Thought you might like them hot."

"Mm, yes. Know what? Some hot berry juice might even go good mixed in that whiskey. What do you think? Want to try it?"

"No, I really shouldn't."

"Why not?"

"I've already had some whiskey today."

"So?"

"So, I shouldn't have any more. We need to conserve it." She couldn't bring herself to enjoy a drink when its effects may have been what led to her taking off on a whim and leaving Abby all alone. No, she shouldn't have any. She needed to stay clear-headed from here on out.

Abby shrugged. "Okay."

They sat in silence for a while while the fish and the berries heated up. Whit was careful to avoid her quiet regard, still too afraid she'd see right through her and down to her very insides where all her pain and vulnerability were housed. So she perused her book, pretending to read here and there until the fish began to smell, letting her know it was warm.

She reclaimed it from the stove and then used the sleeve of her coat to grab the ceramic mug. She set both the stick and cup on the table. "Careful, that mug is hot."

"Pass me the whiskey?" Abby asked.

Whit did and Abby poured a good amount in to mix with the cooked berries.

"Hand me a stick?"

Whit handed her a thin stick and Abby stirred her concoction well before taking a hesitant sip.

"Mm," she said, as if surprised. "It's pretty good." She slid the cup toward Whit. "You sure you don't want some?"

Her green eyes were hopeful, and Whit thought about how she'd been disappointing her lately. So she took a swallow, agreed with her on the taste, and passed it back to her.

"It's good, right?"

"It is."

Abby smiled and Whit returned it, glad she seemed momentarily pleased.

"Now, how about sharing some of that fish?"

Whit inched over the food so Abby could help herself. As she watched her do her best to act like the fish didn't bother her, Whit thought again about what had happened and how she should do better in keeping them both safe.

She turned to glance back at the door, the word carved in it playing in her mind.

The word she knew would remain on her mind deep into the night.

DIE.

CHAPTER TWENTY-ONE

The rest of the day went by without any further events. When it came close to sunset, Whit stood, stretched, and glanced at Abby's leg, which she'd kept propped up on the table.

"I need to go get you more rocks."

"Whit, I'm fine. There's no need to leave."

Whit held up the water bottle which was only a quarter of the way full. "We also need more water."

"Fine, but I'm coming with you."

"You can't. Walking that far will ruin the little progress you've made with your knee."

"Whit, I stink. I desperately need to wash."

"I stink, too. But it's just something we're going to have to deal with for the time being."

"You don't stink," Abby said. "I think you've been bathing down at that creek." She grinned. "You have, haven't you?"

"I've rinsed off."

"I knew it!"

"How about this? I take the pot and bring back some extra water for you to heat on the stove? That way you can at least wash your face and hands."

"And my pits."

"Sure."

"Deal."

"Alrighty." She emptied the remaining berries on the table and shrugged into her coat. "I'll be back soon."

"I know I don't have to keep telling you to be careful, but I will anyway. Please, be careful."

"Ditto."

Abby rose to lock the door behind her, still terribly unnerved at the haphazard-like carving on the door. So much so, that she couldn't bear to even look at it. She bolted the door and then sat on the bed to wait for the banging to commence. She sat for what felt like close to an hour, with nothing but the sounds of the wind trying to creep in through the thread-like slits in the walls. Eventually, she fell asleep, and when she woke, Whit was at the door, softly rapping and calling her name.

"Coming." She shuffled to the door and unlocked it. Whit rushed in from the oncoming twilight, carrying the shirt full of rocks and the pot with the lid tightly secured.

"It's freezing out there," Whit breathed.

Abby could feel the cold pressing in and it caressed her skin as Whit drifted by with cheeks colored a deep crimson. She set the pot on the table and then brought the bundle of rocks over to Abby. "Lie down," she said.

"But I want to wash up."

"You can, but it's going to take a while for the water to heat. So you might as well ice your knee while you wait."

Abby reclined on the bed and Whit positioned the bundle on her leg. She hesitated a moment when finished, then gave a brief smile, and headed back to the table where she unbound the vine from the pot and placed the pot on the stove.

Then she sat to nibble on some fish.

"You look chilled to the bone," Abby said.

"I am." She sniffled and rubbed her face with her coat still on, trying to warm herself. "But it feels good in here." She paused and looked to Abby. "Did you have any visitors while I was gone?"

"Surprisingly, no. It was as quiet as a church mouse."

"Really?"

"Go figure."

Whit popped some food in her mouth and chewed. "I hope it stays that way."

"Me, too."

Whit carried a handful of berries over to her.

"Thanks. And I appreciate you bringing me the water. It's going to feel so good to bathe a little."

"It sure beats bathing in the icy water of the creek."

Abby laughed. "Is that why you're so cold? Did you take a quick dip?"

"A very quick dip. I didn't want that freak who's bothering us to get any ideas."

"God, I don't know how you did that. The frigidness of that water alone would've kept me rinsing off from the shore."

"I didn't fully submerge. Just enough to get the job done with a few brisk splashes."

"And you didn't see or hear anyone while you were out?"

"Nope, not a peep."

"Maybe he got scared off."

"More like he got bored and wandered off after our lack of reaction to his message on the door."

"We didn't really react, did we?"

She shook her head.

"And we certainly didn't tuck tail and run." Abby smiled. "Sounds like maybe we won."

"Possibly. But I wouldn't get my hopes up if I were you. He could still be lingering, working out his next move."

"You would think he would move on since we might get snow soon. He'd said he wanted to find somewhere to shelter in town for the winter."

Whit shrugged. "Apparently, he's having more fun harassing us."

"What a weirdo." She shivered as the damp from the wet rocks penetrated her skin. "That water hot yet?"

Whit checked it. "Almost."

"Good, because I'm cold." She removed the bundle and swung her legs over the side of the bed to stand. Then she stumbled over to the table to sit and warm herself by the stove.

Whit was looking at her with concern.

"You don't have to say it, Whit. As soon as I wash up, I'll ice my knee again."

"I wasn't going to say a word."

She laughed. "Yeah, right."

Whit settled down next to her and then went ramrod straight as a crashing noise came from outside.

Abby too, froze. "What the hell was that?"

"Something is moving through the brush."

"Sounds like King Kong."

"Whatever it is, it's close. I bet it's him, trying to scare us."

"Could be more deer."

"Not a chance."

Whit rushed to the door, and before Abby could stop her, she'd unlocked it and thrown it open to step out onto the porch and yell. "You might as well give it up! We're not afraid of you!"

Abby hurried outside to join her, curious to see if Boyd was within sight. She focused on the tree line to the right, along with Whit, where the noise was coming from. The thick brush shimmied and shook. Then, as if on a mission, a giant brown bear, not a man, emerged. Abby gasped, and upon seeing them, the bear rose onto its haunches and let out a ferocious roar.

"Whit," Abby whispered. "That's a bear."

"Not just a bear. A male grizzly." Whit raised her arms, spreading the back of her jacket out like a kite. She shouted. "Go away bear! Go away!" She flapped her arms.

"We should run," Abby said, tugging on her jacket. "Whit."

"No, don't run."

The bear woofed and gnashed its teeth. Then it lowered to all fours and began to charge.

"Whit!"

"Inside, now."

Abby about-faced, stepping past the threshold, but then tripped and thumped to the floor. Whit hastened to her and dragged her farther in, then slammed the door and slid the wooden beam into the brackets. She helped Abby to her feet and they both stood very still, listening keenly, breathing hard.

The noises of the bear grew closer, until they heard his heavy footfalls on the whining boards of the porch. Abby tried to swallow, but a ball of sheer fear lodged in her throat, causing her to choke.

"Shh," Whit said, easing her onto the bed. But Abby wasn't sure what remaining quiet would do. The bear was already aware they were inside.

Abby did her best to stifle her coughs nonetheless, as her heart thrummed like the blinding wings of a hummingbird. She heard the beast huff and knew he was dangerously close. A loud boom resonated, and the door warped inward, the bear wailing as it rocked against the weathered wood. Abby clung to Whit and they kicked their way back against the wall, huddled on the bed.

"He's going to get in," Abby said.

"No, that beam should hold." Whit didn't sound convinced and neither was Abby.

"The cabin's too old, Whit. He's going to break through. What will we do?"

The bear continued to pummel the door, and a sickening splintering filled the room as the braces holding the beam began to pull away from the wall.

"Shit," Whit said, untangling herself from Abby. She went to the window and tried to jostle it.

"What are you doing?"

"Looking for an escape. We need to get out."

More splintering came from the doorway and one of the brackets gave and clanged to the floor. The left side of the door caved in, and the roar of the bear reverberated. Abby could see the glistening bronze of his fur, smell the foulness of his breath, and hear the scratch of his powerful claws as he tried to fight his way in.

As the door and walls shook from the bear's massive weight, Whit's fishing spear timbered and ricocheted off the floor.

"Whit, the spear!"

Whit scrambled to it, snatched it up, and charged the door just as the Grizzly broke completely through. She cried out almost as loud as the bear's roar as she plunged the sharpened prongs deep into the bear's chest, causing a deafening silence. The animal leveled to all fours and moaned as it reversed. Thick shoelaces of drool hung from its mouth as it let out another noise, this time, a painful sounding cry. Then it stumbled off the porch and walked slowly away.

Whit followed it outside. Abby remained on the bed, still too terrified to move.

"Where is it?" she breathed.

Whit continued to watch, quiet, with her back to Abby.

Abby scooted to the edge of the mattress. "Whit?"

She came back inside, face completely ashen. "It's gone."

Abby nearly sobbed with relief.

Whit doubled back to the doorway and stuck her head outside, checking again. Then she knelt and studied the metal braces that held the wooden beam securely across the door.

"Can you fix it?" Abby asked.

"Not without tools."

The cold evening air began to penetrate, and Abby hugged herself, shivering from more than just the cold as their new reality began to set in.

"We have to leave, don't we?"

"We're no longer safe here without an adequate door."

"Will the bear come back?"

"No. It went off to die." She tossed the bracket aside. "I can't understand why it was so aggressive." She glanced at the doorway. "I need to go investigate."

"I'm coming with."

This time Whit didn't argue. Instead, she unsheathed her knife and waited for Abby before they both exited. A few of the porch beams were distorted, so they carefully sidled around them and stepped onto the ground. They followed the steady trail of blood until just before the edge of the woods where Whit suddenly stopped. She bent and lifted up a piece of fur-covered flesh.

"What is it?" Abby asked, afraid to know.

Whit carried it along as she stood and continued on. As they stepped into the brush, Abby smelled, what could only be, rotting flesh. She gagged as they neared a partially skeletal carcass.

"Is that a...deer?" Abby asked.

"Was. And this is just a piece of it," Whit said as she kept Abby back with her arm. She looked around intently, as if checking for other animals. When she seemed satisfied, she examined the carcass closely. "That bear didn't tear it apart though. It's been quartered. And cleanly. I'd say someone else did the killing."

She followed more blood and pieces of flesh, and pointed to a wider track. "And they dragged the carcass here, close to the cabin."

"To what, attract the bear?"

"Precisely."

Abby's heart fell to her stomach. "He wanted it to come after us?"

"To have some sort of an encounter, yes."

Whit walked on, knelt, and lifted up more remnants of the deer. "See here? He left a trail of deer meat leading right to the cabin."

"But aren't bears supposed to be hibernating about now?"

"Not until October/November."

Abby folded her arms across her chest, once again chilled.

Whit, meanwhile, took the small sections of meat and threw them as far as she could before facing Abby once again. "I need to wash my hands."

They headed back to the cabin and Whit cleaned her hands in the hot water she'd heated for Abby. Then she packed up the fish and berries into the pot and secured it. Abby watched with her hands clasped in front of her at the table, at a loss as to what to say or do. They were exposed to danger now. Both from the wildlife and from Boyd.

Whit seemed to be pondering the same thing. "We'll stay in the cabin tonight. I'll position the door as best I can, but it won't be protection enough from anything with the slightest inkling to come inside. It should help keep us warm enough until sunup, though. Then we need to head out."

Abby didn't respond, but Whit didn't seem to need her to.

"I'll stand guard," she added.

"Whit, you need to sleep too. We both need our strength."

"I'm too concerned about Boyd. He has to know we're vulnerable now."

RONICA BLACK

Abby released a breath. "Okay. I'll go along with whatever you think is best."

"Why don't you go ahead and turn in, in case we need to leave sooner than dawn."

Another chill shot up Abby's spine as she considered what reason that might be. She went to bed in silence and curled up on her side, forgoing the cold rock bundle. Tonight, nothing could help soothe her knee, or her mind for that matter. Tonight, all she could do was pray for sleep.

CHAPTER TWENTY-TWO

W hit roused as her head bobbed and sleep tried to overtake her. She palmed her aching neck, having fought sleep all night as she'd sat motionless at the small table, listening to Abby's rhythmic breathing from the bed.

Dawn seeped in through the edges of the damaged door. She'd propped the fortress up as best she could, but the damn thing was barely remaining upright, much less giving them any sort of respite from danger. So she'd remained awake, keeping watch, while trying to find a way out of their predicament. They needed to reach some sort of help, that much was obvious, but how they were going to do that with Abby's injury was the real brain tickler. She'd debated making her some sort of stretcher that she could then drag behind her like a makeshift sled, but she wasn't sure she was strong enough to gain enough ground on such a low quantity of food. Not to mention that Abby would fight her on it and probably wouldn't allow her to do it. So that idea went out the window, along with a few others that involved her in some way helping Abby walk.

Their best bet was to take it slow and steady and forge their way through the forest until they hopefully hit the highway or came across a hiking trail. But also, along the way, they could check out that other X, to see if it would in any way help them. According to the map on the wall, it should take them about seven days' time to reach the highway, if they took it slow, and a little over a days hike to that X. She could only hope that it wouldn't snow until after they'd reached safety. Though she didn't care for Boyd, he'd been correct when he'd said he could smell the oncoming snow. She could feel it looming as well, and last night's temperatures had plummeted, leaving her to stare at the mist of her breath in the faint firelight from the stove.

She stood and stretched and then stirred Abby awake. She was curled in a ball on her side, obviously trying to keep warm. Whit gently shook her.

"Abby," she said. "Time to wake up."

Abby groaned as she turned, slitted eyes searching for focus. "What time is it?"

"Early."

"Ugh, too early."

"You know what they say about the early bird," Whit said, bringing her the water bottle. Abby sat up and took a few sips.

"Yeah, I do. And the early bird can kiss my ass. I'm not into worms."

Whit chuckled. "Noted. Now come on, we need to eat and get going."

She helped Abby to her feet, and they sat at the table. Whit opened the pot and served them both cold fish and berries. She didn't even want to take the time to heat up their breakfast, she was so anxious to leave. Boyd had left them alone all night, but that didn't mean he would continue to do so. So she wanted to try to get as much of a head start on him as she could.

"Nothing like cold fish first thing in the morning," Abby said with a grin.

"At least you can joke about it."

"Joking is about all I can do."

They continued to eat, with Whit pushing more fish Abby's way as she noticed she was mostly consuming berries. Abby didn't fuss, but ate the fish in silence, making subtle faces as she did, the taste obviously disagreeing with her.

"We'll find more berries today," Whit said.

They packed up to leave as soon as they finished eating and drinking, and then headed out front to glance back at the cabin one last time before they slowly walked away, with Abby wiping at a tear.

"Sad to say goodbye?" Whit asked as they proceeded through the forest.

"It was a good little cabin," Abby said soberly. "Protected us as best it could."

"Yes, it did."

They walked on at a snail's pace for about twenty minutes before Abby was able to pick up the pace. Whit, alarmed at her increasing speed, stopped her.

"You're going too fast. You'll hurt yourself."

"I feel good, Whit. Really. I think I just needed to warm up a bit." She started off again and Whit caught up.

"You're sure?"

"Yep."

"The second you're not, you slow down, okay?"

"Yes, ma'am." They wound through more trees and Abby covered her mouth and nose as the strong scent of death slammed into them for the second time.

"Oh, God, Whit, it's that smell again."

Whit stilled and motioned for Abby to do the same. Then Whit knelt and crept forward until she came to the carcass of the bear she'd stabbed. She scanned the surrounding area, searching for animals feeding, but spotted nothing. She gave Abby the signal that all was okay and then stepped on the bear for leverage so she could extract her spear. Gases escaped the brown heap of the body and Abby turned away and vomited.

Whit held her blood-soaked spear proudly, like a triton, but the stench was starting to get to her too. "You okay?"

Abby waved her off. "Give me a second." She threw up again, this time much less, and then brushed her hand across her mouth. She faced Whit with an ashen look of despair. "Can we go now?"

Whit motioned for her to lead the way, and they continued with the quicker stride until about two hours later, when Abby halted.

"Time for a break." She placed her hands on her hips and took some deep breaths.

"You've done really well," Whit said, checking the time.

"I'm pretty much just stiff-legging it."

"I've noticed."

"Worked great for a while, but now my hip's starting to hurt." She winced as she straightened and then bent her leg. "Not sure which causes the most pain at this point. The knee or the hip."

"Do we need to stop for the day? Make camp here?"

"Of course not. I just need to rest a moment."

Whit wasn't apt to believe her. She knew Abby had a tendency to put on a brave face, and she worried she would further injure herself if they continued on as they had been.

"I think we'd better call it and just start early again tomorrow."

"Whit, no. We can't afford to stop now."

"You're not okay and—"

"I'm fine."

"Abby—"

"We're going and that's final."

Whit blinked. Abby was demanding her way. It was new and unexpected. Whit wasn't sure what to say.

"I said I'm fine and you need to believe me," Abby said. "Okay?"

Whit agreed, feeling like she had little choice. Arguing with Abby would get them nowhere, and if Abby said she was alright, she had to let her be to make up her own mind. After all, Abby had to know what was best for Abby.

"Good, let's get back to it," Abby said, suddenly in charge. She stiff-legged it for a short while before changing to bend her knee, walking at a slower speed than previously. Whit fell in next to her and they forged through the forest for the next couple of hours, taking a few short breaks to garner breath, get their bearings, and take sips of water.

Eventually, they came across a narrow, trickling creek. Whit set down the shirt bundle and pot of food and began rinsing the dark smears of blood off her spear, while Abby went upstream and began undressing. Whit watched as she knelt at the shore to wash her face and hands, wearing only her jeans and a red, lacy bra. She glanced over at Whit once, as she was starting to scrub beneath her arms, and Whit quickly refocused on her already clean spear.

"You're right, it's super chilly," Abby said.

Whit rubbed down her spear again, feeling prudish. "That it is."

"You should join me. It's cold but it feels refreshing."

"Maybe later. I need to build a shelter first."

"You're going to go to all that trouble to make a shelter? Just for one night?"

"We have to have cover. Too cold now not to."

Abby straightened and rubbed her hands on her jeans, taking Whit's breath away as her hair lit up like fire against the backdrop of the deep green forest and her alabaster skin glowed in the fall sunlight. "I'm going to help this time," she said, matter-of-factly.

It took a moment for Whit to concede, she was so flustered from Abby's appearance and nearly nude form. But after Abby dressed, Whit managed to give her instructions on what kind of branches to gather for the shelter. They worked quietly, with Whit collecting and fashioning the heavier pieces of timber and Abby dragging over more heavily leaved branches than they ended up needing. She seemed proud of herself regardless, and Whit then gave her the task of starting a fire as she finished up with the dwelling.

Half an hour later, all was complete and they sat by the tranquil fire, warming their fish and berries on a slab of rock. Whit felt almost numb as she relaxed in the heat, and her eyes had just started to drift closed when Abby spoke.

"Think Boyd's nearby?" She mindlessly poked at the logs with a stick.

"Hard to say."

"At this point I don't even care. After the bear, what's the worst he can do?"

"Don't say that," Whit said. "There's always something worse."

"I just want to kick his ass," Abby said, setting her jaw to stab at a big piece of burning wood. "You know, really pummel him good."

Whit laughed. "You're not the only one."

"That bear," Abby said. "We could've been killed."

"I think that was the intention."

"Then I really really want to kick his ass."

"I'm afraid I want to do worse," Whit confessed.

Abby grew quiet for a moment. "You know what? Me, too. Me, too, Whit. And I'm usually a pacifist. So, damn him for making me even contemplate violence."

Whit hugged her knees and stared up at the materializing stars. Thousands of tiny flickering diamonds set upon the backdrop of a frigid, glowing sky, lulling her back to relaxation, Boyd all but forgotten.

"He won't try that again, right? The bear thing?"

Whit wanted to comfort her and tell her surely not. But she honestly had no idea and tonight, unfortunately, she really needed to get some sleep. She couldn't stay awake all night keeping watch.

Abby was studying her closely. "You look beat, Whit."

Whit smiled, her eyes feeling heavier by the moment. "I think I am."

"Go on to bed then," Abby said sincerely. "I'll stay out by the fire."

Whit started to argue but then realized she was too damn tired. She turned to crawl into the shelter. "Night, Abby. You were a real soldier today."

Abby smiled back at her, sentimental-like. Whit paused briefly, wondering what the look represented, but then proceeded into the shelter without saying another word. She settled on the mound of crisp-smelling pine needles and sighed, crossing her hands over her chest. She was beyond exhausted and grateful for Abby volunteering to take up the watch. Even if it was only for the time being. At least she'd be able to get a little sleep.

She closed her eyes and thought of the brilliant stars twinkling above. What a beautiful sight. What a beautiful night. If only Boyd would leave them be so it could be a peaceful one as well.

CHAPTER TWENTY-THREE

Abby sat straight up in the dark and tried to focus. Next to her, the fire subtly crackled, barely producing enough light to see. She could make out the dark forms of the nearby trees and the black star-studded sky, but little else. She wasn't sure what woke her, but something had shaken her to the core, causing her heart to race. She pushed herself to a stand, took a few soft steps away from the flames, and squinted into the vast night.

"Hello?" Her breath was a white cloud, and she hugged herself from the intense chill. Her nose and ears were numb, her hands the same. She'd fallen asleep outside the shelter. Whit would say she needed to warm up and fast.

Seeing and hearing nothing suspicious, she walked back to the fire and, after giving the embers a thorough rousing stir, added more wood. She warmed herself in the growing heat and considered joining Whit in the makeshift abode. It would be warmer inside, with the heat reflecting off the fire wall Whit had built, and of course, with Whit herself. Perhaps she could snuggle into her again and perhaps Whit would wrap her arms around her as she'd done before, making her feel not only noticeably warmer, but also tremendously safer.

The chill left Abby at just the thought alone, and she smiled, already feeling better. But then she heard something. A loud clang. She froze for a split second, feeling completely exposed and frightened, but then kicked into gear and rushed into the shelter to wake Whit.

"Whit! Whit, get up! Someone is here!"

Whit grumbled awake and, upon registering Abby's words, sat up and crawled from the dwelling.

Abby followed and they both stood motionless in front of the fire, breathing heavily.

"Where?" Whit said.

Abby pointed. "I heard a noise. It came from over there where you hung the pot of food."

Whit pulled out her phone and tried to switch on her flashlight. "It's dead." She looked at Abby. "You stay here. I'm going to go take a look."

"But you can't even see."

"Just stay back, okay? It's probably just an animal, going after the fish."

"What if it's a bear?"

"It would be making a lot more noise."

Abby let her go and remained by the fire. She heard Whit's footfalls for a while, until she got too far away, then she heard nothing at all. And just as she was beginning to panic, she heard footfalls again and Whit reappeared, grimacing.

"Well?" Abby asked.

"Whatever it was stole our pot."

"What? Are you sure?"

"Positive. Took the vine and everything."

"So we're out of food again?" Now the panic really did set in, churning her gut.

"Yep."

"What are we going to do?"

"We'll scavenge and try to fish, just like before. But try not to worry, we can survive a while without food. It's water we mainly have to worry about. Let's go back to bed."

"I don't think I can. I'm too…on edge."

Whit caressed her hand. "It was probably an animal."

"An animal? Wouldn't that have made a lot more noise than just a single clang?" She shook her head. "I'm not buying it, Whit."

"Come on." She gently tugged her, trying to get her back into the shelter. "Let's talk about it away from the cold."

Abby reluctantly followed but Whit halted at the entryway.

"What?" Abby asked.

Whit moved aside to show her. Abby leaned forward to observe something hanging from one of the branches on the dwelling. "What the hell is that?"

Whit held it in her palm and angled it toward the firelight.

"Oh, God," Abby said, as she studied the figure. "That looks like a person. A stick figure."

"I think that's what it's supposed to be."

"What does it mean?"

"Well," Whit said. "Considering the fact that it looks like a person and it's hanging by a noose, I'd say it's another threat. Especially since it was put on our shelter."

"But how could he have put it there? I didn't even hear him," Abby said as shivers overtook her. "Oh, my God, Whit. He was so close. We were so…vulnerable."

"He's trying to scare us."

"He's succeeding." She turned to face the fire. "I'm scared to death, Whit. This is some straight up Blair Witch shit and there's no way I can sleep now."

"Me neither." Whit yanked the stick figure off the branch and tossed it into the fire, along with more wood. "Guess we better settle in by the fire." She sat lotus-style and seemed to be watching the human-like figure as it burned.

Abby approached slowly, still deeply uneasy. Holding herself, both from the chill and the anxiousness she felt, she stared into the dark shapes of the forest, anticipating when Boyd would make his next move.

"What if it's not Boyd?" she asked.

"I've considered that too, but honestly, who else would it be?"

"I don't know. Another stranger?"

"Who just happened to stumble upon us to stalk us?"

Abby dropped down next to her. "This is just getting crazier by the second and it doesn't seem to fit Boyd's MO."

"What does, Abby? Remember you hardly knew the man."

"I know, but I think I got a good feel for him. He—wasn't like this."

"He stole all our food. Don't forget that."

It still didn't make sense to her, but there was little more she could say. Whit was right, he *did* steal from them. And most likely lied about things he'd told her. Maybe it really was Boyd. He was the only one they'd encountered and he did kind of sneak up on them at first, claiming he'd only just then seen the smoke from their fire.

"He tried to kill us," she said softly, thinking aloud.

"He did."

An image of the bear rocking against the door to the cabin filled her mind. It still horrified her to imagine what would've happened had he made it inside. Boyd had done that. Had wanted them to die in an awful, gruesome manner. "How could I have misjudged someone so drastically?"

"It happens sometimes," Whit said. "Don't beat yourself up about it."

More unsettling feelings fluttered in her chest as memories from the past surfaced. "Seems to be happening to me a lot."

Whit glanced at her. "It does?"

Abby nodded, wishing she could get lost in the hypnotic dance of the flames. Whit didn't say anything more. She seemed to know that whatever she was referring to was something deep and most likely painful. She was respecting her privacy and Abby appreciated it. But it didn't make the memories any less agonizing. She wasn't sure what would, but she knew she'd do anything to make the fluttering anxiousness dissipate.

"I met her five years ago," she started, almost in a daze. "I thought she was the most charming, most captivating person I'd ever met."

"What was her name?" Whit asked.

"Daphne. Daph for short. God," she breathed. "She was beautiful, funny, witty. And dynamite in bed. I thought I'd met the woman of my dreams." She stared into the fire. "But, as I soon learned, nobody's that perfect. Dream women do not exist."

"What did she do?"

Abby let out a laugh. "What didn't she do? She was extremely self-centered, and I had no clue. I mean, she lied to me about love, Whit. Why lie about love? I'll tell you why. To take advantage of you, that's why. And to take everything they can from you."

Anger welled up inside her, killing the fluttering in an instant. Now her chest burned and her throat ached like acid had risen to eat away at it.

"She stole from you?" Whit asked.

Abby nodded again, brushing a stray tear from her eye. She refused to cry over Daphne. Refused to cry over her again. "She did," she said. "And she lied to me and to my family both. Tried to take from them too with some fraudulent business deal. But luckily my mother caught on to her before it was too late."

"That's good."

"Ha. Yes. Good for them. But for me, not so much. Because I didn't believe my own mother. I didn't believe what she said about Daphne. So, unfortunately, I was duped. And duped badly."

Whit reached over and covered her hand. "I'm so sorry, Abby."

"Don't you want to know how much I lost?"

"Only if you want to tell me."

"Thousands," she said.

Whit squeezed her hand.

"I'm sorry," Abby said. "I still can't bring myself to verbalize the total amount out loud."

"I understand. You don't have to."

Abby met her gaze. "Don't I need to in order to fully heal?"

"Maybe. But you shouldn't force anything."

"You're so kind, Whit." She squeezed her hand in return. "So decent."

"Decent," Whit said and chuckled.

"What's wrong with decent?"

"Nothing. It just doesn't sound very exciting."

"I've been with exciting. Trust me, it's not all it's cracked up to be." She looked back to the dancing flames. "Sometimes you just long for decent. And kind." Her gaze returned to Whit, who was watching her closely, warming her just like the heat from the fire with her smoldering eyes. "You understand what I'm saying?"

"Yes. Question is…do you?"

Abby focused on Whit's luscious-looking lips and leaned in to kiss her, taste her, savor her. But just as their mouths were about to connect, Abby felt an icy tingle on her cheek. First one, then another. And another. She looked up to where it seemed to be coming from, and saw lazy white snowflakes drifting down from the sky.

"It's snowing," she said, truly moved by the wondrous sight.

Whit blinked up at the night as flakes landed on her dark lashes. Abby smoothed them away with her thumbs and Whit caught her by the wrist as the downfall increased. "We need a good shelter, Abby. One better than this. It's going to get cold."

That panic feeling came rushing back, making Abby nauseous. "We should go, shouldn't we?"

"As soon as dawn breaks." She checked her watch. "In a couple of hours."

"We'll have to move quickly," Abby said, already dreading the pain that would cause.

But Whit shook her head. "No, we go slow and steady. Just like we've been doing. Rushing will only cause problems. We need to remain calm, think positive, and just do the best we can."

"But—"

"Shh." She touched her lips. "No worrying. Just doing." She gripped her hand. "Come on, let's wait out the rest of the night in the shelter, away from the snow."

"I hope it slows soon. Otherwise, we'll be trekking through several inches of snow come dawn."

"I have a feeling it'll just be a light dusting," she said, gently urging her inside.

"How do you know?"

"I live here, remember? And you're not supposed to worry."

"I'm not sure I know how to stop." She sat on the pile of pine needles and waited while Whit crawled in behind her and pulled the door into place. Then Whit surprised her by embracing her, holding her tight.

"I'll take your mind off everything."

Abby's pulse jumped to her throat. "How—will you do that?"

"By telling you a story."

Abby relaxed into her. "I could use a good story."

Whit rested her head on top of Abby's. "I thought you might."

CHAPTER TWENTY-FOUR

Abby fell asleep before Whit even finished her story. She'd fought it for a while, wanting to hear more about Whit's grandmother, but her fatigue had finally taken hold, and she dozed off in Whit's arms, snoring ever so slightly. Whit didn't budge, enjoying the feel of her warm body against her own and the way her thick hair smelled of pine needles. She could get used to this. Abby in her arms on dark, cold nights, just the two of them.

"Don't get your hopes up," she whispered. She was very much aware that once this trek was over, she'd probably never see Abby again. They'd both go their separate ways and Abby would return to the Lower Forty-eight, most likely never to venture to Alaska again. The thought was depressing, one she didn't want to let fester. So she eased Abby off her and pushed out the door. Dawn had broken and the sky was a deep pewter, the snow having stopped. There was a bit more than a dusting, with about an inch on the ground. And the temperature felt like it was just below freezing. She bounced on her toes for a few seconds to try to get her blood flowing before trying to restart the fire. She wanted it to be nice and hot for Abby when she woke, which needed to be sometime soon if they wanted to get a move on.

She knelt at the fire pit and agitated the coals before tossing on more wood. Then she went to where she'd hung the pot of food the night before. The fresh snow was crunchy under her boots and she walked about halfway before she spotted someone else's tracks.

It looked as though they'd come to check on the campsite, halting about halfway and then turning to head back the way they'd come. She wished she could follow the footprints and see where they led, but she knew she couldn't leave Abby. And she didn't really know what she'd do when she came upon Boyd anyway. Other than give him a piece of her mind. The real question was, what would he do if she surprised him? Kill her?

It was best if she didn't find out. Because some questions were best unanswered.

"Good morning."

Whit turned. Abby stood close to the fire, stretching. Her fiery hair was mussed and she looked like death warmed over, but Whit still thought she was damned beautiful.

If only I could wake up to her every morning.

She shook the thought away, displeased. Where were all these thoughts of wanting to get with Abby coming from? True, she hadn't been with a woman in some time, but these desires were about more than just sex. These were real yearnings, deep desires. She wanted Abby, yes. But more than that she *really* wanted her. To be with her. For an extended period of time. Maybe even forever.

Whoa.

What the fuck?

She trudged back to the fire, more than just displeased with herself. Now she was downright unsettled.

"You okay?" Abby asked, retrieving the water bottle from the shelter to take a few sips. She passed it to Whit, who waved it away. "You look upset."

"I'm fine." She stabbed a log until it broke into pieces.

"Bullshit. Something's wrong. Is it Boyd? Did he come back?"

"He did. But he didn't come close. His tracks end back a ways."

"What does he want?" Abby asked, looking disturbed. "Hasn't he done enough? Jesus."

Whit kept poking at the fire. "Just be glad he chose to leave us alone."

"Yeah, *after* he chose to take our food *and* our pot. He really screwed us this time."

"But we're alive. And we have water."

Abby was about to take another sip, but then thought better of it. "Yeah, lucky us," she said.

Whit threw the stick she'd been using into the flames. "You ready to get going?"

"Can I pee first?"

Abby disappeared behind some brush and Whit quickly did the same. When they finished, they stood around the fire for a few more minutes before extinguishing it. Abby didn't ask her any more questions and Whit was thankful. She wasn't sure how she'd respond to her if she did. What would she say? *I'm pissed because I'm fantasizing about spending forever with you?*

That was sure to go over real well.

"Ready?" Whit said as she stomped out the last of the flames.

Abby followed her quietly and they set off through the white coated forest. As the morning progressed, the snow began to melt, and icy rain began to fall. Whit paused beneath the protection of a tree. They were already soaked to the skin.

"We should stop," she said. They should've reached the other X by now, whatever it was, but as far as she could tell, they must've missed it.

"We haven't gone far enough yet," Abby said. But she'd been limping already, and badly. Not to mention shivering.

"Abby, we'll freeze."

"What do you propose we do?"

"We stop here and shelter up. Wait out the rain."

"I think we should go on. Then stop and shelter up. What's the difference if we do it now or later?"

"Hypothermia," Whit said. She was already worried about Abby. Her jacket wasn't as good as Whit's, which was made specifically for inclement weather. Nor was it as warm.

Abby sighed. "Shit, I hate it when you're right." She set down the water bottle and pulled the hood up on her jacket. "I have to pee again." She walked off into the brush and Whit slid out of her jacket to give to Abby. Then she started looking around for dry timber to make a fire with. She was exhausted, and freezing, but she had to get them warm and into adequate shelter. It was hard telling how bad or how long this storm was going to be.

Abby returned with a fury, nearly bumping into Whit. She was gasping with excitement. "Whit, you were right! There's a cabin!"

"Where?"

Abby dragged her into the brush and they walked until they came upon a clearing. Abby pointed to the tree-covered hills beyond. "See it?"

It was an A-frame cabin, nestled atop the nearest hill. Whit exhaled and nearly collapsed with relief.

"Can you make it?" she asked Abby.

"Damn right I can. I'll drag myself up that hill if I have to."

Whit grabbed her jacket, insisted on Abby wearing it, and they headed off toward the hilltop cabin. Whit led the way and Abby kept up well at first, but by the time they reached higher ground, she was breathless and really struggling with her knee. She was better protected from the sleet, which was slamming down on them at an angle, smacking them in the face. Whit though, was completely soaked, her sweater now weighted and cold, hanging from her body. She was shivering along with Abby, and fatigue and delirium were settling in.

"Hold on to me," Whit said, hooking her arm into Abby's. Though really it was Whit who needed the support. Her body was beginning to fail her. They needed to reach the cabin and soon.

They began to ascend, and Abby cried out in pain.

"Come on, Ab-by, you can—do it," Whit stammered.

"Whit, I can't. It's too much. The angle of the hill is killing me."

"P-put all your weight on me. All your weight, Ab-by. Come on, now. Use me as lev-e-rage." She shook her head, as if that would help with the stuttering. Her limbs were stiff and they ached from the cold. And she was using all her strength to virtually carry Abby up the hillside.

"I'm too heavy," Abby said. "You'll never be able to help me. Just leave me here."

"Not a chance."

"I'm serious, Whit. Just leave me."

Whit pivoted and held her face. Her skin was glacial and slick with rain, her lips pale and quivering.

"I'm n-not leaving you. Got it?"

Abby blinked up at her and nodded.

"Let's go." Whit pulled her closer and she felt Abby shift her weight. They took one slow step at a time, climbing the hill, grabbing onto branches and bushes as they went. Whit's breathing felt slow and shallow, as she tried her best to propel them upward. Abby's weight was crushing and she realized that while she might have been able to easily help her on level ground, trying to go uphill was a far greater challenge. She wasn't sure if they were going to make it. She paused, struggling for breath. She coughed up rain, a sizable amount having streamed into her mouth.

"Whit," Abby said. "You're too cold and I'm too heavy."

"Don't," Whit said. "Just stop it." She tried to walk again, but she slipped on the slick ground.

"Whit!" Abby clenched her by the sweater and helped her to her feet.

Whit struggled to remain upright, the urge to collapse overwhelming. "Come—on. We—have to keep going."

"No, we're done for. We should go back down."

"Just—a f—few more yards." Whit linked their arms again and started walking the incline. Abby followed suit, but the trek was trying and treacherous, with heavy brush. Whit searched for the trail. They'd just been on it, where did it go? Why were they clawing through all this brush?

"The trail," she said. "Where is it?"

"There is no trail," Abby said.

"But there is. We were—just on it." She couldn't locate it, regardless of how hard she scanned the area against the slanting sleet.

"Whit, there's no trail."

They forced onward and Whit fell again, losing her footing. She slid back a few feet, leaving Abby to clamor after her.

"We're going back down," she said when she had her by the sweater.

"No, we have to find the trail. It leads to—there! There he is. Dad!"

Abby stared at her, mouth agape, obviously opposed to them making their way to her father. He was standing right there, just in front of the cabin. They couldn't turn back now. No fucking way.

Whit regained her traction and continued on. She heard Abby follow, but she stayed behind her. "Whit, we're going to die."

"My dad will—save us," Whit said. "Just you wait and—see. He's just up there. Just a ways away." She pushed on, but her eyelids were growing heavy and everything was getting fuzzy. Like the torn edges of a page.

If she could reach her father, he'd be so proud. They'd celebrate and get warm and he'd share tales of expeditions over warm sips of whiskey. If only—

"Oh, thank God," Abby said as they crested the hill. She rested her hands on her knees and tried to catch her breath. Whit lunged forward, trying to run toward her father who stood waving at them.

"Come on," she said. She reached the stairway to the cabin, but he vanished. Somehow, she knew he was inside. She climbed the steps and shoved open the door. It was dry inside but not considerably warmer. That didn't matter though. All that mattered was her father. And there he was, standing by the stove, waiting.

She turned and smiled as Abby entered behind her.

Then, as she turned back to face her father, to tell him how much she'd missed him, the world suddenly faded to black.

CHAPTER TWENTY-FIVE

Oh, my God, Whit!" Abby rushed to her side and palmed her face. Her skin was slick and slimy from the rain, and icy to the touch. Her lips were a pale blue and Abby quickly palpated her neck for a pulse. She had one, but it was slow and thready.

"Okay, what to do, what to do?" Panic set in and she surveyed the cabin for anything that could help. She saw a simple stove in a makeshift kitchen, a worn couch, and a table with two chairs. There was also a loft, but she wasn't sure what was up there. She'd seen a sign outside, stating that this was a public use cabin, so surely there was something in there that could be of some use. She saw a door nestled in the corner. She opened it and found folded wool blankets. She brought them out, set them down next to Whit and stood still to ponder.

"What do I do?" Then it came to her. What would Whit do if it were her, which, in all honesty, was getting very close to happening. Soon they'd both be in trouble.

With that in mind, she stripped out of the two jackets and her pants, boots, and wet socks. Then, in her underwear and sweatshirt, she began to undress Whit, working efficiently to get her out of the soaked clothes.

"I don't know what I'm doing, but I'm doing my best." Once she had her stripped down to her underwear and bra, she removed her shoes, socks and sock liners, and dragged her over to the couch. With all her might, she lifted her and laid her on the cushions and then wrapped her tightly in the wool blankets.

"Okay, now what?" she said as she glanced around with her hands on her hips. The cabin was cold and close to barren as far as supplies, so very little help. Why couldn't she think?

Because Whit is comatose and we're both freaking freezing, that's why.

Again, she asked herself what Whit would do. Then the stove caught her eye. "Ah-ha." Her teeth chattered as she dug in the pocket of Whit's pants and pulled out the fire starting kit. Hastily, she piled some wood, which was stacked neatly next to the stove, into the hatch and struck the ferro rod. Only the wood wouldn't catch. So she searched for something else to light and found a calendar on the wall above the kitchen counter. She tore off the previous month's page, wadded it up and shoved it beneath the wood. She got the fire going, blew on it some, and then shut the door to return to Whit.

"Whit," she said, shaking her. "Wake up. You're scaring me."

Her eyes fluttered but did not remain open. "Whit, come on." She shook her again, but Whit only moaned and mumbled something again about her father.

"No," Whit said, grimacing. "Don't let him hurt him. Don't let him hurt, Dad."

"Who?" Abby asked, gently rousing her. "Whit, tell me who?"

But Whit fell silent and Abby carefully drew the blankets back to crawl in with her, skin to skin, and then pulled the covers over them. She shifted for comfort, and then sighed with relief as their skin began to meld together in growing warmth. She rested her head in the crook of Whit's neck and inhaled her damp, earthy scent.

"Who knew it would take us both nearly freezing to death before I'd get to lie with you like this?"

Whit moved slightly and moaned.

"Yeah, I didn't think it possible either. But here we are. Lying together nearly nude, in a desolate cabin in the middle of Alaska. No Boyd within sight and no bears either. Just you and me and you're missing it all."

She hugged her tighter and closed her eyes, the heat from their bodies now lulling her to sleep. "We'll talk later," she slurred. "When you feel better."

❖

"Abby, Abby, wake up," a soft voice said.

"Hm?" Abby's eyes flitted open and she lifted her head to focus.

"Hi," Whit said.

Abby blinked down at her. "Hi."

"We must've fallen asleep together."

Abby crawled from her to stand beside the couch. "Yeah, I guess so."

"Only," Whit said, her eyes scanning Abby's body. "We're undressed."

"Yeah. About that."

Whit kicked the blankets off and sat up to rub her face. "Any particular reason why?"

Abby grabbed her clothes, realized they were still soaked, and dropped them.

"We were, uh, wet. To say the least." She should've thought to ring their clothes out and hang them near the stove.

"I see," Whit said, rising to examine her own pile of cold, drenched clothing. She carried the lump of clothes over to the kitchen and began ringing them out in a bucket which had probably been used as a bin. Abby did the same and when they finished, they hung the clothes over the backs of the kitchen chairs and angled them closer to the stove.

"I seem to have lost some of my memory," Whit said as she settled back onto the couch. Abby joined her and offered her one of the blankets to cover up with. Whit took it, thanked her, and draped it over herself. Abby did the same with her own blanket.

Outside, the rain continued to pour, beating against the side of the cabin and the large windows. Abby shivered, imagining being back out in it, and snuggled deeper into her blanket.

"You got cold," she eventually said. "Hypothermic I think."

"Really?"

"You started talking about your father and you came in here, inside the cabin, and just passed out on me."

"I passed out?"

"Mm-hm."

She studied her hands. "I was talking about my father?"

"You kept saying, 'Don't let him hurt Dad.'"

Whit's face went even more ashen than it already was from the cold.

"What did that mean?" Abby asked.

Whit toyed with the fuzz on the blanket. "That was quick thinking, getting us out of those wet clothes," she said. "Sounds like you saved our lives."

Abby didn't respond, but rather scrutinized her own blanket. "You don't want to talk about it? The things you were saying?"

"Not especially."

"Why not? Does it pertain to his murder?"

Whit tossed the blanket aside and stood.

Abby hurried to calm her. "I'm sorry, I shouldn't have asked. It's just that—well, the things you said—I thought maybe—"

"You thought?"

Abby swallowed, disliking the pained look on her face. "Yeah, I just thought that maybe, you know, you were reliving it or something,"

"And you think I would want to talk about that?"

"It might help."

Whit shook her head. "No. It won't."

"How do you know?"

"Because I know, alright?"

"But how?"

"Jesus, Abby, give it a rest, will you?"

Abby closed her mouth, intent on doing just that. But her heart ached for Whit and she knew, just knew that if she shared whatever was troubling her so much, that she'd feel better. "I just know that when I shared some of my past with you, I felt relief. And I thought that maybe, you'd feel the same."

"But we aren't the same, Abby. We're different. Very different people. And I know it won't help because…I've talked about it before. Or tried to at least. And it didn't do anything but make things worse."

"When was that?" Abby asked, treading carefully.

Whit ran her hand through her dark mane and the sinewy muscles in her torso flexed. Abby had to swallow down her rising desire and focus instead on the continued pain she saw in Whit's fleeting gaze.

"Years ago. Soon after it happened. Law enforcement, they suggested I see someone. A shrink."

"And it didn't help?"

"I was a child for God's sake. So, what do you think?" She grabbed several pieces of wood and yanked open the door to the stove to shove them inside. It didn't need to be done quite yet, but she forced them in anyway, as if she needed to keep her hands busy.

"You were a child?"

"Yes. And what child wants to talk to a shrink?"

Abby shook her head. "No, I meant...when your father was murdered."

Whit's face fell and she bowed her head. Abby went to her and gently placed a hand on her arm, almost afraid to touch her, fearing she'd startle and run away.

"I'm so sorry, Whit. I had no idea. You...I'm just so sorry. No child should have to go through something like that. Death is traumatizing enough as it is and—"

"Yeah, well try witnessing it." She pulled away and went to stand near the door, crossing arms over her chest to stare out at the rain. Her jaw was set and her eyes intently focused. Abby thought that she saw them begin to pool with tears. She moved toward her again but stopped herself short of touching her.

"You saw it?"

Whit sniffled. "Yeah. I saw it."

Abby was at a loss for words. It took her a moment before she spoke, as she searched for the right thing to say. "That's terrible, Whit. And something you shouldn't have seen."

"Shouldn't have seen?" She turned to glare at her. "I should've stopped it!"

She pushed past Abby and crossed to where their clothes hung on the chairs. Abby watched helplessly as she frantically began to dress.

"Whit, what are you doing?"

"Leaving."

"To go where exactly?"

"I don't know. I need some air."

"It's pouring down rain, Whit, and you've literally just recovered from what I fear was a hypothermic episode."

"Yeah, well what do you know? You're just a city girl."

Abby didn't let the comment sting. "I know what you taught me these past few days. And I watched you pass out after nearly freezing to death in the cold, relentless rain."

"I need some air." She struggled but managed to pull on her wet pants, then examined her heavy looking sweater, and tossed it aside. She shrugged into her jacket wearing only her bra and then stepped into her boots without socks. She knelt to lace them up, then seemed to think better of it, and walked back to the door where she pulled it open, letting in a rush of cold, damp air.

"Whit, don't." Abby tried to stop her, tried to grip her coat, but Whit hurried out to the steps where she tripped and tumbled down, landing hard on the ground below.

Abby ran down after her, hysterical. "Whit, oh, God, no." She cradled her head, searching for injury. She fingered a cut on her brow and a scrape on her lower lip. Whit opened her eyes and winced.

"Ow, Christ." She touched the cut on her head and eyed the blood on her fingertips. She sat up. "Fucking A, I fell down the stairs, didn't I?"

"I think you tripped over your laces." Abby sat back on her haunches, relieved that she was mostly okay.

Whit sighed and slapped her hands on her thighs. The rain pummeled them, icy and fierce. Whit began to laugh as she angled her face toward the crying sky. "I fell down the fucking stairs. Can you believe it? Of all the things to kill you out here, including a fucking grizzly, I go and fall down the stairs."

Abby stared at her in disbelief. But then she, too, began to laugh, because it *was* rather ludicrous.

"Crazy, right?" Whit said. "And you're nearly nude." She helped Abby up, despite having been the one who fell. Then they walked arm in arm back up the slick steps, supporting each other. Once inside, Abby closed the door and they stood still for a moment, glancing at one another awkwardly.

"Guess I should get out of these clothes again," Whit finally said.

"Guess so."

Slowly, Whit undressed, wrung out her clothes, and placed them back on the chairs near the stove. Then Abby, after drying with a blanket, tried to examine Whit's cut, but Whit drew away with a scowl.

"It hurts," she said.

"It needs tending to." Abby recalled seeing a first aid kit mounted on the wall above the kitchen counter. She retrieved some supplies from it before returning to Whit who was sitting on the couch, covered in a blanket.

"It's fine," Whit said, dodging her touch.

"It's not, and I'm doing this, whether you like it or not."

Whit stilled and Abby first cleaned the wound and then covered it in a butterfly bandage. "There. Was that so bad?" She grazed her fingertips along her cheek and down to her lips. Whit inhaled audibly but didn't try to escape.

"This looks painful too," Abby said.

"It's not so bad."

Abby dabbed it with gauze, but Whit stopped her, clenching her by the wrist.

"Am I hurting you?"

"No."

"Then what?"

"That's not going to make it feel better."

Abby got lost in her heavy gaze as it seemed to draw her closer and closer. So close she could feel the warmth of her breath. "What will?"

"This." Whit tugged on her and pressed her lips to hers, gently, tentatively. Abby allowed the meeting of their mouths to linger, thoroughly enjoying the feel of her warm, velvet-like skin.

"Did that hurt?" Abby asked, remembering her wound.

Whit smiled. "No." She brought her back in, this time for a more heated kiss. One where she openly and eagerly explored Abby, framing her lips with her own, while sneaking her tongue out to caress.

"Whit," Abby whispered, her heart pounding. "You feel so good."

Whit chucked the blanket aside and encouraged Abby to straddle her. As Abby did, Whit buried her face in her chest, where she grazed her awakening skin with kisses.

Abby sighed and knotted her hands in her damp hair. She met her mouth again, this time for a searing, deep kiss, where tongues both welcomed and explored. Whit moaned up into her, digging her fingers into the flesh of Abby's back before quickly unclasping her bra to free her breasts. She burned a stare into her as she flung the bra aside and then fully took her in.

"You're more beautiful than I imagined," she breathed, lightly running her hands up and down Abby's torso, teasing her.

"You've imagined me?"

"Oh, yes. Many times. And the red bra, it didn't help my self-control any."

Abby laughed and stroked her face. "I've thought of you, too. Especially when we were in the shelter together and I was lying in your arms."

"Why didn't you say something?"

"Why didn't you?"

Whit shrugged. "Fear."

"Of what?"

"Rejection."

Abby traced her sore lip, wanting to kiss it once again. "I would've never rejected you, Whit. I've...developed strong feelings for you."

Whit blinked up at her, her expression softening with deep resolve. "Abby, I—me too." She smiled, all starry-eyed, and then winced, reaching up to touch her lip.

"It does hurt," Abby said.

"Only when I smile."

"Not when we kiss?"

"No way." She started to smile again but seemed to think better of it, which caused Abby to laugh.

"So, I can do this again?" Abby leaned in and placed a soft kiss on her scrape.

"Yes," Whit said. "Please, do it again and again."

Abby did as instructed, thoroughly enjoying the tease. Whit couldn't take it, and she pulled her in for a deeper, more thorough probe of her mouth, while her hands massaged her breasts.

"Whit," Abby said. "I'm getting really excited." Her skin was on fire and she could feel her pulse between her legs.

"Something wrong with that?" Whit asked as she breathed upon her nipples, bringing them to a firm head, which she then lashed with her hot tongue.

Abby moaned and gripped the back of her neck. "Nothing at all," she said. "I just—ah Jesus—wasn't sure if you were okay enough—to continue. You did just fall down the stairs, you know."

"I'm perfectly fine."

"Thank God. Because I really, really don't want to stop."

Whit responded to that by pressing her hand against the throbbing flesh between Abby's legs. Abby hissed and rocked into her, the pleasure mounting quickly.

"Whit, oh, God. Oh, my God. I'm so close."

Whit enveloped her nipple with her mouth and sucked, nibbling the tip ever so slightly. Abby arched her back and cried out to the rainy Alaskan sky as she spilled over into oblivion, thrusting madly in Whit's arms.

"Yes, baby," Whit whispered, providing just enough pressure to finish her off nicely.

Abby went limp and Whit held onto her, dragging kisses across her collar bone. "That was wonderful," she said.

Abby palmed her forehead, suddenly embarrassed. "Sorry it was so…quick."

"Mm, it was perfect. Just as I imagined you."

"You imagined me climaxing within seconds, did you?"

Whit chuckled. "I did, actually."

"And why is that?"

"Because you're so fiery and passionate about everything. I just assumed you'd go off like a firecracker in bed."

"Oh, I see." she said. "And I just proved you correct, didn't I?"

"You did."

Abby kissed her and relished her briny taste. She wasn't sure if it was the scrape or the rain making her taste so salty, but she loved it either way and she was longing to taste her in other areas as well for comparison. She skimmed her fingers across her back and gripped her bra strap to unfasten it, but a noise made her pause.

Whit, too, heard it and looked up at her.

They sat very still, listening to the falling rain, waiting. Abby was just about to tug on the strap again when they heard it a second time.

"What is that?" Abby asked.

Whit tapped her hip, signaling for her to rise. Abby crawled off her, and Whit went to the window, searching for the source of the noise.

"It's got to be the rain," Abby said.

"That's what I was thinking. But it's not. It's different. It almost sounds like—"

Another quick tap against the wall sounded and Abby froze.

Whit faced her. "Is that what you meant by knocking when you heard it at the other cabin?"

Abby shook her head. "No. It was more continuous than that."

"It sounds like—" Whit started. "A rock hitting the wall."

Another rap came, this time making contact with the window. Abby jerked and Whit jumped back, alarmed.

"Motherfucker," she said as she hurried over to her shoes.

"Whit, don't. You're not even dressed."

"He's out there. Probably watching us. Watching us, you know…do stuff."

"I don't like the idea of that either, but you can't go running after him half naked and in the rain. Besides what will you do if you catch him?"

"I don't know. Beat the shit out of him?"

"As good as that sounds, it's not very realistic. You'll never catch him. Think about it. He wants us to react. That's why he's doing it. But I guarantee you he's already five steps ahead of us."

Whit paused, shoe in hand. Abby could almost hear the cogs of her mind turning.

She dropped her boot and placed her hands on her hips. "You're right. Chasing him is exactly what he wants." She sighed.

"I'm not the only one who's fiery, am I?"

Whit ran a hand through her hair. "Guess not."

"You were ready to tear off after him and kill him."

"Can you blame me?"

"Absolutely not. But I don't want to see you get hurt. That would devastate me."

Whit held her hands and they eased onto the couch. "Creeps me out that he probably saw us," she said.

"Me, too."

"He's beyond a stalker at this point. He's...deviant."

Another object hit the window, and a crack veined out in the glass. Whit stiffened but kept control of herself.

"We have to ignore it," she said.

Abby touched her face. "We do. After all, we're in here where it's warm and dry, and he's out there in the storm, probably soaked to the gills like an idiot. Let him get hypothermia this time."

"I wish he would. I wish he would wander off somewhere never to be found again. Let Alaska have her way with him."

"Maybe she will. In due time." Abby rested her head on her shoulder and Whit wrapped an arm around her and relaxed back into the couch. More things were thrown, some banging into the window, some against the walls, but all were ignored.

"This is almost nice," Abby said. "If it weren't for Boyd and his annoying little tantrums."

"It is."

The rain stopped and they both glanced out the window at the silence. They saw a figure standing out by the trees, wearing a dark green hooded slicker. Whit stood, ready to give chase, but Abby grabbed her.

"No," she said. "Remember it's what he wants."

"But he's right there."

"He's taunting you, Whit. Daring you to go out after him."

"I wish I had a gun. I'd open the door and shoot him."

"Just sit back down and relax. Try not to think about him."

"What if he comes up to the door? You want me to ignore him then?"

"He won't. He knows what you did to that bear."

"But he's getting more and more brazen, Abby. And I don't want him to hurt you."

"He won't. We won't let him. If he comes to the door, we'll fight. But otherwise, we ignore him."

Whit released a long breath. "It's going to be a long night."

Abby pulled her close. "At least in the dark, he won't be able to see us."

Whit returned the embrace. "Does that mean more kisses?"

"Mm, it does."

"Well, I'm all for that, then."

"Boyd be damned?"

"Boyd be damned."

CHAPTER TWENTY-SIX

If only Whit could relax and truly ignore the fact that Boyd was standing right outside the cabin.

"Hey, where are you?" Abby asked, holding her face. They'd been kissing and watching as the storm continued to calm and the sun began to disappear behind the mountains.

"I'm sorry," Whit said. "I just can't stop thinking about him out there."

Abby sat back. "Me neither."

"Really?"

"Well, yeah. He's tried to have us killed and now he's showing himself? Of course I'm unsettled by it."

"But you talked me down and sounded so blasé about it."

"I was trying to keep you here and keep you levelheaded. It worked, didn't it?"

Whit stood and draped one of the blankets over her shoulders. "For the time being."

"You mean you're still going to go out after him?"

Whit checked her clothes, found them damp, but dressed anyway.

"Those can't be dry," Abby said, snuggling beneath the other blanket.

"They're close enough."

"Whit, you'll get a chill. You should let them dry."

"I don't want to get caught off guard," she said, standing by the window. She looked out to where Boyd had been standing near the tree line and scanned the area several times before she felt satisfied.

"You're worried he might do something else?"

Whit turned to face her. "Like I said, it's going to be a long night."

She walked into the tiny kitchen, grabbed a couple of mugs, and rummaged through the cabinet. She found a bottle of rum and a sealed container of instant coffee. There was also a box of herbal tea. She held them up for Abby to see.

"Pick your poison."

"Coffee."

"Spiked okay?"

"Definitely."

Whit used the last of their water for the kettle and placed it on the wood stove to heat. When it signaled that it was hot, she made the coffee and added some rum to top it off. She brought both cups over to the couch where she joined Abby to sit and sip.

"Mm, this is great," Abby said, taking a drink of the steaming liquid.

"Hits the spot, doesn't it?" She leaned back and extended her legs to cross her ankles. Her clothes felt cold against her skin, but she felt more at ease being dressed with Boyd lingering nearby. She was really surprised that Abby wasn't. Not that she was complaining.

She was just getting ready to take a sip of her coffee when she heard something else outside. She and Abby both turned to look and to their astonishment, they saw an SUV driving up to the cabin.

"It's the Forestry Service," Whit said, reading the side of the vehicle.

"Like a forest ranger?" Abby asked as they stood.

Whit grinned. "Looks that way. You better get dressed."

Abby hurried to the chairs and pulled on her clothes while a man, who did indeed appear to be a ranger, stepped out of the car and climbed the steps.

He took his broad-rimmed hat off before he knocked.

Whit opened the door immediately.

"Oh, hello. I saw the smoke and thought I'd come by," he said. He offered a polite smile, which caused the wrinkles around his dark blue eyes to crinkle.

"You have no idea how glad we are to see you," Whit said, welcoming him inside.

The ranger entered and spotted Abby, who thankfully, was fully clothed. "You wouldn't happen to be my my missing travelers, would you?"

"Yes!" Abby said. "We've been walking for days, trying to find help."

"We've been searching for you two for a while." He stuck out his hand. "I'm Jackson. Jackson Jessop."

"Whit." She shook his hand. "And this is Abby."

Abby went to him and did the same. "Did you..." she started, looking dismayed. "Find Junior?"

Jackson played with his hat. "The man in the vehicle?"

Abby nodded.

"We did."

Abby wiped away tears. "We didn't want to leave him like that, but—" She turned away and her shoulders shook with muffled sobs.

Jackson pressed his lips together and scratched his graying temple. He looked as solemn as Abby. "I'm sorry for your loss, ma'am. But I am glad you two are okay."

"We're a little worse for wear," Whit said. "And Abby has a pretty significant knee injury. But other than that, we're okay."

"She forgot to tell you that she hit her head falling down the stairs out front," Abby said, after composing herself. "And she also forgot to mention that we have a man after us."

"A man?"

Whit motioned Jackson toward the table and offered him a seat. He slowly sat and deposited his hat on the table.

"He said his name is Boyd Laird," Abby said, settling in across from him. "He came into our camp a few days ago and acted friendly enough."

"But then we woke the next morning and he'd stolen all our food," Whit continued. "After that, strange things began to happen and we just assumed it was him harassing us."

"What kind of strange things?"

"More things taken," Abby said. "And while we were holed up in another cabin, he lured a grizzly in and it nearly killed us. He also carved the word DIE in the door."

Jackson's brows knitted. "Sounds serious."

"He's been throwing rocks at us here today," Whit said. "Cracked the window." She motioned toward the vein-like crack. Jackson looked and then slid a notebook out of his jacket pocket. He tapped a pen on the table and then poised it over a blank page.

"You said his name is Boyd Laird?"

"That's what he told us," Abby said.

"But we think he lied about almost everything," Whit added.

Jackson massaged the stubble on his chin. "We've heard of a few guys moving through these parts here recently. Found one of them dead yesterday."

"Jesus," Abby said.

"Someone killed him by the looks of it."

"Oh, my God," Whit said. "That's terrible."

"And scary," Abby added.

Whit continued. "This guy Boyd said he's been living off the land. And that he's heading back to town to find somewhere to stay for winter."

Jackson nodded, contemplating.

"You think he could be your killer?" Abby asked.

"Hard to tell. But it's possible." He continued to make notes. "You got a description?"

"He's scrawny," Abby said. "A little taller than Whit with salt-and-pepper hair and a long beard."

"And he stinks," Whit said. "Badly. Not sure if that's important to know or not."

Jackson scribbled some more. "Every little bit helps."

"Can we go now?" Abby asked. "Not to rush you or anything, but I'm dying to get back to civilization and away from Boyd."

Jackson closed his notebook, put it away, and set his hat back on his head. "Sure, just let me take some photos to document your claims while I'm here."

Abby smiled broadly and looked to Whit. "We're saved," she said. "Finally!"

Whit returned the smile as best she could. She was happy to be rescued, but she was sad that her time with Abby was coming to an end. Uncertainty stained their future and she was feeling anxious about it already.

Jackson walked to the window and began to take pictures of the noticeable crack. Then he opened the door and stepped outside to take pictures from there, careful to get several different angles. Whit watched as he descended the stairs and began searching the ground for what she assumed were the rocks or objects that Boyd had thrown. She saw him kneel to take more photos, then straighten and turn to search the forest. He headed back up the stairs and tugged on his hat, as if in deep contemplation.

He waited a moment before he spoke. "I've taken some photos of both the window and what appears to be some sizable rocks at the base of the cabin. You mentioned that you assumed this was the Boyd fellow doing this to you, but did you actually see him do these things?"

"Yes," Abby said. "We saw him today. He stood right out there at the tree line."

Jackson looked back behind him. "Out there?"

"Yes."

"Well, we saw *someone,*" Whit said. "He was covered in a hooded green slicker."

"It was Boyd," Abby said. "Who else would it be?"

"Like I said," Jackson said. "There have been reports of several hikers working their way through these parts."

"You really think it could be one of them?" Whit asked.

"I honestly have no idea, ma'am. I'm just playing devil's advocate here. Seems to me that a man wouldn't come into your camp and introduce himself, allow you to see his face, and then decide to harass you. It would be pretty stupid on his part."

"I didn't say he was smart," Whit said. "And I'm pretty sure he didn't like the fact that I didn't fall for his bullshit. My attitude toward him was noticeably hostile."

Jackson seemed to ponder that bit of information. Then he looked behind him once again. "Let me go see if he left any tracks back by the tree line, then we'll close up shop and go."

Whit nodded and she and Abby cleaned up and extinguished the fire in the wood stove. By the time they were finished, Jackson had made his way back to the SUV. He sat behind the steering wheel, waiting patiently for them, engine idling. Whit crawled in the back, allowing Abby to sit up front with Jackson.

"Find anything?" Abby asked. She'd perked up considerably since Jackson's arrival and Whit knew she was more than excited to get to Cozy. She'd mentioned contacting her editor while they were straightening up, and Whit could sense her dogged determination to finish the article she'd been sent on assignment to write. Even after the past few days of notable hell, she was still thinking about her article, with recovery seemingly the last thing on her mind. She really was a fighter.

"I found a few tracks," Jackson said, turning the vehicle around to drive away from the cabin. "Got some pics. Not sure how well they'll turn out. I radioed in a report, though. Gave an update on your status and on your claims about Boyd Laird. They're going to send someone out at first light to do a more thorough investigation."

"Think they'll be able to find him?" Abby asked.

"Not if he doesn't want to be found. Alaska has an innate ability to swallow people whole sometimes. Those that want to disappear and those that don't. She's not very picky and she can be more than accommodating."

"I hope they find him," Abby said. "He doesn't deserve to just get off scot-free. Not after all he did."

"If I were him, and I saw my vehicle pull up, I'd get gone real quick like. Get gone far away from here."

Whit wouldn't care if he disappeared and Abby was able to go back home to the Lower Forty-eight, far away from him. Of course, that meant she'd be far away from her as well. The thought hurt, but she knew her safety was more important than her growing feelings. Regardless of how special they were.

No, her wants, needs, and desires, she had a feeling, were about to be put on the back burner. She just hoped it wouldn't be for good.

CHAPTER TWENTY-SEVEN

It had been three days since Abby had last seen Whit and she was beginning to wonder if she'd already forgotten about her. If maybe she had returned home to the someone she had waiting for her and had put Abby far from her mind.

I should've known better than to have gotten involved with a taken woman.

But Whit had seemed so genuine, and so kind. Abby should've allowed her to explain her situation when she'd tried. Maybe it would've helped her to have made sense out of all this. Now it seemed as though it was too late. Whit was presumably back home with her woman, and Abby was alone and getting ready to return to Phoenix. As nice as Cozy was, and it was a quaint, nice little Alaskan town, she felt incredibly isolated and alone in her little two-room rented cottage house. She almost preferred to be back in the hospital, where at least she was around more people. She and Whit both had been admitted for a night to receive IV fluids and to get checked out.

She'd learned that she needed to see an orthopedist for her knee, that she may need surgery, and that she needed to consume more calories to replenish her nourishment requirements. The latter was obvious, but the doctors had told her to take it slow, so she wouldn't make herself sick. So, she'd been eating a few small meals a day, just so happy to have real food once again. She'd mainly been sticking to soups, with lots of cooked vegetables and beans, and she was already feeling a whole lot better. And frankly, she didn't care if she never saw another fish again as long as she lived. Just the smell of them made her nauseous. She'd discovered that when her guide had shown up with some sockeye salmon for her the previous evening. Abby had had to make a beeline for the restroom where she dry-heaved, leaving her guide staring after her questioningly at the door.

I wonder if Whit's having similar issues?

She thought about calling her, but she didn't have her number and she wasn't sure where she lived. While it wouldn't be difficult to find out in a place as small as Cozy, she thought it best to steer clear. After all, how would it look if she showed up on her doorstep and her girlfriend answered the door? What would she say? What would she do?

So, she let things be, knowing that if Whit truly wanted to see her, she'd get a hold of her somehow. She'd better hurry though, because she was leaving in two days' time.

Abby walked to the thermostat and adjusted the heat. She couldn't seem to get warm enough, despite being dressed in layers. Her clothes, she'd noticed, were all fitting looser upon her return, and she wondered if she'd have to buy a new wardrobe or if she should wait to see if she'd regain the weight she'd lost. As it was, she could see the indentation of her abdominal muscles and she'd never been able to see those before. And her breasts, well, they were smaller, which unnerved her. Why did women lose in their breasts and not in other places?

She adjusted the belt on her pants once again and settled down on the couch to sip from a steaming mug of hot cocoa. Her laptop was open and sitting on the coffee table, the cursor blinking at the end of her document. She'd just finished her article on the Alaskan small towns and though, in her opinion, it was relatively good, she knew her heart wasn't in it.

Something was missing.

It just wasn't the article she wanted to write.

She'd loved the small towns she'd visited, so that wasn't the problem. It was just that…the story no longer seemed relevant to her. And Whit's words kept playing over and over in her mind. About how she didn't want any more tourists in Cozy, that she preferred to keep Cozy just the way it was. Now that Abby had been to Cozy and experienced it firsthand, she could understand why. The town was small and, well, quite cozy, with a population of under three hundred, and only one stoplight which swung on a wire down on Main Street. The buildings were colorful and period-style, some restored, some in need of restoration, set against the backdrop of the snow-covered Ridgeline peaks. The people were quiet, though friendly, and helped each other when needed. There was an understanding here, an ambience of quiet resolve, of live and let live. A sudden throng of tourism would tarnish that and, Abby suspected, send most of these townsfolk back into their homes to wait out the influx of visitors.

Yet Abby had a deadline and a responsibility. Her editor and her magazine were expecting the article. She wasn't sure what to do.

She set down her hot chocolate and lifted her laptop. After staring at her document for a long moment, she re-saved it, and closed the top to put it back on the coffee table. She'd deal with it later.

Right now, she wanted to relax, sip her drink, and think about… her mind kept returning to Whit and the way her lips had felt against hers, the way her warm skin had caused hers to tingle. And then there were her eyes and their endless depths the same color as the creek dependent upon the position of the sun. Sometimes a dark maple syrup, sometimes a coppery whiskey. But every time beautiful and soulful and seemingly full of words she so desperately wanted to share, but ultimately shied away from.

A knock came from the door, and she nearly spilled her cocoa. She was still unusually jumpy from the ordeal with Boyd, who, as far as she knew, still not been caught. She put her mug down and walked hesitantly to the door. She wasn't expecting her guide again until tomorrow and with the exception of her one neighbor, no one else had come calling.

She peered out the side window. A uniformed policeman was standing at the threshold. She unlocked the door and opened it.

"Miss," he said, by way of greeting.

"Yes?"

"I'm Deputy Misgreaves with the Ridgeline Department of Public Safety. I've been ordered to notify you that one Boyd Laird has been located and questioned."

"He has?" She gripped the door frame, suddenly dizzy.

"Yes, ma'am."

She took a moment to control her breathing and noticed that the deputy seemed to be waiting for her before he continued.

"You said questioned. He wasn't arrested?"

"No, ma'am. May I...step inside a moment?"

The chill of the air outside began to seep in, suddenly noticeable to her, and she moved aside to allow him entry and quickly shut the door. She motioned toward the chair next to the couch. He removed his knit cap and settled while she sat where she had before.

"Would you like some coffee?" she asked, feeling like she had to be hospitable.

"No, thank you."

Abby clasped her hands and waited.

The young deputy appeared uneasy, as if he were about to deliver some bad news. "The suspect in question, Mr. Laird, was located here in Cozy early this morning."

A shiver ran through her, and she hugged herself. She didn't like hearing that he had been so close. Had he been looking for her, or for Whit? She didn't ask, but rather waited for the deputy to continue.

"He was taken to a holding cell here in town and we were notified and came directly. We questioned him thoroughly and well, ma'am, it seems that Boyd Laird could not have been your perpetrator."

"What?" She felt dizzy again.

"He claims he's been here, in Cozy, for days and we've corroborated his story with witnesses."

"But that doesn't make sense. We saw him. He was there, in the woods."

"I'm sorry, ma'am, but it wasn't Mr. Laird."

"So you let him go?"

"We had nothing to hold him for."

"He stole all our food!"

"He admitted to that, ma'am, but it's hardly anything we can charge him with."

She stood. "But we nearly starved. He—tried to have us killed."

"Ma'am. I understand it's upsetting. What you went through and all. But it couldn't have all been Mr. Laird." He pulled his cap back on and stood to look at her somberly.

Abby panicked. "Wait, you can't just tell me that and leave. What about the investigation?"

"We haven't been able to locate any other suspect."

"So what does that mean?"

"We've moved on from the case."

She blinked, disbelieving. "Is it closed?"

"Not officially." He headed for the door. Abby followed him, feeling completely lost and helpless.

"But that's it?"

"If you can think of anything else," he said. "Let us know and we'll look into it."

He opened the door and walked away. Abby watched him go, wanting to call out to him, to tell him he was wrong and that it *was* Boyd, that he was just a good liar. But she knew she'd sound ridiculous. She closed the door and went back to the sofa where she collapsed and cried.

❖

The next day, when Abby still didn't hear from Whit, she decided to call her guide to see if she knew where she could find her. Turns out she did, and she gave her the address. Abby told herself, as she was walking through town, past the old buildings, listening to the ATVs driving by, that she was going to see her solely to discuss Boyd and her visit from the police. And not for any other, more personal, reasons. Her heart still raced with anxiousness nonetheless, even as she stopped at the town's one and only small grocery store to get some more hot cocoa.

The clerk greeted her politely and sold Abby the box of hot chocolate for twelve dollars, a steep price she was expecting considering it was Alaska and things were harder to come by.

"Can I get you anything else?" the clerk asked.

"Oh, no thanks. This is good."

"You the writer everyone's been talking about?"

"Am I that obvious?" Abby chuckled.

"In these parts, all new faces are obvious."

"Well, I'm leaving tomorrow, so I'm afraid I'm not here for too much longer."

"You out exploring the town? So you can write about it?"

"I've already done that. I'm actually on my way to see a friend. Her name's Whitley Travers. Do you know her?"

"Sure, I know Whit. She's good people. Although…"

"Yes?"

"She just seems to work so much. Always taking off to go fly people around. I don't see much of her. Not even when she's home. She just holes up in that house."

It took a moment for Abby to comprehend what she was saying.

"Seems to me she's a bit lonely. I mean how could she not be? Working all the time and you know, her home life—"

The bell above the door jingled as another patron walked in. The clerk greeted her with a smile and the two women began talking about someone else in town. Abby excused herself and exited the store. She stood in the early winter sun, got her bearings, and then headed for Whit's house one street over.

When she reached the tiny home, painted a robin egg blue, she stood at the door and observed a wind chime made of small rectangular mirrors and bird feathers. It made a delicate noise in the cold but gentle breeze, and she allowed it to relax her enough to ring the doorbell.

It took a moment for someone to answer, but when they did, they pulled the door just slightly ajar. Abby couldn't tell who it was peering out at her.

"Uh, hi, I'm Abby. I'm looking for—"

The door inched open wider, and Whit's face appeared. She had a dish rag in her hand and Abby could smell the distinct scent of frying onions and peppers wafting from inside.

"Abby, hi. How did you...find me?"

"Small town."

"Right."

When Whit didn't say anything more, Abby continued. "I came to talk about Boyd."

Whit's face contorted. "What about him?"

"Did a deputy not come and speak to you?"

"Someone stopped by earlier, but I wasn't here. Why? What's going on?"

"They're saying that they've questioned Boyd and that he's not our perpetrator. That he's claiming he's been in Cozy for days and that he even has witnesses to back up his story."

"That's bullshit."

"That's what I said."

"It's impossible. He's just so—fucking manipulative."

"I know! So we have to do something. Say something. Anything. We have to get them to believe us. Boyd—he could've had those people cover for him. I mean, we don't know, do we? So how can the cops be so sure?"

"They can't. I wouldn't put anything past that guy."

"I'm so glad you agree with me. I've been so torn up over this. I've—"

Someone came into view behind Whit and Abby stopped talking. It was a woman, close to her own age, and very attractive with long black hair down past her waist. She placed a hand on Whit's shoulder.

"I need you," she said.

"Can it wait?"

The woman's dark, obsidian eyes flicked to Abby. "No."

Abby's heart lodged in her throat. She began to back away. "That's okay. You're busy. We can talk another time." She turned to leave, tears burning her eyes. Whit did have someone waiting for her back home. She wasn't lonely at all and when she was holed up at home, she was holed up with another woman. A beautiful woman, who wanted and needed her attention.

"Abby, wait," Whit called.

But Abby kept walking, quickening her pace. When she reached the dirty, snow-encrusted street, she started to run. She ran until she reached her place and hurriedly unlocked the door to go inside and collapse back onto the couch.

And once again, she buried her face in the cushions and cried.

CHAPTER TWENTY-EIGHT

It took Whit less than an hour to find out where Abby was staying. She called around, spoke with a few friends, and learned that she was renting a small home through someone in town. It took less than half an hour to walk to her place. Whit thought about taking the ATV, which was what she drove while home, as did most folks in Cozy, but she decided she wanted some fresh air and some time to think.

Abby showing up when she did had been unfortunate, and the way she'd left even more unfortunate. Whit knew it was time to explain things, whether Abby wanted to hear it or not. Whit had to say her piece. What happened from there, well, that would be up to Abby.

The rented house was painted a pale yellow with dark blue trim. Whit recognized it as the home where one of her long-time friends grew up, but had long since left. Now it was owned by Gemma Ulrich, a Cozy native, who rented it out to tourists when they came through in the summer. As it was, Cozy didn't have many visitors, but those who did make the trip, came predominantly in the summer months. Abby being able to get into the house in late September, spoke to the summer tourists already having taken off back to warmer climates. Soon there would be nothing but the Cozyites to welcome in another long winter.

Whit walked up to the door and gave a gentle knock. "Abby, it's me, Whit. Can you open up? We need to talk."

"I don't want to talk," she said, her voice muffled through the door.

"We need to, Abby. Please. Things can't continue like this between us. We need to air some things out."

The door opened and Abby stood there with a pinched look on her face. "Okay, Whit. You win. Let's do it. Let's air some things out." She made air quotes with her fingers and Whit knew it was going to be a trying conversation.

"May I come in?" Whit asked. She really preferred not to have the discussion out where others might hear. The town was small enough as it was, and rumors were known to spread like wildfire. She didn't want to be the subject of them.

"Suit yourself," Abby said, walking away from the open entryway. Whit stepped inside, closed the door, and joined Abby in the living room where she sat with her face in her hands on the couch. The house was pleasantly warm, so Whit tugged off her knit cap and shrugged out of her coat. She tossed both on the chair, but remained standing.

"Abby, I need to tell you something."

"No need. I already know."

"What do you know?"

"That you and your girlfriend live together and you can't, for whatever reason, leave her."

Whit sighed.

Abby glanced up at her through her fingers. "I'm right, aren't I?"

"Yes, you're right."

"I knew it. Damn it, I knew it." She slapped her hands on her thighs. "Why then, did I get involved with you? Was it because I thought I was going to die? No, that's no excuse, is it?" She laughed. "You know what it was, Whit? I had real feelings for you. Silly me."

"I have real feelings for you, too, Abby."

"You can't. You have someone. So don't tell me that."

"Abby…you're misunderstanding."

"Misunderstanding? That's an interesting way of trying to explain things. Do you not live with your girlfriend?"

"I do but—we are no longer together. Not in that sense."

"Oh, so it's a shared home with an ex-lover kind of thing." She again made air quotes with her fingers.

"Yes," Whit said. "But again, it's not what you think. Bobby—that's her name—is ill, Abby. She has ALS. And she lives with me so I can help care for her. Her family, they're in the Lower Forty-eight and they pretty much disowned her years ago for choosing to be with me. For being gay. So I'm all she has."

Whit paused and waited for Abby to respond. It took her a while, and when she did she sounded truly upset. Her voice cracked and she wiped at her tears.

"I'm so sorry," she said. "I had no idea, Whit."

"I know. That's why I wanted so very much to explain."

"I should've let you. I just assumed—God, I can be so hard-headed sometimes."

"You just thought like anyone would in your position."

"But the woman I saw. She looked fine. She looked rather beautiful and healthy, in fact."

"That's Nancy. She's the home health nurse and a good friend. I've known her for years. Bobby, she wasn't in your line of sight. She's pretty much bed-bound now. She doesn't have much time left. So, I'm not going to be working again anytime soon. I need to be at home with her. Nancy and I both."

"Of course. I understand."

"But I meant what I said, Abby. I do have feelings for you. Deep feelings. Real feelings. I just—don't know what I can do about them right now."

Abby went to her and took her hands. "Don't worry about it," she said. "You have enough on your plate."

"But I need to worry about it. I don't want to lose you."

Abby smiled and skimmed her face. "I can't stay, Whit. I have to go."

"I know."

"So how could we ever make this work? Even if Bobby was okay?"

"I don't know." Whit palmed her cheek. "I just know what I feel. And that's not going to go away when you do."

"No, it's not, is it?" Abby closed her eyes, leaned in, and kissed her. "Mm, this is crazy," she said, continuing to plant soft, luscious kisses on her. "We shouldn't be doing this."

"No, definitely not." Whit wound her hands around her waist and pulled her closer. "But I'm more than willing to break the rules if you are."

"Oh, God, yes. Let's break all the rules. Even if it's just for tonight."

"You got it." Whit then eased her back down onto the couch and pressed her body between her legs. Abby welcomed her by encasing her with her legs and gripping the base of her head to hold her firm while she slid her hungry tongue inside her mouth. Whit answered with a vengeance, meeting her tongue with her own while rocking herself into her. Abby made a noise of sheer delight and lifted her hips to meet Whit's rhythm. She then began to claw at Whit's back, dragging her nails down her shirt, grazing her flesh, causing Whit to shudder.

"Nothing and no one can stop us now," Abby whispered.

"No."

"We're all alone and safe and warm."

"We are."

"Then make love to me, Whit. Please. Make love to me."

Whit trailed her mouth down to her neck where she gently sucked and nibbled as Abby arched herself, making an offering. Her green eyes seemed to burn as they watched Whit make her way farther down her body, inching up her sweater bit by bit as she went. When she had it up around her neck, Abby sat up briefly to slip it off and toss it aside, before she gripped Whit's face and brought her in for another searing kiss, one that Whit had to fight to draw away from.

As she did, she moved even lower, and this time tugged on Abby's pants, quickly unfastening the button to bring them down over her hips. Then she paused at her knee to carefully remove the brace she wore and then proceeded to strip off her pants the rest of the way. Abby sat up once again to take off her bra and then helped Whit out of her hooded sweatshirt and thermal undershirt. She was braless and the air teased her nipples, instantly hardening them. Abby seemed to delight in seeing them and she immediately grazed them with the back of her hands.

"My God, you're breathtaking," she breathed. "Come here." She pulled Whit back onto her and they once again deepened their kisses until Whit managed to separate from her to drift down between her legs. After holding her gaze for just a moment, she then snuck out her tongue and rimmed the edge of her panties and Abby squirmed beneath her, unable to take the purposeful tease.

"Jesus, Whit. You're—killing me."

Whit continued the tease, until finally, and at the behest of a very vocal Abby, she flattened her tongue and licked her dead center through the satin material. Abby arched up into her, grabbing her head, pleading for more.

"Please, Whit. Please."

Whit conceded, unable to wait longer herself. She had to taste her. Relish her, marinate in her. She yanked her panties aside and attached herself to her swollen clit.

"Whit! Oh, my God. Yes!"

Abby knotted her hands in her hair, holding her fast to her as Whit furiously fed. She sucked hard and slow, then fast and tender, driving her into a frenzy. At last she came and cried out in a guttural voice for more and then hoarsely for mercy.

Whit stopped only when Abby went limp and then softly spasmed every second or two until she stilled completely. She sat up and tugged Whit into her arms, while carefully slipping her hand down the front of Whit's pants to caress her through her underwear. Whit shook and shuddered, so very close to spilling over herself. Abby seemed to sense this and she laughed deviously while toying with her flesh through the fabric.

"You're so wet I can feel it through your panties," she said.

"That's what you do to me."

"Do I?"

"Ye-es."

"What else do I do to you?"

"Drive me mad."

"Yeah?"

"Uh-huh."

"Let's put that to the test, shall we?" She slipped her hand into her underwear and into her aching flesh. Whit stiffened, groaned, and nearly came on the spot. But Abby, wise to her, stilled, then slowly, oh so slowly, began to play her like the finest of instruments.

"You're beautiful," Abby said into her ear. "So very fucking beautiful, Whit. And I wish I could pleasure you like this forever. Do you know that? Forever. To feel you on me and in my hand, the very center of your being. Your most precious of places. I love it, Whit. And I..." her voice cracked, and Whit saw the rest of the words in her eyes and she came, hard and fast, powerful and slow, wave after incredible wave as Abby stroked her expertly.

"Abby," she cried. "I—" and she broke into uncontrollable spasms, unable to finish her sentence as the orgasm continued to surge through her.

Abby watched her closely, rubbing her until she eventually collapsed atop her. Then they both remained silent, gathering breath.

At last Abby spoke as she ran her fingers through Whit's hair. "I loved every second of that," she said.

"Mm, me too," Whit said.

"And as much as I love having my hand right where it is, I believe I need to move it as it's falling asleep."

Whit chuckled and shifted so Abby could slide her hand from her pants. She quickly embraced Whit and they held one another in languid silence again. Until eventually, Whit closed her eyes and didn't open them again.

CHAPTER TWENTY-NINE

When Abby woke it was dark, save for the electric fireplace burning beneath the television set. The heat was thick, and she was sweating, and Whit was lying on top of her. They were still on the couch where they'd promptly cuddled after lovemaking. She smiled as she recalled that rather enjoyable lovemaking and she reached down to stroke Whit's temple, relaxing in the sounds of her sleep.

"I love you," she whispered, glad she was finally able to say it. Whit didn't hear it, but maybe that was for the best. They'd agreed to this one night together and nothing more. At least not for the time being. While the thought saddened her, she was hell-bent on making it the best evening ever. She wanted to show Whit just how much she cared for her and she was going to thoroughly enjoy doing so.

But just as she was about to wake her, to indeed show her, there was a knock at the door. She stiffened, alarmed. A quick glance at the clock showed her it was nearing eight o'clock. Who could it be? The police again? Maybe they'd come to her place to talk to Whit. Or maybe they had more news concerning the investigation.

"Whit, wake up." She gently shook her and Whit came to as another knock sounded.

"Someone's at the door and I bet it's the police." Whit crawled from her, and they both rose, dressed, and made their way to the door. Abby, feeling safe with Whit by her side, and still feeling rather groggy, pulled the door open without peering out the window.

A figure stood in the dark wearing a rain slicker, his face obstructed. And before Abby or Whit could react, he brandished a curved blade and spoke.

"Inside, now."

Whit tried to slam the door, but the man managed to wedge his boot in the doorway. Then he shoved his way in and slammed the door closed behind him. Abby searched for something to grab, anything that she could use against him. But there was nothing. He took a step toward them and she gripped Whit's hand.

"What do you want with us, huh?" Abby demanded. "We've done nothing to you."

"He's sick," Whit said, her gaze intently focused on the knife. "He gets off on this kind of thing. Don't you, Boyd? You fooled the cops and now you've come to finish the job, haven't you?"

The man laughed and then slowly pulled down his hood. Abby gasped as the man before her was not Boyd, but someone else altogether. Someone she didn't recognize at all.

"Who the hell are you?" she blurted.

"Not Boyd," the man said. He rubbed his balding head.

"What do you want with us, then?"

His steely gaze slid over to Whit who was standing in apparent shock and silence.

"You know, don't you, little Whitley?"

Abby blinked, confused.

"Whit, do you know him?"

Whit swallowed. "I do."

"Who is he?"

"An old acquaintance," he said, showing off a sinister, almost bucktoothed grin.

"They should've never let you out," Whit seethed.

"Thanks to you, they almost didn't. And that's why I'm here. To show you my appreciation for your efforts to keep me locked up. And for your testimony against me all those years ago which got me locked up in the first place."

"Whit, what's he talking about?"

"Oh, I'm sorry," he said. "Allow me to introduce myself. Since Whitley obviously isn't going to. I'm Stanley. Stanley—"

"His name is Otter," Whit growled. "And he's the one who murdered my father."

Otter took a bow and grinned. Abby felt bile rise from her stomach as Whit squeezed her hand and spoke.

"You were the one following us the day of the accident," Whit said.

"I was."

"And you drove off and left us to the wild."

"I did."

"But then you decided to follow us on foot."

"I did indeed. I thought about killing you there, in the woods, and leaving you to rot and never to be found, like I did that poor hiker, but then I just had so much fun playing with you both that I changed my mind. I didn't expect the ranger to show up when he did. That ruined all my plans for the two of you. So I've had to... improvise." Again, he grinned, brandishing his awful, yellowing teeth.

Whit cried out and lunged at him and Otter quickly dodged her and shoved her into the wall. Then he charged Abby and before she could turn to escape, he hit her hard and an awful searing pain shot up from her side. The next thing she knew she was on the ground and Whit was screaming, crying out, "No, no, no!" She scrambled to her side while Otter stood there laughing.

"Oops, it's happened again. I've accidentally stabbed someone."

He held up the blood-caked knife and Abby grew dizzy. She pulled her hand away from her torso and saw more of the dark blood. "Oh, God," she said. "Oh, no."

Whit pressed her hand into the wound. "You're okay," she said. "It's okay."

Otter tsked. "I don't think it's okay, Whitley. I think she's in a lot of trouble. Just like dear old dad. You better do something. Quick."

"You son of a bitch," she said, spittle flying from her mouth. "I'll kill you."

He laughed. "Now that I'd like to see."

She left Abby to lunge at him again. Otter swung to his left and grazed her with his knife as she soared past him. She braced herself against the wall, trying to catch her breath. Her outer thigh stung, and she knew for certain that she'd been cut. But there was no time to think about that. She had to help Abby. She couldn't lose her. Not her too.

She pushed away from the wall and grunted as she went at him again, this time grabbing his wrist to control the weapon. He gritted his teeth and struggled against her, both of them fighting for power. Though she was strong, she was no match for his six foot plus frame and sinewy build. He'd no doubt worked out while incarcerated too, and struggling with him using all her might was getting her nowhere. So when she had the chance, she relaxed her stance and he closed the gap between them, thinking he had the upper hand. But she quickly kneed him in the groin and then held his head as he bent over in pain and slammed that too into her knee. He collapsed onto his side, groaning in pain. Blood surged from his nose. Whit moved as quickly as she could, going to Abby who was still conscious but paling by the second.

"Hang on," she said, hoisting her up from under her arms. "We're getting out of here." She dragged her toward the door as Otter continued to writhe on the floor. Whit opened the door with one hand and slid Abby outside onto the front stoop. Otter managed to stand. He wiped his nose with the back of his hand. His other gripped the knife.

"You bitch," he said, showing off his now blood-stained teeth. "You'll pay for that."

Whit hurriedly pulled Abby down the stairs and onto the dirt path. But Otter pursued them, rushing out of the house with the look of death in his crazed eyes. Whit released Abby and stood before her, putting herself between her and Otter. She was not going to let him near her. He was not going to hurt her again.

"Sorry about your girlfriend." He grinned. "It's a shame, isn't it? That you're going to lose her too?"

"What are you waiting for, Otter? Afraid I'll punish you some more?"

His grin vanished and he thrust his knife at her, threatening. Whit focused solely on the blade. Otter she could handle. For the most part. But the knife was a different story. From behind, she heard an approaching vehicle. And though Otter looked behind her, searching for the source, she kept her eyes on the blade.

"Someone's coming," she said. "Might as well give it up, Otter. It's over."

"It's not over until you're dead."

"Then come on. Do it. You don't have much time now." Her blood was thrumming and her senses were on overload as adrenaline surged through her. She was waiting for just the slightest movement from Otter, praying she'd be able to react in time. The oncoming vehicle slammed on its brakes behind her, gravel crunching. A door opened and a man called out, "Police! Drop your weapon!"

Whit nearly relaxed with relief, but Otter still held firm to the knife. It seemed he wasn't going to give up or give in.

"Time to die, little Whitley." He lunged at her and tried to plunge the knife into her midsection. But she shifted sideways, just as he'd done to her, and grabbed him from behind, spinning him away from Abby who remained on the ground. Whit then punched him hard in the jaw, sending him spinning back the other way, the knife still in his grip. She hit him again, on his opposite jaw, and he rotated again, this time falling into a heap in the dirt. He groaned and stirred as she stepped over him, ready to pry the knife from his bony hand. But as he rolled over, she saw that the knife was embedded in his gut, his hand slowly sliding it out. He grunted as he got the blade free, but black-looking blood surged from the wound and he touched it, fingers trembling.

"I'm hurt," he said, almost child-like. He looked to Whit. "I've been hurt. I need help."

Whit stared at him a moment, thinking that nothing she could say would ever make a difference. Nothing at all. Her father was dead and gone and Abby, she was badly injured. She went to her and pressed into her bleeding wound.

"Did he—get you?" Abby asked.

"No."

The police officer ran up to them, shoulder mic held to his mouth. He was calling for help. Whit tuned him out. Her only concern was for Abby, whose eyes were drifting closed.

"No," Whit said, gently shaking her. "You can't fall asleep, you hear? You have to stay awake. Stay with me."

"I need help," Otter cried.

The policeman knelt next to him and plucked the knife from his grip. He set it out of reach and then came to her and Abby.

"She needs help, now. Call a care flight."

He nodded and stepped back to speak into his mic once again.

Whit held her close, trying to keep her awake, but she was fading fast. The last thing she said, before falling unconscious were three little words.

"I love you."

CHAPTER THIRTY

Congratulations. The article is a big hit," her editor said. Abby smiled and held the phone snug to her ear. She sat back on her couch and squinted against the afternoon sunlight streaming in through the window. Her phone had been ringing off the hook with her friends and family calling with congratulations in regards to her story. She'd managed to answer most of them, but some of them she had to resort to texting, because the biggest call, was the one she was on now. The one with her editor.

"The magazine would like to offer you another exclusive. Anywhere you want to go. Anywhere at all."

Abby held her cheek, overwhelmed. "You're kidding."

"It's your choice. All expenses paid of course. Only…you have to go within the year. Think you'll be up for it?"

She'd had surgery on her knee two months before and she was healing nicely. But nevertheless, physical therapy was a bitch, and she was still not walking normally. "I hope so. With the knee and everything."

"Well, how about this for incentive? You get to bring a companion."

"A companion?"

"A travel buddy. Don't tell me you haven't got anyone in mind. Especially a certain someone from Alaska?"

Abby sank lower into the cushions. "I haven't heard from her. Not since my surgery."

"She hasn't called to check up on you?"

"It's been radio silence for months now."

"Have you tried reaching out to her?"

"Once. No response."

"I'm sure she has her reasons. I wouldn't take it personally. You said she has someone she cares for, right? Maybe it has something to do with that."

"Maybe." But still, why couldn't she at least say hello, how are you? It wasn't that difficult. She rested her hand on her abdomen and then lifted her shirt to caress her scar. Whit had been right by her side in the hospital when she'd awakened from surgery. She'd been there until she'd been released and given the all clear. And then, after Abby left to return home…virtually nothing, save for that one text the night before her knee surgery, which had simply read, *GOOD LUCK*.

She didn't pretend to understand. The whole thing was crazy and though she knew Whit to be more of a quiet, reserved person when it came to her feelings, she never expected to get the cold shoulder from her.

"She'll call, Abby. In the meantime, think about your story and your next destination. And oh, yeah, enjoy the heck out of this one's success."

"Thanks."

"I'll holler at you later."

Abby ended the call and checked her messages. A text had come in while she was on the phone, but her heart sank as she realized it wasn't from Whit. She tossed the phone aside and sighed. She should be ecstatic right now with all the praise the article was getting, but all she could do was think about Whit.

She picked up the phone again and typed quickly with her thumbs, writing Whit another text. This one asking if she was okay and why hadn't she heard from her. But then, right before she sent it, she changed her mind and tossed the phone away once again. She wasn't going to text her and then wait on pins and needles for a response that most likely wouldn't come. She just wasn't going to do that to herself. If Whit wanted to contact her, she would.

A light knock came from the door and Abby tensed. She'd developed quite the nervousness to people arriving at her door, thanks to a visit from a grizzly and a crazed killer back in Alaska. She rose, took the time to pull back the curtain to peer out the window, and then did a double take before opening the door.

Whit, in all her glory, stood on her stoop in a pair of worn jeans and a tight T-shirt. Her black hair hung below her shoulders, glimmering in the sun, while her whiskey eyes flashed. She looked so good Abby stumbled for words.

"Whit—you're—a—"

"Here?"

"Yes. You're here."

"I am." She briefly glanced down at her boots as if nervous. "Aren't you going to invite me in?"

Abby blinked. "Yes, yes. Please, come in."

Abby moved aside and Whit entered, shoving her hands into her pockets as she did. She stood there in the foyer, looking uncomfortable.

Abby escorted her inside, and led her to the couch before sitting opposite her on the adjoining chair. She looked down at her tank top, suddenly mindful of her appearance. She hadn't expected company, much less Whit. She must look a mess.

"Sorry, I wasn't expecting anyone," she said as she brushed imaginary crumbs from her top.

"Don't apologize," Whit said. "You have no reason to."

"I just look—"

"You look beautiful. As always."

Abby blinked some more. Whit continued, glancing at the glossy magazine on the coffee table.

"Read your article," she said. "It's good."

"You read it, really?"

"I like what you wrote about Cozy. You really did it justice, without selling it as a tourist destination."

"I tried not to. I fell in love with it, you know. Or maybe you don't know," she said softly, referring to more than just Cozy. "And I tried to respect the townspeople and their wishes."

"You did."

Silence.

"I also like the way you told our story. You were real. Honest. Even when it didn't paint you in a good light. Even though bits of it were difficult to read. You still told the truth."

"That's my job."

"Well, you're good at it, Abby. Really good."

"Thanks."

Whit clapped her hands together and stared out the window and into the bright sunshine. Her irises lightened, and Abby was reminded of the color of that coppery creek. She suddenly longed to be back there, if only to sit and watch Whit fishing again.

Whit cleared her throat. "What you said about me. The way you painted me...I didn't deserve all that. You made me out to be some sort of hero."

"You are, Whit."

"No, I'm not." She met her gaze and Abby could see the pain there. The immense and terrible pain. She tried to touch her hand, but Whit drew away and stood. "I let him hurt you, Abby. And you almost died."

Abby stood alongside her. "Whit, that wasn't your fault. The police, they didn't get to us fast enough. They'd found that body in the woods and then that stolen vehicle with Otter's prints. They just didn't get that information back in enough time to help us before Otter got there."

"I should've stopped him. I should've protected you. Just like I should've done with my father."

Abby did touch her this time. She gripped her hands. "Hey, I didn't die. He didn't kill me. I'm here and I'm okay. And your father...Whit, you couldn't have saved him. You were a child and in the middle of the woods. There was nothing else you could've done."

Abby had been told by one of the detectives just what all had happened to Whit all those years ago on that excursion with Otter and some other hikers. Her heart had broken for Whit, and she'd tried to talk to her about it, right after they'd learned that Otter had died, but Whit had refused.

"Whit, are you hearing me?"

Her shoulders fell and then shook. She tried to turn away to cry, but Abby wouldn't let her. Instead, she pulled her into her arms.

"It's not your fault. None of it."

"I'm just so sorry, Abby," she sobbed.

"As I said, you have nothing to be sorry for, Whit. Nothing. Got it?" She held her tight and let her cry. She knew it was a long time coming, wondering if Whit had ever cried over anything before.

They stood like that for what felt like an eternity, with Whit crying and Abby holding her. When she eventually stopped, she sniffled and wiped her eyes before speaking.

"I'm also sorry for not keeping in touch. I just—felt so responsible for you getting hurt. I couldn't bring myself to speak to you."

"Oh, Whit." Abby wiped her tears. "You're here now, and that's all that matters."

"Yes, I'm here." She held her hands. "About that." More tears flooded her eyes. "Bobby passed away."

"Oh, no. When?"

"Last week. I've been…pretty upset over it. Wishing I could've done more for her, you know?"

"Of course. But you did all you could."

"Did I?"

"Yes, Whit. I know you and I know you did."

She sniffled some more. "I hope so. Anyway, I came to see you, soon after we had the service. We couldn't bury her yet because the ground is frozen. But we had a service."

"Was it nice?"

"It was. But her family didn't come. Not even in death."

Abby stroked her face. "Yes, they did. You were there. You were her family."

"Yeah. Nancy and I were, you're right."

"See?"

Whit took a big breath and managed a smile. "It's good to see you, Abby. Really fucking good to see you."

"You too, Whit. I've missed you so much."

"I've missed you."

Abby held her again and then drew back to kiss her lightly on the lips.

Whit moaned softly, signaling her approval. "So, what do we do now?"

"I don't know. You got any plans?"

"No, not a one."

"You don't have to be back in Alaska anytime soon?"

"Not if you aren't going to be there."

Abby smiled. "Well, then how about another adventure?"

"Another adventure?"

"This one, say in Egypt?"

"With you, Abby, I'd go anywhere."

THE END

About the Author

Ronica Black lives in the desert Southwest with her menagerie of animals and her menagerie of art. When she's not writing, she's still creating, whether drawing, painting, or woodworking. She loves long walks into the sunset, rescuing animals, anything pertaining to art, and spending time with those she loves. When she can, she enjoys returning to her roots in North Carolina where she can sit back on the porch with family and friends, catch up on all the gossip, and relish an ice cold Cheerwine.

Ronica is a two-time Golden Crown Literary Society Goldie Award winner and a three-time finalist for a Lambda Literary Award.

Books Available from Bold Strokes Books

Coming Up Clutch by Anna Gram. College softball star Kelly "Razor" Mitchell hung up her cleats early, but when former crush, now coach Ashton Sharpe shows up on her doorstep seven years later, beautiful as ever, Razor hopes the longing in her gaze has nothing to do with softball. (978-1-63679-817-2)

Firecamp by Jaycie Morrison. Going their separate ways seemed inevitable for two people as different as Fallon and Nora, while meeting up again is strictly coincidental. (978-1-63679-753-3)

Fixed Up by Aurora Rey. When electrician Jack Barrow and artist Ellie Lancaster get stuck on a job site during a blizzard, close quarters send all sorts of sparks flying. (978-1-63679-788-5)

Stranded by Ronica Black. Can Abigail and Whitley overcome their personal hang-ups and stubbornness to survive not only Alaska, but a dangerous stalker as well? (978-1-63679-761-8)

Whisk Me Away by Georgia Beers. Regan's a gorgeous flake. Ava, a beautiful untouchable ice queen. When they meet again at a retreat for up-and-coming pastry chefs, the competition, and the ovens, heat up. (978-1-63679-796-0)

Across the Enchanted Border by Crin Claxton. Magic, telepathy, swordsmanship, tyranny, and tenderness abound in a tale of two lands separated by the enchanted border. (978-1-63679-804-2)

Deep Cover by Kara A. McLeod. Running from your problems by pretending to be someone else only works if the person you're pretending to be doesn't have even bigger problems. (978-1-63679-808-0)

Good Game by Suzanne Lenoir. Even though Lauren has sworn off dating gamers, it's becoming hard to resist the multifaceted Sam. An opposites attract lesbian romance. (978-1-63679-764-9)

Innocence of the Maiden by Ileandra Young. Three powerful women. Two covens at war. One horrifying murder. When mighty and powerful witches begin to butt heads, who out there is strong enough to mediate? (978-1-63679-765-6)

Protection in Paradise by Julia Underwood. When arson forces them together, the flames between chief of police Eve Maguire and librarian Shaye Hayden aren't that easy to extinguish. (978-1-63679-847-9)

Too Forward by Krystina Rivers. Just as professional basketball player Jane May's career finally starts heating up, a new relationship with her team's brand consultant could derail the success and happiness she's struggled so long to find. (978-1-63679-717-5)

Worth Waiting For by Kristin Keppler. For Peyton and Hanna, reliving the past is painful, but looking back might be the only way to move forward. (978-1-63679-773-1)

Flowers and Gemstones by Alaina Erdell. Caught between past loves and present secrets, Hannah and Vanessa must each decide if the other is worth making difficult changes for a shot at happiness. (978-1-63679-745-8)

Foul Play by Erin Kaste. Music librarian Kirsten Lindquist knows someone is stalking the symphony musicians, but can she prove that a string of murders and suspicious accidents are connected, all without becoming a victim herself? (978-1-63679-689-5)

Hollywood Hearts by Toni Logan. What happens when an A-list actress falls for a paparazzo, having no idea her love interest is the one responsible for the photos in a troublesome tabloid scandal targeting her? (978-1-63679-695-6)

Ride It Out by Jenna Jarvis. When the COVID-19 lockdown traps Mick and Katy in situations they'd convinced themselves were temporary, they're forced to face what they really want from their lives, and who they want to share them with. (978-1-63679-709-0)

Scarlet Love by Gun Brooke. Felicienne de Montagne is content with her hybrid flowers and greenhouses—until she finds adventurer Puck Aston on her doorstep and realizes nothing will ever be the same. (978-1-63679-721-2)

The Hard Stuff by Ana Hartnett. When Hannah, the sales manager for a big liquor brand, moves to Alexandra's hometown and rivals her local distillery, sparks of friction and attraction fly. It turns out the liquor is the least of the hard stuff. (978-1-63679-599-7)

The Hunter and Her Witch by Rachel Sullivan. When an ex-witch-hunter falls for a witch, buried pasts are unearthed, and love is placed on trial. (978-1-63679-830-1)

Trustfall by Patricia Evans. Devri and Shiv never expect their feelings for each other to linger, but sometimes what you've always wanted has a way of leading you to who you've always needed. (978-1-63679-705-2)

All For Her: Forbidden Romance Novellas by Gun Brooke, J.J. Hale, Aurora Rey. Explore the angst and excitement of forbidden love few would dare in this heart-stopping novella collection. (978-1-63679-713-7)

Finding Harmony by CF Frizzell. Rock star Harper Cushing has to rearrange her grandmother's future and sell the family store out from under her, but she reassesses everything because Gram's helper, Frankie, could be offering the harmony her heart has been missing. (978-1-63679-741-0)

Gaze by Kris Bryant. Love at first sight is for dreamers, but the more time Lucky and Brianna spend together, the more they realize the chemistry of a gaze can make anything possible. (978-1-63679-711-3)

Laying of Hands by Patricia Evans. The mysterious new writing instructor at camp makes Grace Waters brave enough to wonder what would happen if she dared to write her own story. (978-1-63679-782-3)

Seducing the Widow by Jane Walsh. Former rival debutantes have a second chance at love after fifteen years apart when a spinster persuades her ex-lover to help save her family business. (978-1-63679-747-2)

The Naked Truth by Sandy Lowe. How far are Rowan and Genevieve willing to go and how much will they risk to make their most captivating and forbidden fantasies a reality? (978-1-63679-426-6)

The Roommate by Claire Forsythe. Jess Black's boyfriend is handsome and successful. That's why it comes as a shock when she meets a woman on the train who makes her pulse race. (978-1-63679-757-1)